IN HIS ARMS

"Thank you," Timona whispered, and he took it as an invitation to move.

He wanted this to last at long as possible, for he would not feel the like of her again. But he'd been craving her too long. Too many long hours.

She arched her back and he stopped for a moment in a last desperate attempt to hold back.

"Ah, no, Timmy, God, don't," he groaned into her fragrant hair, and he nearly blacked out with the pleasure.

Thoughts of any other woman vanished with Timmy in his arms. He rolled away from her and fumbled around for the candle.

"Mick," she said, and he could feel her skin as she moved close and brushed against him. "I don't think you have kissed me enough. I do like your kisses." Her soft hands lightly stroked up his belly and across his shoulders.

In the dark, Mick found her mouth and he kissed her. His tongue traced her lips. The tender kiss deepened and bloomed into something demanding and rich. He ripped aside the last scrap of linen that was once a lacy petticoat he'd caught glimpses of, and there was nothing but sweet bare skin between them. He forgot about light.

Somebody
Wonderful

Kate Rothwell

ZEBRA BOOKS
Kensington Publishing Corp.
http://www.zebrabooks.com

ZEBRA BOOKS are published by

Kensington Publishing Corp.
850 Third Avenue
New York, NY 10022

All Kensington titles, imprints and distributed lines are available at special quantity discounts for bulk purchases for sales promotion, premiums, fund-raising, educational or institutional use.

Special book excerpts or customized printings can also be created to fit specific needs. For details, write or phone the office of the Kensington Special Sales Manager: Kensington Publishing Corp., 850 Third Avenue, New York, NY 10022. Attn. Special Sales Department. Phone: 1-800-221-2647.

Zebra and the Z logo Reg. U.S. Pat. & TM Off.

First Printing: July 2004
10 9 8 7 6 5 4 3 2 1

Printed in the United States of America

*To Margaret R. with love and gratitude;
And I owe more than a measly lunch
to Linda Ingmanson and Nan.*

Chapter 1

Mick had finished his beat and was strolling home from the precinct when the ruckus broke out. He could ignore it, the shouts and running footsteps echoing from the dark alley. God knew he wanted to ignore it. He'd had a hell of a couple of days on duty, and all he wanted was ten or twenty hours of uninterrupted sleep.

Someone howled, a wordless cry of wild, gleeful menace.

He stopped undoing the tight top button of his wool frock coat, and peered down the street into the shadowy corner. A pack of scruffy, mostly grown boys scrambled out of the alley. Probably the newly formed band of street arabs, all the big talk in McFee's tavern. Nothing so tough as a real gang, but worth keeping an eye on.

On the corner, the ragged boys shuffled forward, circled, closed in, thin shoulders hunched up, the air electric with anticipation before an attack. What had they found? A cat stupid enough to venture from a shadowy basement? A near-starved dog?

In the center of the circle, an arm flashed out. A shout twisted into a scream, cut unnaturally short.

Not an animal. A human.

They must have trapped an off-streeter, a stray who didn't move fast enough or pay whatever fine they demanded. Lone idiot, thought Mick, disgusted.

A brick smashed into the gutter. With a resigned growl, Mick yanked out his club, and took off at a run. "Get the hell off o' him." Mick pounded over the cobblestones toward the boys. "Beat it."

The leader turned to watch Mick, probably waiting to see if a cop was willing to go one on six. Damn. The boy had to know police didn't generally bother with street urchins' fun. Not unless they troubled members of the tax-paying public, which didn't include other shabby lads.

As Mick got close, the ferret-thin leader jerked his head, signaling his troops. The gang scuttled away.

"Yah, dirty mick," they jeered as they scattered.

A couple of years back, Mick would have been startled to hear them yell his name. It hadn't taken him more than a day in this country to figure out "mick" was a slur for all Irish. But when he donned the double-breasted, brass-buttoned coat and strapped on the truncheon of the New York Police Department, the name calling stopped. Usually.

The off-street kid sprawled in the gutter and across the stones of the filthy, manure-strewn street. He didn't moved and his eyes were closed.

For a moment, Mick's heart plummeted. *A Dhia.* God.

Another corpse. He never got used to the corpses, especially the young ones.

But no, the kid moaned faintly.

Mick hitched the knees of his blue serge trousers and squatted to check him. Still out cold. When Mick glanced up, a pale face disappeared behind the corner of a building.

The gang's lookout, likely the youngest, watched to

see if Mick'd go after them. He knew if he did, they'd split up and some would double back and harass the off streeter. Nuts to that.

He touched the back of the unconscious lad's head behind the gray tweed cap that was jammed on at a rakish angle. His hand came away covered in blood. The boy had a cut gaping wide on one shoulder, too.

Mick sighed. He wished he could shake the lad awake, walk him to some safer street, all the while administering a stern warning to be more careful. Then he could get himself home at last. But the lad looked too beaten to abandon, even if he was led off the gang's turf.

Mick leaned over to examine the cut on the kid's shoulder. Hard to ignore the reek of putrid vegetables—the young idiot had landed in a pile of garbage. Mick pulled aside the blood and filth-covered jacket.

His heart took another, unpleasant jump.

This was no boy. Under the jacket, the victim's shirt had ripped, exposing a lacy chemise and the curve of a breast.

Blessed saints. A female left here in this state would be a fine time for the older gang members, once they noticed her. What kind of a fool of a girl, or woman, rather, would run around the streets dressed up like a boy?

"Hell," Mick muttered. The public hospital? A good half mile. After thirteen hours in hobnailed boots, he was reluctant to take a single extra step.

And he couldn't forget the last urchin he'd left at the hospital. The boy had died there, though it was a matter of a simple break in the leg. Mick still berated himself—he should have set that leg himself, even if he had been on duty.

His flat was nearby. And he'd brought home strays before. Most of them stayed for a few days, then roamed off, though they'd come back now and then, to beg an occasional meal. But this would be the first female he'd brought home, unless you counted the dog that had been hit by a cart and later had puppies on his frock coat.

The woman's eyes half-opened.

She started to sit up, and Mick hauled her to her feet. Her eyelids fluttered shut. She began to collapse. Mick caught her under the arms before she hit the stones again. Looking at her from above she looked entirely feminine—hard to imagine how anyone missed those obvious curves. Most of her skin, and even her fingernails, were fairly clean, so she hadn't been traipsing around the streets in this disguise for long.

"Hell," he muttered again. He did not need this.

Mick leaned forward and tossed her onto his shoulder. She weighed no more than a sack of feathers. As he made his way down the sidewalk, he gave an easy heave and shifted her to his other side. Might as well keep her off her injured shoulder.

A few passersby gave Mick curious glances. One gaunt neighborhood drifter strolled past. He had employment today: a sandwich-board advertisement for a tobacconist hung from a yoke on his shoulders.

He stopped to holler, "Hey, officer! That package what you coppers're gettin' for pay these days?" The vagrant cackled at his own wit. Mick ignored him.

His block was by no means the worst in the city, but that was the best that could be said of it. Gargoyles glared down from his apartment building's façade. Other than that touch of whimsy, the place was as grim as all the buildings crammed uncomfortably on the crowded street.

Still, Mick made an effort to keep it clean. He absently brushed the worst of the filth off the breeches the girl wore and plucked a rotting lettuce leaf off her hip. He pushed open the front door with his large, booted foot. The ghosts of thousands of boiled cabbages, flavored with a hint of raw sewage, drifted to his nose.

Home sweet home.

"Mr. McCann," fluted the widow who lived on the bottom floor. She leaned against her open doorway and smiled at him. The smile vanished when she saw the body flung over his shoulder. "Mercy!" she cried. "Is that the boy what caused the racket out there?"

"More likely the lads after him."

With his free hand, he tilted his helmet politely at the widow, who wore nothing more than a chemise above her corseted waist. She scowled and slammed back into her apartment.

He wasn't just imagining it, then. The ill-tempered widow clearly had an eye on him. For the first time, Mick was almost glad he had the kid—no, woman—over his shoulder.

He carefully bounded up the creaking steps two at a time, skirting the trash, chairs, washtubs and baskets that cluttered the hall.

In his dimly lit, one-room flat, he laid the woman onto his bed and stepped back to look at her. Delicate lines to her face, and high cheekbones and small nose. Italian? Jewish? Maybe even black Irish. Her skin was creamy pale, though the hair jammed under the tweed cap was dark, almost dark enough to hide the color of blood.

Oh. The cut on the back of her head. He looked down at himself. Christ, his coat was shoulder to waist in her blood. Fear jolted though him. Was she so badly hurt?

The woman's breathing was steady enough. He gave her a quick examination. The blood had come from her head; he'd seen enough of those cuts to know they could bleed impressively. He could leave her for a few minutes.

Mick took down the large pot he used for washing, and trudged up a flight to the working pump for water. It didn't take many days on the job for him to learn cold water was best for getting out blood—good thing, to be sure, since the building had no hot.

Botty must have heard his steps. The scruffy little mutt came careening down the stairs, a misshapen cannonball of a dog. He'd lurked up in the top floor, probably hiding from the widow.

Mick put down the full basin and bent to scratch the dog's remaining ear. Botty pushed at his hand with ecstatic wheezing growls. When Mick opened the flat's door, Botty clicked into the room and settled on a rag under the bureau with a contented sigh.

Mick poured some water into a clean saucepan to use for the woman. Then he stripped off his coat and shoved the most badly stained sleeve into the large pan. He'd see about the female after he got the damned boots off.

He pushed down the straps of his braces and plopped down on the sagging bed next to her.

She moaned. Then spoke. "My God, no. Not again." The five words made her origins clear. An English-woman.

A pity. He didn't think much of the English.

He swivelled around, one boot dangling from his hand. Horrified green eyes stared up at him from a pale face. The woman didn't seem particularly happy to see him either.

She groaned. "Hell's bells. All that effort, wasted. Did the boys on the street tell you where to find me?"

"Hey?"

"I should not have riled the man," she murmured.

"My God, this one's much. My head is so wobbly, it will fall off. Oh, blast. I give up."

"Aye?" Mick rubbed two fingers across his unshaved chin. Maybe she was a criminal who'd caved at the sight of his helmet hanging on the chair. "Right. What did you do, then? Were you going and asking for trouble from those lads?"

"No." The woman sounded tired, but testy. "As I told the man in charge, someone will pay for my return. A good amount, no questions asked. He didn't seem to care. I should have known better than to wander, but the light . . ." Her voice died away.

Perhaps she had suffered some kind of brain injury. He studied her pale face; her eyes were closed again. He'd check her pupils later. "The man in charge?" he prompted.

"Oh, I don't know." A definite peevish note to her tone. "Perhaps he's not in charge. He claimed he was. Perhaps some other beast is the owner. Perhaps you are. I don't truly care. I said I give up, so go on then."

Mick dropped the boot he held onto the floor. He stood up, lit another candle and peered down at her. "Here, now. Are you all right, miss? You do know you got a nasty cosh on the head?"

She opened her eyes and looked at him again, glaring, for pity's sake. Her blood-streaked brow furrowed in regal disdain. "And would that make the slightest difference to you?"

"What?"

"I mean, do you rougher types actually care if the girl is injured or unwilling? I tried drooling and crooning like a mad-woman and that didn't stop the first man. Then they said that rough types get the girls who act up." The woman gave a small moan. She examined him. "Though I must say you have a kind face. Does it help my—ah, me—if I say I give up? I will apologize to the men I injured if it is necessary. Might I be given a different sort of, ah . . ." She flushed.

Mick began to suspect he understood her too well.

"Jesus," he said at last. "What the hell do you think I am?"

She blinked at him. "A customer?"

He couldn't hold back his whoop of laughter. "Look around, woman. Does this look like a whorehouse?"

The woman pulled herself up. She squinted around the dark, shabby room. Mick grimaced when he considered what she saw. There was the sagging bed she lay on, a chair and a bureau. The paper on the walls that might have had pink roses a decade ago. He had given up trying to thoroughly clean the place, though he kept it neat.

"Yes, from what I saw of that bordello, it does, rather," she said timidly. "But from your manner, I- I appear to be mistaken. Oh. Good. Very good." Her eyes rolled up, and the touch of pink in her cheeks drained away. She fell back on the bed in a faint.

Sat up too quickly, Mick supposed, and felt for her pulse in her neck. Strong and even. He stared down at the little whore for a moment. Strange to think that if she came from his village, her choice of profession would mean she'd cease to exist. Her picture would be turned to the wall, and no one would utter her name again. He hoped her people were more tolerant.

He sat back down to take off his other boot. After he washed his hands in the pot of perishing cold water, he examined the wound on her head. It still oozed. He gently felt it again. No sign that the skull had been injured. He'd have to give her stitches, though, and the gash on her shoulder did look nasty enough to leave a scar. He'd ask her about it when she came round again. For a moment he considered doing the stitches while she was out cold, but she'd probably appreciate knowing what he was about before he started.

English. She'd like a cup of tea, perhaps, but he wasn't going to waste fuel until he was sure.

He carefully slid his arm under her and hoisted her close. And froze.

A waft of the woman's scent hit him, and he just about swooned himself as he breathed in. Under the dust, the stench of the street and perspiration he smelled a complex fragrance of flowers, absurdly out-of-place in his back tenement. And in the mix, a sweet but musky scent he thought might be called sandaltwig. No, sandalwood.

He leaned closer and sniffed again. The flowers and sandalwood were overlaid with another impossibly delicate essence. A man could spend a day doing naught but breathing this in . . .

"*Sguir,*" he said aloud. Stop it.

Still holding her cradled against him with one arm, he reached for the dipper of clean water. No point in soaking the bed. He pushed the dipper toward her lips. When that didn't rouse her, he dipped his fingers into the water and dribbled some down the side of her face.

"Wake up, then, miss. We got some work to do on you before we get you on your way."

The cold water did the trick. She stirred and her eyes opened. For a moment, horror flashed into her face, but then as quickly disappeared.

"Hallo," she said. "Now I remember. I saw you getting undressed and thought . . . Ah. Well. I do apologize. Now I understand you are not a customer or a boss. Thank heavens."

He grinned. "That about sums me up."

He peered into her eyes. Green, though not a true green, a rather mossy green speckled with gray. She looked back. Their gazes locked, and his breath caught in his suddenly tight throat. He grew entirely aware of her body leaning against his chest. Stop it, he warned himself, silent this time, and he loosened his grip on her.

Her eyes. Right. The pupils looked the same size. "You look better already I'd say. Can you tell me what year it is?"

"1882."

"Good. The day of the week?"

"Wednesday?"

"Right. Have you done any vomiting?"

"No."

Her interesting shape still rested against his arm. He lowered her to the bed and smiled reassuringly down at her.

"But listen, miss, you're bleeding all over me bed. I'm thinking your head requires a stitch or two, and maybe your shoulder. I'll do that and you can tell me about yourself to keep your mind off the stitches, all right then?"

He bent down and hauled out the medical kit stashed under the bed. He pulled it onto his lap and unbuckled the top.

She felt the top of her head gingerly as she watched. "You've got a strange bedside manner for a doctor. Not to mention a strange surgery, or rather, office." She looked him up and down. "No, I do not believe you are a real doctor either."

"I'm no boss, no customer, nor doctor. I've stitched up plenty of wounds though, on our farm. My father taught me and he learned from a doctor. D'ye want a real doctor? I can take you over to the hospital or I'll go search for Dr. O'Toole."

He sighed and put the kit back down on the warped floorboards. He looped his braces back onto his arms and started to fasten the top of his shirt.

"No," she said suddenly. "I trust you. I believe you know what you're about. I dislike doctors, actually, and would rather have you."

"That's the spirit," said Mick, who was thoroughly knackered and did not want to jam his feet back in the boots and tramp the half mile, probably carrying the woman most of the way. He knew he wouldn't simply dump her to wait alone, and the wait was always long.

He opened the bag and took out the needle, gut thread, and a bottle of spirits. "So, miss. What's your name?"

She eyed the scissors he fetched from the bottom of the bag. "I should tell you, shouldn't I? Very well. I am Miss Timona Calverson." She paused a long moment. "Do you think you have to cut my hair?"

"Pleased to meet you, Miss Calverson. I'm Michael McCann. I only have to cut a bit of it. Not the whole head of hair. Otherwise can't see what I'm doing with the needle."

"Oh, I see." She reached up and pulled off her cap. About three feet of dark brown hair tumbled down, along with two hairpins.

Mick almost jumped back. "Aye, but that is a lot of hair."

She pushed it back from her face. "I can't bring myself to cut it, though it's a difficult vanity to indulge whilst traveling." She slowly leaned over and bent her head so he could see the cut. "Go on, Mr. McCann."

He stared down at the oozing gash on the back of her scalp. "I won't have to chop off a great deal, since the cut isn't large," he said soothingly. "And it's in the back so you'll be able to cover up the spot. Oh, it's thick stuff," he murmured as he carefully trimmed around the spot, blotting up the blood every few seconds. The strands were surprisingly thistledown soft for such substantial hair. "Lovely."

"Thank you."

He hadn't noticed he'd spoken aloud. He spent enough time alone in the flat he tended to talk to keep himself company.

She twisted round to look over her shoulder at him, nervous. Couldn't blame her. From the sound of it, she'd had quite an adventure, poor little whore.

He washed the wound, then briskly poured the spirits onto a clean cloth and lightly clapped the cloth to her head.

"Ow!"

"Sorry, miss. I'd offer you a spot of gin for the pain, but I believe you're not supposed to drink when you have head wounds."

Her mouth curled into something between a smile and a grimace. "I was merely surprised. Go ahead, do your worst and I shall hold steady."

"I don't doubt it, miss."

He had her lie face down across his lap, as if she were a sewing project. That's the way he dealt with most of his "patients." Easier to work on the quiet woman than on the squirming dog that Paddy, a neighbor, had brought him the week before, but she was more distracting. With her astonishing hair down and spread across his lap and thighs he couldn't help but get notions. The weight and warmth of her made it worse. And when he caught her scent again, he knew the notions weren't going to abate.

Hell, he only hoped she didn't notice his reaction. Just what a nervous woman recently roughed up by thugs did not need.

"I think only a few will do the trick," he said.

She gave a soft yelp when he began. He stopped to give her back what he hoped she interpreted as a friendly pat. He grinned at his instinctive move; many of his patients liked a good back rub. The grin faded as he imagined stroking other parts of the delicate body sprawled across his lap.

Stop it.

He got back to work.

At the first stitch, he noticed her hand on the bed was clenched so tight he worried she'd hurt herself with her fingernails. He leaned over and shoved a bit of a blanket into her fist. "Squeeze this when it hurts."

After a few minutes, he clipped off the final stitch. "Good then." He sprinkled some powder on the wound, then reached down to her armpits and hauled her body sideways up and off him.

Perhaps he moved her too quickly for someone in her condition. But this one had to get out fast. He didn't need her around, and God knew what Daisy would say if she found out.

"My shoulder isn't bleeding as much now." She sat up and tucked back her chin to examine herself. "But it hurts. And it looks dreadful. Ugh."

True enough, the gap in the flesh should be closed. "Hell," he muttered. He cleaned the needle, thread, scissors and wound with the spirits, then tried to position her on the bed. He knelt on the floor next to her, but he wasn't used to working that way.

He cleared his throat. "I'm afraid it'll, er, be best to do it the way I did your head."

"I don't mind," she said brightly. "I expect I shall find it easier to breathe face up." She gingerly pulled off the jacket, then unbuttoned the shirt and started to pull it off too.

"Good enough," he yelped at the fascinating and unwelcome glimpse of her milky smooth skin. "Just the shoulder, eh?"

She gave him a small, odd grin and arranged herself across his thighs, scooting herself around on his legs more than was necessary. Even through the thick cloth of his trousers he felt the warmth of her brushing against his erection.

The sly smile of hers told him the little wretch knew what she was doing to him. She was enjoying herself, Mick thought crossly. Damn prostitute. He scowled down at her, but then felt sorry for it when he glanced at her face again. She watched him, distress in the odd eyes.

"I- I am sorry about causing all of this trouble, Mr. McCann," she said as she stared up at him. "I appreciate all that you have done for me. And I shall leave as soon as I can."

Maybe she wasn't toying with him, then. It wasn't her fault he was starved for a female. He avoided meeting her eyes, and studied her shoulder. He smiled to ease her worry.

"If you're going to dress like a boy, Miss Calverson, I suppose I ought to accompany you. Just so's you're safe when your disguise is discovered."

He leaned closer to look at the wound near the delicate line of her collarbone. When he made the mistake of glancing over at her face, he could see the gray-green eyes watched him. Her warm breath fanned the side of his face. His own breath came fast and unsteady.

She wasn't the only one who needed distraction.

He cleared his throat. Again. "But will you tell me why are you dressed so odd, miss?"

"I needed some clothes because they left me with only a chemise. Annie, one of the girls, found these clothes in her closet. I suppose some of the customers liked girls dressed as boys, or perhaps just boys. Annie and I thought I'd be less conspicuous in them."

"And where is this marvelous place you escaped from?"

"I don't think I heard the name. I believe it is a few blocks from the river." She groaned and closed her eyes. "The only thing I am certain of is that I do not know the area, and, oh, the day is a jumble."

She flinched when he cleaned the wound, and then again when he put the first stitch on her shoulder. She gathered up a handful of the bedding to clutch again, but she didn't move or cry out. A brave creature.

He finished another stitch. "You weren't there long then?"

"A couple of hours at most," she said.

"Which house were you in before they got you? Or were you on the street?"

"What do you mean? Oh, no, you think I've been a . . ." She snorted. "No, I did not come from another one of those houses, Mr. McCann. I dressed rather shabbily, which probably was a mistake. Perhaps I walked too far alone, another mistake. But the light was so wonderful and I was admiring the views when I was grabbed. I think they used chloroform on me. The next thing I knew, I was lying on a filthy bed in a filthy room with a man ripping at my dress."

She drew in several deep breaths and he could feel her shudder, her first sign of distress. A moment later she continued, her tone ridiculously matter-of-fact again. "I acted queerly, and then I screamed. And when that didn't help, I fought him."

"Did you, now." Mick meant the words merely to soothe her, but she must have thought he wanted an explanation.

"I used my knees. My brother, Griffin, has shown me ways to defend myself. I managed to hurt the man."

Mick winced.

"He shouted about the dreadful things he planned to do to me. Then he limped out and locked the door. When he came back he was accompanied by another man and they had some rope. They told me that since

I was difficult I would get plenty of what they called, ah, rougher customers."

"I saw they intended to tie me to the bed. And that was when we started up the most absurd game of round and round the cobbler's bench—they chased me around the bed. I shouted the same things I told you. That people would pay for my return and so on. They probably shouted too, but I was too agitated to listen." She made a small noise, something like a laugh and said, "What a ridiculous scene."

She flinched again as Mick made another stitch, then remarked, "Really, if it was money they wanted, they might have just tried for a ransom." She gasped. "Oh. That hurt."

Mick had pulled the thread too hard and fast. He wondered how she could remain so entirely collected. A couple of years ago, he would have trotted her straight to the police station. Or told the woman she was a daft, fanciful female who missed her calling as an authoress of penny dreadfuls. He'd seen a lot in two years.

"So you got away then?"

"Soon after that. I am afraid I hurt the larger man rather badly, which made him angry. He attempted to pick me up. I used my heels on his private parts, and my fingers in his eyes. Griffin showed me that, too. The man was screaming when I ran down the hall. I found Annie sitting in her room and she helped me. I was trying to find my way back to the pier when I came across that group of ridiculous boys. They kept asking me about which street I was from. Then I woke up and there you were."

Pity for her twisted his gut, though she undoubtably lied about being a prostitute. He knew she was evading the truth somehow. Her unruffled manner revealed she couldn't be an innocent—an inexperienced young girl in such circumstances would not be so calm, nor understand so much of what she'd seen. But he'd lay odds she hadn't made up the whole of it.

Part of her story had to be lies. What were her first words when she saw him? "Not again." A small woman wouldn't have a chance against two large bordello hoodlums. Wishful thinking, he supposed.

"It sounds mortal dreadful, Miss Calverson. I shall make a report, of course," he said at last. "So then. Is this the last of your cuts? Are you, ah," he hesitated, "ripped or injured elsewhere?"

"I should think this is more than enough to go on with."

He certainly wouldn't press the issue. "Aye, well, I'm nearly done then. Considering all you've been through, I am surprised you're so calm as you are." Surprised was an understatement.

"Good God. I was anything but calm when I got out of there. I shook for a long while. And then I got lost. I keep telling myself it could have been worse. They didn't steal anything but my clothing. I hadn't brought any equipment with me. Or my compass. Oh, no."

"Ah now, lass," he soothed. "Done in a tick. I'll tie this last stitch and the nightmare is over. We'll take you back to where you belong."

Mick made his final clip and started to bandage her up. He carefully wrapped the clean strips over the soft skin.

She groaned. "No, oh, I have just recalled the worst of it. My father will have left. He will imagine I meant to meet him ahead, because we once discussed that. Good lord, what might he do without me?"

He laughed, incredulous. "Miss Calverson. You tell me you've been kidnapped, imprisoned, ah, nearly raped and yet you're most worried about your father?"

She exhaled a long breath as she slowly sat up. "I can

usually take care of my self. My father is often another story. He is supposed to be going to Minnesota but heaven knows if he'll make it there. He might end up in Montana or . . . or some other place that starts with 'M.' Michigan. Mongolia. Anywhere. Will you help me get back to him?"

Mick opened his mouth, then closed it again.

She gingerly pulled the dirty urchin's blouse up over her shoulder. "No, no. I can see you're tired, Mr. McCann. It must be late. Perhaps in the morning? You can help me then?"

"Good idea," he said, relieved. "'Tis my day off tomorrow. I am busy in the afternoon, but I can help in the morning." He put away the medical supplies, rinsed his hands in the water, and, after a moment's hesitation, wiped them on his blue trousers.

He walked to the small stove. "A cup of tea for you, miss?"

"Yes, please."

She lay down again. He could feel her steady gaze on him as he shook out the last few grains of tea into the pot. There was only enough for one cup. Just as well since Lex had broken his only other mug the week earlier.

"What about you, Mr. McCann? Aren't you having any?"

"Oh, I don't care for tea in the evening," he lied cheerily. "I'll add sugar, shall I? Good for you just now."

When he held out the chipped mug she sat up and curled her legs under herself. She watched him over the rim as she sipped. He sat back in the chair and smiled encouragingly at her as she gulped down the tea. For a moment she stopped drinking, and eyed him intently. With all her hair tumbled around her and the big greeny eyes she looked like a pretty little witch about to cast a spell.

He raised his eyebrows. "Something amiss?"

"No. Not now." She touched her head. "This already feels better. I don't even have a headache."

He fished his memo book from his back pocket. "Since you feel better, would you mind if I asked you some questions then?

She nodded.

"Could you describe the first man?"

"American accent. Balding, large build, small brown eyes, several teeth missing, mostly in the back of his mouth."

As he listened and jotted notes, he reflected that it was too bad he and Miss Calverson were wasting their time. From her description of the men and the house, he narrowed it down to one of two places in Satan's Circus, the area more lately called the Tenderloin. The man could be Two-Punch Jack from the Lucky Flower. Scotch Alfie and his house fit the description, too. Both men were major contributors to the police sugar pot.

Mick had long understood that his first job was to protect the system. And its corruption. Public safety came in a distant second.

Mick survived his month as a rookie and took the required secret oath never to peach on his fellow cops. But the first time Mick tried to refuse his small share of the precinct's "sugar," his friends warned him he'd be pegged as a troublemaker. He'd be off the force fast, unless he pocketed the graft.

Little chance a copper would even question the man who attacked this Calverson girl. The first time Mick tried to bust a pimp because the man had beaten a girl, he was made to understand Baboon Harris paid big money to avoid overzealous cops.

Mick assuaged his conscience by using some of his share of the graft to buy food or coffee for the off-duty—or used up and tossed out—girls. He'd give this girl some of the dollars in the drawer to at least buy herself some decent clothes.

"Thank you, miss. That's enough to go on for now." He flipped his book closed and stood. Mick would hand the report to his sergeant and no doubt it would get "lost." If Mick complained, he'd likely be hauled before the loathsome Captain Johnson as a potential squealer.

She handed him the empty mug, and gave a little sigh. "Thank you. I feel like a new woman. And if you could just lend me a blanket I shall be set for the night."

Ah. No, no. Bad idea.

"I'm thinking we should find another place for you to stay tonight."

"Do you suppose that is wise when I am dressed so, er, peculiarly?" She looked up at him expectantly. When he didn't say anything, she added, "Really, I only require a blanket and the floor. I have slept in worse conditions."

Stifling a yawn, he forced himself to his feet. "I'll get the blanket. And the floor."

"We shall share the bed," she said decisively. "Each wrapped in his own blanket. So there will be no impropriety. You see? It will be absolutely fine."

He was too damned tired to argue.

He snapped his fingers and Botty scrambled out from under the bureau.

The woman stared at Botty. "Is that your dog?"

"As much as he is anyone's," Mick said.

"What on earth happened to him?"

"Some kids got hold of him. I was all for putting him out of his misery, but a boy from the alley wanted me to try to save him."

"Does he belong to the boy from the alley?"

"Nah. Eddy can't keep a dog." Mick bent down to rub

Botty's back. "Not supposed to have a dog in here, either. So old Botham's often got to fend for himself."

"Bottom? You call him that because he has no bum?"

"You English say Bahth-ham."

"Why'd you name him that?"

"That's the name of our landlord. In Ireland. First time I picked up the dog, he bit me hard. And he's horrible ugly, too. Aren't you," he murmured fondly to the mutt who'd never been a beauty. Botty's looks weren't improved by the fact that he was missing part of a foot, all of his tail, a chunk of his backside, and an ear, and patches of pink skin showed where the black fur had been stripped away.

Mick opened the door, signaling that he was done with conversation. He led the woman out back to the outdoor privy.

Walking carefully through the narrow dirty yard, she paused and looked up. She gasped. "It is beautiful—as if it has been decorated for a celebration."

Above them, row upon row of laundry hung from the lines stretched between tenements. Mick glanced up for a moment at the clothing snapping in the evening breeze. Hard to see Mrs. Welty's knickers as any sort of decoration. This Miss Calverson had an odd way of looking at things.

Mick sniffed, amused, then went back inside, Botty at his heels. He heard the woman's light step as she tentatively made her way up the back stair and he pushed opened the door so the light in the flat would show her the way through the dark hall.

After they made do with the last of the clean, cold water for a wash up, she climbed onto the bed. She picked up the smaller gray blanket and rolled herself into it like a stuffed cabbage. Then, with her back to him, she perched her body at the far edge of the old, sagging mattress. She probably had to hang onto the edge of the thing to keep from falling into the crater.

She twisted around and beamed at him. "I have completely forgotten to thank you Mr. McCann. You are my savior, sir. Thank you. I shall always be grateful." She turned away again, wriggled around for a minute or two and fell still.

Nonplussed, he reached for the other blanket.

Mick yawned. He'd had only six hours between shifts and last night he had made the mistake of trying to catch a nap in precinct barracks rather than walk home. That meant he spent six hours trying to ignore the stench of smoke and unwashed cops. And he had yet to figure out how to block out the shouts and howls from the jail cells and shelter in the basement below the cops' dormitory.

And now this daft woman had stumbled into his life. He took a deep breath, and caught the faint whiff of her. Trouble, he thought vaguely, as his eyes closed. Big trouble.

Despite the facts that he was filthy from his beat, still nearly fully dressed, and lying next to an utterly desirable female when he hadn't had a woman in half a year, he was asleep in a few minutes.

Timona was hungry. Mr. McCann probably was too, but if she mentioned food, he might talk about making her leave again. Anyway, she suspected he was already asleep.

She knew she had best keep her mind busy or she'd think about food. Or, far worse, about the horrible bordello.

First she would find out if anyone at the company knew if her father made it onto the train. With Papa traveling by himself, who knew what might happen between New York and Ohio? Mr. Blenheim, Papa's secretary, was to meet them somewhere in Ohio. She had already asked the gentleman from the New York Calverson Company office to send a wire to Mr. Blenheim concerning their train schedule. So that *should* be all right.

If she could confirm Papa had gotten on and stayed on the train, and had met Mr. Blenheim, she would be free to spend some time in New York.

She would buy another camera and some dry plates.

She would write to her best friend, Araminta. She might eventually go to Minnesota and join her father.

And, at some point, she would marry Michael McCann.

If he wouldn't marry her, perhaps she could hire him. Or if he wouldn't work for a female, perhaps her father could hire him as a bodyguard. She wasn't sure what Mr. McCann could do, other than reassure lost females and a practice a bit of useful doctoring.

Funny that her heart could travel so far in a matter of an hour, much further than she had in any of her other journeys.

At first she had thought he was a beastly huge redhaired monster. His reassuring manner had soon comforted her. She perceived the next transformation when her heartbeat increased markedly as she lay across his thighs. She had listened to his deep, soft voice. Then she noticed his smile.

And now she understood that Araminta had been right all along. After years of wondering if she had a defective core, Timona had found a cure for herself. A large, calm, magnificent cure. No money. Irish. Gentle, deft, talented hands. He had a face that belonged to sun and wind, not the crowded streets of New York. He mentioned a farm, so perhaps he was not well educated, at least in terms of formal schooling.

What else did she know about him? He was kind, and slow to take offense. Generous enough to give his last cup of tea to a woman he thought was a runaway whore. Compassionate enough to house what had to be the ugliest dog on the face of the earth.

She knew he was attracted to her, but he was not pleased by that fact. He seemed to think she truly was a prostitute. Not an auspicious beginning.

His steady breath confirmed that he was asleep. Good, he didn't snore. She would be able to sleep for the next fifty or so years.

Though she did not dare to climb out of his dreadful bed, she carefully sat up to look around the room. In the dim light of the candle he'd forgotten to blow out, she spotted the frock coat mostly jammed into a capacious pot and the helmet dangling from the chair.

A policeman then. She'd seen the uniform on her two other visits to New York. Did he like the work, she wondered. Would she like being married to a police officer? She hoped so, though she rather doubted it. Too much worry.

She lay down, facing him this time, wishing she could study his face. She could barely make out the vague shape of his large, sleeping form, rising like a dark, gently sloping hill beside her. The candlelight created a glowing nimbus around the edges of his soft, curling hair. Not carrot, a paler shade that she imagined turned bronze in the summer sun. The light flickered over the golden stubble of his beard.

She closed her eyes, wishing she could see him smile again, a broad smile that did more than show white teeth. A smile that brimmed with humor and warmth.

He had saved her. Now according to some tradition or another that she hazily recalled, she was his responsibility for the rest of their lives. Thank goodness. She was tired of being the responsible, solid member of her father's entourage.

Mr. McCann seemed better at responsibility, a true professional. Though it hardly seemed fair to put all the burdens of caring on him.

Perhaps, she thought as she smiled into the darkness, they could take turns.

Chapter 2

The train heading to Chicago boasted a first-class Pullman Palace car adorned in bright blue velvet with heavy, carved mahogany furnishings. Two men sat at a table in the overheated compartment. Both smoked cigars, both were dressed in quiet, expensively tailored tweed suits.

Mr. Blenheim, the taller of the two, felt it his duty to read aloud notes to old Sir Kenneth, a short, stout Englishman. Blenheim ignored his employer's inattention and read in his strong tenor voice, with an accent and inflection that had been nurtured at Eton and Cambridge.

He ended with, "And so I can only conclude The Westland mining contract is in good hands. Mr. Calverson hired a most respectable individual."

"Eh? Westland? Useless property that. Waste of time."

Blenheim did not bother to reply. Under the best of circumstances, Sir Kenneth didn't listen to the notes of any non-paleontological meeting. And just now, the old man had the light of potential discovery in his eyes. Traveling to the next dinosaur dig, he was lost to anything that lived or breathed less than 65 million years ago.

Still, Blenheim needed to know the answer to another question, even if it meant reaching forward and physically shaking the old bustard. "Sir Kenneth, I was wondering—when will Miss Timona be rejoining us?"

"Eh? Hand me that pencil, Blenheim."

"Miss Timona, sir."

"Miss . . . Oh. Last I saw her, she was going out to plan more photographs of buildings. She made some fine pictures of the last dig. Fine shots. Must say, she keeps stopping and hauling all that cumbersome equipment out. Damn nuisance. It's become her obsession."

No more than you have for lizards, Blenheim thought, but did not say. He leaned back in the plush seat to pull his gold watch out of his waistcoat pocket. A few more hours to Cleveland.

Blenheim thought about the woman he privately referred to as his beloved. Miss Timona was damnably independent, but surely she was responsible enough not to allow Sir Kenneth out of New York alone.

Blenheim had been taken aback when he found the old man on his own.

Sir Kenneth at a dig, no one need worry. Sir Kenneth wandering one of his properties, again, not a problem. Only when he traveled did Sir Kenneth constitute a hazard to himself and mankind.

Blenheim smoothed back his already smooth blond hair as he pictured his reunion with the delectable Timona. It would be a touching scene, yes, but somewhat fraught with delicate difficulties. He would have to gently remind Miss Timona that he, Blenheim, could not be in two places at once. She knew he had to meet with the agents in Pennsylvania concerning her family's affairs. He was not yet on familiar enough terms with her to berate her, but the gentle reminder should be enough. She would blush and laugh and perhaps make a pretty apology for not being on the train with her father.

And she would mention her photography only after

she had listened to his account of his travels in America and after she asked a few intelligent questions about company business.

He would not worry about Miss Timona. Yet.

But what if she grew as impossibly single-minded as the old buffoon for whom he worked?

Blenheim admired her form and pretty, gamine face. He respected her lively intelligence. He adored her vast quantities of money. His own fair good looks and her darker beauty would, he hoped, combine to make attractive little Blenheims someday.

Yet there was only so much eccentricity a man could tolerate. Was it possible that as she grew older she would be more like the old man in front of him? He closed his eyes. Dreadful thought.

"Porter. Whisky and soda at once."

The deferential porter rushed to obey. Only the whisky, and the thought that Timona might become more like Griffin, her decidedly clearheaded older brother, kept Blenheim cheerful.

Mick was having a wonderful dream. A lovely, soft woman floated in his arms. This was the kind of dream he did not want to wake from.

He woke up. A lovely, soft woman was in his arms.

She faced away from him and a vaguely familiar scent filled his nose. Maybe the scent lingered from a dream he'd forgotten, a haunting recollection of the country, a sunny meadow.

No. The fragrance came from the woman's hair and skin. Half awake, he leaned forward into the sea of dark hair and sniffed. *A Dhia*, this put sweet clover to shame. He'd never drunk in anything as simply wonderful in his life.

Jesus.

Miss Whatever-her-name. Started with a "Cal." He instantly inched away from her. But she moved right along with him. Her sweetly rounded rear end wiggled against him and she murmured a happy, sleepy noise. Saints, no wonder he was having one of those dreams when her bottom rubbed against him like that.

Daisy would skin him alive.

But then again, he argued with himself and the absent Daisy, a man did have needs. Daisy was a good girl and had made it very clear that she would submit to a man only if his ring was on her finger.

Daisy had also made it clear that what she didn't know about would not harm her. She said as much in the park one day, when he tried to give her a kiss. She added something like men have needs virtuous women didn't even know about.

It wasn't entirely nonsense, he decided as he breathed in the little prostitute's fragrance. He definitely had needs.

He'd test her a bit. If she jumped, acted skittish, he'd know she wasn't ready to take on more men yet. He'd stop, right away. He hoped.

Of course he would stop. No point in patching up creatures if you only injured them yourself.

Some of her hair lay across her face, so he carefully pushed the strands back. The hair was as silky as he recalled from the night before. He leaned over her and pressed his face close to hers. Not quite a kiss, but he hovered close, nearly touching, breathing in her sweet meadow scent.

Mick had shared his bed with other people; at home he'd awakened with one of his younger brothers more often than not. But never in his life had he slept the night through with a woman in his bed.

Beyond his hunger for her, he was enchanted by the

cozy warmth of her and sight of the flushed, vulnerable face asleep in the gray dawn light.

Then she opened her eyes and smiled. No shock, no backing away. A large smile. Just like the small one he'd seen the night before, but with gleaming white teeth added to the knowing look. He felt a trifle let down. He didn't want her to act entirely shy and foolish, but somehow, he wished she didn't look so sly.

"Good morning, Mr. McCann," she whispered and twisted towards him. "Are you about to kiss me? I should like that."

Not what you'd call a worldly remark, he reflected. He leaned forward and obliged her. Did prostitutes kiss? This one didn't even seem to know how. Her mouth was too tight, lips all stiffly puckered.

"Come on now," he whispered. "Don't give me a smack like you do your da." He glided a finger over her lips to smooth them. "Soften them, like so."

He leaned towards her again, and she seemed to have learned the lesson remarkably quickly. Her mouth was velvet and succulent. A few minutes later, when he slipped his tongue between her lips, she opened for him. And pushed her whole body towards him.

"Ah, much better, much," he murmured. He reclaimed her clean-tasting, sleep-warmed mouth as he ran his hands over some of the best curves it had been his privilege to touch. Her skin matched her scent: delicate, rare. And softer than anything he'd imagined. His own body shouted in silent, yearning joy, more than ready for a good, long drink of woman after a drought.

His head pounded with blood—since the moment he'd first caught the scent of her, he'd felt as if he'd suddenly begun to produce far too much blood.

"Jesus," he whispered. "I want you something fierce."

"Jaysus," she imitated softly.

They whispered as if a third person lay in the room. Someone they must not disturb. Daisy, perhaps.

Mick felt another twinge of guilt. He'd only met Daisy a month ago, but already had vague ideas of a future with her.

Miss Cal-whatever whispered hesitantly, "Yes. It is quite all right. I mean, this is different, isn't it. This is not at all the same as yesterday. Um. So it would be a good thing to do, wouldn't it?"

"Oh, no, no." He felt as if his heart would break. He'd grown too cynical. Despite the too-sly smile, despite her sins, she was a fellow human and perhaps as lonely as he often felt.

"No, no? As in you don't want to now?"

He grinned at her. "No, no. As in this must be different from those men or I will shoot meself."

Her face emptied of all smile and she suddenly looked blank, almost afraid. "Jaysus," she whispered. "You have the loveliest smile I have ever seen in my life, Michael McCann."

His was gripped by another qualm at her words. And she seemed too intent as she examined him. He could feel her warm breath coming fast on his face, as if she panted. How those mossy green eyes stared at him. He couldn't make out their odd color in the pale dawn, but he could see they were serious. Would she somehow latch on to him after they made love?

It was one thing to adopt a kitten. But this one would require more than an occasional bit of fish. He had to smile at the ridiculous thought of this woman hanging around his door. For one, she was too cool a customer. She obviously took care of herself, as well as a harebrained old father.

Calverson. That was her name.

Her accent was not like the working-class English he'd met in New York. Her scent, her looks were so alien to him—the thought struck him that she might come from money. But she was far too worldly to be a pampered rich girl. Likely she worked at one of the better bordellos, and had been taught to speak like a lady.

Then she chased away all thought when she lowered her thick dark lashes over the greeny eyes and leaned towards him, with her lips slightly parted. Maybe some other man could say no to that invitation. Mick would sprout wings and fly first. He pushed his mouth on to hers, and slipped his hands up under the shirt she wore. Oh, Lord. Her breasts were warm and fuller than he expected. He gently rubbed the pads of his thumbs across their tips. The soft noise she made between a sigh and groan could have come from his own throat the way it yanked at him.

He pulled her against him. She wedged her leg, still clad in the filthy britches, over his hip, and he hummed his approval as he slid his hand over her leg to her behind. With both hands he cupped the sweet curves of her bottom and pressed against her, hard, rhythmically. She gasped, a soft moan that might have been pleasure.

Or surprise, or dismay.

Gentle. He fought the urgent drive to shove down her britches, and shove into her as soon as humanly possible.

One last try at sanity. He'd come up for air. And introduce the invisible person haunting the room.

Artificially, of course, but he didn't know how else to do it. He said, surprised at the huskiness of his voice, "You are so pretty. Just as pretty as Daisy."

She reacted as he thought she might. She pulled away.

He had to suck a deep breath and remind himself not to go after the tantalizing body that now lay several inches away.

"Daisy. Oh. And she is?"

"Daisy Graves. A girl I know. I'm seeing her this afternoon."

"Are you, are you engaged to her?" He heard caution in her voice and knew he was right to mention Daisy. The woman, despite her fallen state, did have some thought of him beyond a good, friendly bout of sex.

"Not exactly. But there is an understanding, I think."

"That you are engaged?"

"Something like." Not really, but perhaps eventually.

She lightly kissed his cheek, a more pleasant reaction than he might expect. But, oh, blast, perhaps a dismissal. "Will you tell her anything about this?" she asked.

He almost laughed at the idea. "She would not want to know. If you understand me."

"No. I don't think I do, Mr. McCann." She did not sound offended, but actually confused.

Hell. He wasn't certain he understood either. And this woman's warm self so close meant he was having trouble breathing properly, let alone thinking. But he'd try. "A man has needs."

"But what about Daisy Graves?"

"She would not have the same needs."

Miss Calverson shook her head, her loose hair shushed softly against the pillow. "Maybe not yet, she doesn't. She will. I did not think I had those particular needs either."

"What changed?"

"I met you," she said, casual as can be.

Uh-oh. What the hell did that mean? Mick, even in a full blown, painful state of desire, understood he truly had to pull back.

He would remind her about the line. That would be enough to make her either feel ashamed or see red fury.

"No. That's not it at all," he said gently. "Miss Graves is a good girl, you see."

She stared at him blankly, and then groaned. "This might be a problem," she muttered as if speaking to herself. "Your world is divided between virgins and fallen women."

He'd been ready for her anger, but not this. He'd heard that kind of phrase before. "Look here, you think that just because I am Irish—"

"Not just because you're Irish." She shoved up on an elbow to lean close and look him in the eye. "Because you are male."

He had no reply to that. Hell, he wished he'd just kept kissing her instead of introducing so damn many words into the situation. He'd be in her by now, if he'd kept quiet. In her and in heaven. The thought made him dizzy with a wave of raw, heart-stopping, groin-aching lust. He slipped his hands up the curves of her side and tried to pull her back against him.

She made a disgusted noise, and flipped onto her back, out of his grip. Her mouth opened as she took a deep breath. No question, she had plenty to say. He supposed he deserved it.

"I don't think it can be that simple, Mr. McCann. Photography. Now that is a matter of light and shadow."

He frowned. Still clutched by the astounding hunger for her, he wondered how the devil pictures came into the matter.

"Hey?"

"Photography is black and white. Yet even gray is not full color, and you can't—"

A sudden clattering and thumping interrupted her. Someone banged at the door.

"Mr. Mick!"

Timona clamped her mouth shut. Was she really about to blather on about photographs again? Mr.

Blenheim was right. She needed to correct that ten-
dency.

Michael McCann slid away from her. He groaned,
clapped a large hand to his forehead and shoved his
fingers through sweetly bed-rumpled hair. And oh, my,
the man had gorgeous forearms. Muscular and with
red-gold hair.

He shouted, "Rob? What is it?"

There were more thumps coming down the stairs.
"Mr. Mick!" several voices shouted. "Fire!"

He had the door open before Timona, made awk-
ward by her sore muscles, had managed to scramble
out of the crater in the center of the bed. A group of
faces surrounded Mr. McCann, mostly young children,
and one weeping woman.

They stood in a semi-circle looking up at the man,
who already reeled off instructions. "Rob. You'd best
take the pump since it needs strength. It's a bitch to
work of late."

Mr. McCann shoved his billy club toward a boy
dressed only in a long undershirt. "Petey, you go downstairs and wait. Do not bang the curb for help unless
Rob gives you the word. Got it? Only then. Or what happens?"

"Or you'll use it on my behind."

"That's right, boy-o." He snapped his fingers, and
Botty scampered to his side. Mick pointed down the
stairs. "Botty, you can't follow me. Go with Petey. Go
on."

The dog tucked what was left of its rear end between
its legs, and trailed reluctantly after the boy down the
stairs.

Mick shoved his hands into the pockets of his
trousers. "Where is the blasted whistle?"

One of the boys spoke up. "Remember? You gave it

to the leddie in the next door building when she said she feared her old man friend."

"Damn. The stick'll have to do. The rest of you, on the stairs, the way you practiced. Be ready to pass the buckets or bang doors and run when I give the word." He looked around the little group and groaned.

"Aw, saints, Jenny, where's Tuck?"

The stout woman in the hall began to wail "Tuck-uck-ucker."

Jenny pressed close to Mick and a baby started to wail.

"Ho, now, watch Quint, Jen."

He took the infant from the wailing woman and absently passed it over to Timona who held the screaming, squirming baby under its arms, and away from herself. Her dearest friend Araminta was probably good with babies, but Timona wasn't sure what to do with the squirming handful.

Mr. McCann, striding back into the room, stopped to flip the baby onto its belly, so it lay face down on Timona's arm. "Like this, see. Poor mite likely has gas. This eases it."

How on earth did he know about babies? For a moment she wondered if he had a wife and children back in Ireland. No. He would surely have some memento of that other life if he did.

Mr. McCann pulled a rumpled handkerchief out of a pocket of the frock coat, dipped the cloth in water, and then tied it across his face. He grabbed his dripping wet blue coat, and the large pot full of water stained with something dark. With a chill, she realized it was probably her own blood he'd washed from his coat.

He started up the stairs, his strong legs taking the steps three at a time. As he ran he called down, "Jenny, love, stop the wailing. Save your breath. We might need you to wake anyone who miraculously slept through this."

The noise ended at once.

It had been perhaps thirty seconds since the banging and mayhem had started. Mr. McCann had his troops ready and pressed into action. Timona trailed after him, awkwardly clutching the baby, and wondering how she should help. The child stationed in the hall gaped at her instead of watching Mr. McCann tear up the stairs.

A door opened. A fat, unshaven man in an under-shirt glared at the children on the stairs. "Fire? Again?"

The girl nodded.

The man bellowed up the stairs. "Mick? You taking care of it?"

Mick's voice floated down. "Aye, Jim. I'm thinking it's not so bad. We'll knock you up if need be."

The man yawned, then retreated into his flat and slammed the door.

"Why're you dressed like that, ma'am?" the girl asked, but Timona was up the stairs following after Mr. McCann. The fire must be at the top of the building, for the air grew hazy with smoke as she slowly climbed the stairs. The charred, sharp stench stung her eyes and nose.

"I shan't go any higher," she reassured the baby, who seemed to be falling asleep on her arm. "I just wish to know where he is."

She soon reached the next flight, where Jenny stood next to Rob at the pump. "I wondered where little Quinton'd got to," said the plump, dark-haired woman, still sniffing after her bout of tears. She wiped her face with the back of a hand and held out her arms. "I can take him back. I'm fine now."

Timona clumsily thrust the baby towards her.

"You're a girl, ain't you?" said Jenny, as she settled the baby in the crook of her arm. She had a strong southern American accent. "So why are you dressed like that?"

Timona wondered why these people cared more about her clothes than the fire.

A thicker puff of acrid smoke drifted down the stairway.

"It's a long story," she said politely. "Where is Mr. McCann?"

"Our place is the top of the building. One more flight up." The older boy pointed. "That's where the fire is. Don't worry. It's not a bad one, I think. Maybe even I coulda put it out but Ma thought we'd best rouse Mr. Mick. Hey, ma'am,' he called after her, "if you're going up past our Henry, you ought to get down low. That's what Mr. Mick says to do. Air's better when you go on your hands and knees."

Timona climbed past their Henry, who stood at attention and solemnly stared up into the smoky hall above them.

On the top floor, the hot, thick air brought tears to her eyes, and her lungs hurt with every inhalation. Instinctively, she dropped to all fours. Should she bang on the doors before the other tenants suffocated?

The door to the flat was wide open and as she crawled, she could see the dim figure of Mr. McCann stomping on a smoking cloth. His wet coat, she realized. Even as she watched, the smoke began to die away.

She coughed and crawled to the doorway. "Do you need any help?" she called hoarsely.

"I don't. 'Tis out. I'll just be fetching Tucker." The damp handkerchief muffled his voice, but she could hear he sounded almost cheerful.

"What about the Tuckers' neighbors? They might be having trouble breathing."

"You can knock up the neighbors if you think it best, but this time is not bad enough to worry about."

She wondered what the place was like when it was bad enough.

He headed to the back of the room. She couldn't see him in the dark and smoke. She waited and for a long moment her chest hurt with something more painful than the smoldering air. Get out of there, she wanted to scream. She gulped a few smoke-filled, shallow breaths, forgetting that she should not do so, in all the confusion.

Mr. McCann appeared in the door, the lanky figure of an unconscious man draped across his back and shoulders. With one hand he pushed down the hand-kerchief tied across his face. He grinned at her. "Feathers stink something awful, eh?"

She stopped herself from racing to him and throwing her arms around him.

He started down the stairs, and was two flights down, when Timona heard the sound of retching.

Mr. McCann's voice drifted up the stairwell, half-laughing, half-groaning. "God help us, Tuck, couldn't you wait til you got outside?"

Timona thumped down the stairs after him. She felt like laughing aloud. Her hair and skin and clothes smelled of smoke, but Mr. McCann would stink far more.

She slowed her steps as she remembered Daisy. Perhaps she should ignore Daisy's existence? Timona at once amended that thoughtless resolve.

She'd meet the woman first.

If Daisy didn't appreciate the treasure she held, then Timona would work as hard as she could to take Mr. McCann for herself. She'd transform herself into a bandit, a pirate, or even a coquette. Whatever it took.

Chapter 3

Timona spent the first hours of the new day helping to clean the reeking apartment. Mrs. Kelly and Mrs. Hurley, who lived in the building, worked with them for an hour or so, and even the widow on the bottom floor pitched in. She took in the younger members of the Tucker family, which seemed to surprise everyone.

"Her place is the biggest flat in the building," Rob told Timona, as they trailed down the stairs from the Tucker's flat.

Henry, who was ten, added, "We get one room of her place, and she has two more. But it's not for long. She's already told us five times it's just until we get the worst of the smoke out and the place cleaned up."

At the bottom of the steps, they met Mick coming out of the widow's flat, where he'd checked on the still-unconscious Tucker.

Mick looked up at them, his brow furrowed. "Jenny, Rob. It's time to talk, but it'd best be over breakfast at Colsun's. Henry, you come along and we'll get victuals for the little ones and Tuck. And the widow."

"And Botty," added Henry.

"Of course," said Mick and grinned at him. He turned to Timona and gave her a blank look, almost as if he wasn't sure who she was. "You coming along, then?"

Timona touched his arm as the group trooped out the door. "Mr. McCann."

In the small foyer, she pulled him aside. "I, ah, told Mrs. Tucker my name is Cooper. I hope you don't mind calling me that?"

He shook his arm free and scowled down at her. "Are you wanted by the law, Miss Calverson?"

"Nothing like that. No. I will explain later, but I promise you that I am not a fugitive."

He squinted at her for a long moment. "All right then. Miss Cooper it is. And even if you are a hardened criminal, you come on and down a bit of food. You must be half starved."

They walked out the door. On the sidewalk, he stopped for a moment and turned to face her. He pushed back his shoulders, folded his arms and stood, legs apart, shifting from boot to boot. The universal stance of a policeman.

He didn't look her in the face. Instead he gazed over her shoulder, as if searching for something behind her, and spoke in a halting mutter. "Er. I don't know if . . . um. I should apologize for going at you this morning. Even if tis your usual, ah . . . After your rough day yesterday, I didn't think . . . So. I am truly sorry."

She was fascinated to see him blush. Before she could answer, he strode away, so fast she had to trot to catch up with him.

Mick led them to Colsun's Restaurant, a dingy, crowded room in the first floor of a building down the street. It had a stale fug that Timona suspected would cling to anyone who even walked past the place: a mix of cigars, grease, and coffee.

The wooden floor of Colsun's was dark and scarred

and probably hadn't been swept in days. The hard chairs were almost as dirty as the floor they stuck to.

Most of the patrons were laboring men taking a quick breakfast before heading off to work. Rob, Jenny, and Mick settled at a table. Timona had followed after them and sat down, hoping to look as if she belonged.

She now wore a gown that smelled of smoke, hung like a tent on her, and was a purple so loud it gave her stomach pains. But it was a dress, not the boy's breeches she'd worn, and she felt nothing but gratitude to Jenny for it. Her feet fit into a pair of thick leather boots that nobody needed right now. They were too small for Rob and too big for the next boy down.

The two waiters lounged in a corner, chatting and ignoring the customers.

At last one of them ambled over and cleared off their table. He removed his toothpick, rubbed his hands on the stained apron covering his front, then plopped a thick, white mug of coffee down in front of each of them.

"Eggs, please, Teddy," Mick told the waiter, and said to the others, "Be right back." He went to the back of the restaurant and pulled open the kitchen door. He cupped his hands and shouted something over the din into the kitchen.

A burly, scowling man soon appeared with a basket for Henry to take back to the widow's apartment. Mick paid the man and strolled toward the table, stopped by several people along the way. He smiled and shook his head. They'd invited him to sit down.

A popular man, Mr. McCann.

He handed the basket to Henry and gave the boy an affectionate pat on the shoulder. "Not too heavy for you?"

"Mr. Mick!" Henry was scornful. Then he must have caught his mother's eye, for he gave them each a polite nod of the head, and raced out of the restaurant toting the basket with two hands.

When Mick sat down, Rob and Jenny looked over at him expectantly, as if he held the answer to all of their unasked questions.

Timona picked at the runny scrambled eggs and listened.

"Thing is, I think you have to watch Tuck every time now when he smokes his pipe." said Mick, as he spread something that probably wasn't butter onto his toast.

"It's the fourth time the poor man has fallen asleep while smoking." Jenny put down her mug. "You think he'd learn."

Rob glanced around the crowded, noisome little café as if he were afraid someone might be listening. "He can't help it, Ma."

"He was drunk," Jenny said. "That's why."

Timona stopped chewing when she saw that Mick was watching her, Timona, with narrowed eyes.

"Miss Calverson, don't you be thinking Tucker is some kind of drunk just cause he's got no work and is poor," Mr. McCann said in a low voice that only she was supposed to hear.

Honestly, he was touchy. She swallowed the mouthful of disgusting egg. "I didn't think any such—"

"Ma'am, my pa drinks because he is sick." Rob must have overheard after all. "Mr. Mick, it was my fault. He woke in the middle of the night, aching something fierce. So he had me fetch his pipe and gin. I meant to stay awake but I fell back to sleep. Wasn't his fault. Poor Pa is sick as they come, Miss Cooper."

Mick opened his mouth, but before he could speak, Jenny wailed, "Not so sickly. My Tucker is not so ill."

Mick handed her a handkerchief. "Jenny. It's hard, but now's the time we got to figure something out."

We, thought Timona. The man was wonderful.

Mick spoke to Jenny. "You posted that letter to Tucker's brother? Have you got word back yet?"

Jenny sniffed and nodded miserably. "He'd be willing to take us on."

Rob, again acting as interpreter, explained to Timona, "Uncle Dave's our only relative. He's got a farm in Indiana or some such place. Out west of here. Chickens, I think."

"Turkeys. Horrible birds." Jenny clicked her tongue. Her thick, dark eyebrows knit into a scowl. "I hate to leave New York. Won't be no good for Tucker neither."

"The children, Jen," Mr. McCann stroked her shoulder. "They're your first worry and this is no place for them. Look, love, you have had a long night. What do you say you go back to the widow's for a rest, and to see how Tuck is faring. He'd want you there, and anyhow, I don't suppose your young Sarey's up for much nursing. I'll just get Rob another cup, and we'll chat until he has to go to work."

Jenny nodded and pushed back her chair.

Mick got to his feet, too. He picked up her shawl from the floor, and handed it to her.

A gentleman. Timona couldn't remember the last time she watched someone perform an act of kindness without expecting a tip or some other, less tangible reward.

Jenny wrapped the shawl around her plump, disheveled figure. "I'll go to Tucker. Nice to meet you, miss. Thank you for your help."

Timona stood, and offered Jenny her hand. "I am very glad to meet you too, Mrs. Tucker. And thank you again for the use of the gown."

Jenny shook her hand, looked her up and down, and smiled. "Looks pretty on you, I'd say, Miss Cooper. Suits you." She looked at Mr. McCann. "Much prettier than . . . well, least said, soonest mended."

Mick's mouth went tight, and Timona guessed she was talking about Daisy. She'd never competed with another woman before, but she would imagine the good opinion of friends would help her cause.

She sat back down and watched Jenny trail out the door.

Mick cleared his throat. "Begging your pardon, miss, but I should talk to Rob for a few minutes."

"Ah." She stood up again and wondered where she should go.

"No, Mr. Mick. It's fine for her to be here. Go on. I suppose I know what you'll say."

"Aye, well." Mr. McCann turned away from Timona. He put a large hand on the boy's shoulder. "Rob. I'd say it's a matter of days. Maybe weeks at most. Tucker's not going to be with us much longer. When I took a look at him just now, I couldn't rouse him. His heartbeat's even more irregular, too."

Timona gasped, but the boy only nodded, and frowned down at his hands encircling the white coffee mug.

Mr. McCann kept his hand on Rob's shoulder. Timona strained to hear his soft voice. "Thing is, when he goes, Jenny might not do so well for a while. Maybe a long while. She must know he's dying, I tried telling her, so has Dr. O'Toole. But she won't, she can't . . ."

For a moment, the unflappable Mr. McCann stopped talking. He stared at a crust of bread that lay on the table. "She won't admit it and so I reckon she'll have to do all her mourning when he goes. You're the eldest. You'll be in charge."

"That's not fair, he's practically a child." Timona must have been tired or she would never have interrupted. Two pairs of blue eyes looked at her in amazement. She dropped her gaze to the greasy oil-cloth.

"I'm nearly fourteen," said Rob indignantly. "I'm apprenticed to the blacksmith."

"I agree with Miss, er, Cooper. 'Tisn't fair to you."

Timona gaped at Mick, surprised by his agreement. He continued, "But it won't be for long, Rob. Just til you get to your uncle. T'others will count on you. Good thing you're a strong lad. Sarey'll be a help with the youngest ones. You'll get by. But here's the other thing . . ." Mr. McCann cleared his throat. "I wonder if you've seen the letter. Because it might be your ma wasn't entirely . . ."

Rob croaked. "Oh. You mean there might be no letter from Uncle Dave."

"And when your da passes on, you'll have to move fast before you run out of money, and your mam goes back to her old job as barmaid and starts drin—" He stopped talking and coughed. When he darted a quick, wary glance at Timona, she resisted the urge to roll her eyes at him.

Rob said, "I may need some help, Mr. Mick. And I need to borrow money to go out there. And I don't know what all I have to do."

"A' course I'll help," Mick said.

"Me too." Timona piped up. "I'll help."

She looked up from the table and met Mick's blue, frowning eyes. The chilled gaze disappointed her. A few hours before she had practically melted from the heat of those eyes.

He tilted his head and examined her for a long moment, then said, "You'll be back with your da, miss. We're looking into that this morning."

She shrugged. "It appears to me you have enough on your plate, Mr. McCann. I think I worried too much for my father yesterday. I shall make sure that Papa's secretary is with him. Then I need no longer worry."

"Secretary?" Mr. McCann's face puckered as if she

had said something obscene. "I thought your da was some kind of fool, the way you spoke of him. A secretary?"

She picked up her mug and gulped down a swallow of dreadful, boiled coffee. She gathered the man was a tremendous snob about the English and, she now understood, about people with money. She had to step carefully until she had him ensnared.

"Never mind the secretary. A fancy name for a type of caretaker." She would feel guilty about calling Mr. Blenheim a caretaker except, come to think of it, the title often fit the poor gentleman's job description. "We must worry about Mr. Tucker and his family. Not me."

Rob stood up. "It's past my time, Mr. Mick. I'm off to Biggens's shop. Glad to meet you Miss Cooper. Thank you for all of your help with the family and all."

Timona smiled. "It was a pleasure, Mr. Tucker. And I must apologize for speaking out of hand earlier when I said you were practically a child. I was a careless wretch when I was young, and I forget that other young people are far more responsible. If I were your mother, I would thank my lucky stars for giving me a young man like you to turn to."

Rob's young face lit as if she had bestowed a medal on him. He tugged at his wool cap and sauntered out of the restaurant.

Mick laughed. "Now you'll have a slave for life, Miss Calverson."

"I meant what I said."

He studied her for a moment. "Yes, and it's a good thing to have said, at that. Make the boy proud of himself—it'll likely be the only reward he gets." His last words sounded grim and Timona wondered if he spoke of Rob or himself.

"There's the reward of seeing his family thrive," she

ventured, and Mick smiled at her at last. He had the kind of eyes that sparkled when he was pleased.

The crowd in Colsun's had begun to thin out. A scraggly unshaved man walked into the restaurant. He stopped and bellowed across the crowded tables. "You were right about me collywobbles, McCann. That stuff you gave me cleared me runs right up."

A voice from behind the counter shouted even louder. "No talk of collywobbles in my establishment, damn you."

Mick raised his coffee mug to them both. "*Dia duit ar maidin*—Good morning to you, too, gentlemen."

Timona laughed.

Mick shook his head. "A class establishment, eh? Right again, miss." He swallowed the last of his coffee with seeming relish, and rose to his feet. "So now we find your da and his, er, secretary and send you on your way. Mebbe as we go you can tell me why you're parading part time as Cooper, too."

Hell's bells, she thought. This is not good.

Chapter 4

Mick paid Teddy the waiter and they strolled out of the restaurant. As they started towards Park Avenue, Timona decided to resort to basic tactics.

She grabbed at his arm and gasped. "Might we stop for a moment, Mr. McCann. I- I think I feel a little faint."

He looked so worried she felt a trifle guilty. Not ashamed enough to actually change tactics. "Oooo. Mr. McCann, I think I have to return to your flat. The world is spinning."

She made a soft moan. He grabbed her arm, pulled her close and wrapped an arm around her. It felt lovely to be pressed against his warm, solid side. At least she didn't ask him to carry her up the stairs.

The hideous Botty trotted along after them, Mick stopped to rub the dog's back. She figured the injuries extended to Botty's throat, for she already noticed that he didn't bark but made a huffing growl of a sound instead. He made the noise now, and half-closed his one eye in ecstasy as Mick rubbed his fur.

"That's enough now, Botty. I got work to do," Mick said. Botty immediately squirmed into his spot under the bureau.

* * *

The oppressive dankness of the dim room pressed in on Timona as she lay on the bed, watching Mick attempt to wash some of his clothes. What could he do to entertain himself living alone in a place like this?

"Mr. McCann," she said, trying to sound weak, but not desperately ill—the man had worries enough. "What do you do on your free time? I mean other than walk out with Daisy Graves."

He straightened up from the large pan, where he was trying to scrub out a shirt.

"Don't get much free time," he said. He squinted at the shirt and poked it. "Ach. An ash must have landed here. I think this has got a hole burnt clean through. Small at least."

"I can see you are busy." Saving every forlorn creature in his little corner of the world was busy work. "Is there anything you do when you need, oh, I don't know, cheering up? Play cards. Go out for a beer. That sort of thing."

He shook his head. "Can't, often. My family back home needs every spare penny. Debts."

"Do you spend all your time here and at work?"

He squeezed the water out of the shirt, threw it into the other pan, and put some other clothes into the tub.

"I see a show now and then. New York has some fine theater. The library is free and . . ." He hesitated. The way he straightened up and began to fiddle with the cuff of his rolled-up shirt sleeve made her wonder if he was about to confess that he murdered and skinned kittens.

"So I do read. And I, uh, play the flute some."

She forgot she was supposed to feel ill and sat up excitedly. "Oh do you? I love the flute. My brother plays. Do you have one?"

He reached behind the rickety bureau and pulled

out a battered wooden instrument that didn't look like any flute Timona had ever seen.

"It was my da's. He started to teach me, but then he died. I messed about, but never got proper lessons. Back at home, I could screech on it all day long and no one but the sheep and the cow would care. It's crowded here, so I don't like to blow it for too long at a stretch."

"Please, will you play for me?"

"You certain you want to hear?"

She nodded. "Absolutely."

He sat straight-backed at the edge of the bed and put the wooden instrument to his mouth. She was not prepared for the quiet, haunting music he played.

"My goodness," she breathed.

He stopped and grimaced. "I'm not trained, you know, and the animals are not what you'd call good judg—"

"Michael McCann, just play. Please."

He played for about five minutes. Some of it sounded familiar to her, but not the winding, climbing tunes that grew in complexity and then died away. His music was often sweet but she thought she heard hints of wild and wistful sorrow. Timona had heard beautiful music in her travels, but none that had filled her with such longing. She wished someone would discover dinosaur bones in Ireland so she could follow her father there, and find out if Mick played music from his homeland.

"You are wonderful," she whispered when he laid the flute on his lap and gazed at a spot on the bed somewhere near her feet.

She would never allow him to play for anyone else. Women would fall in love with him purely because of that flute. Or whatever it was.

He blushed and started mumbling again, nonsense about lack of training, and she interrupted. "Mr. Mc-

Cann. I have heard musicians from many countries. And I say you are wonderful."

"Eh, thank you," he muttered at last.

She must have been under a spell. "Mr. McCann."

"Mick."

"Mick. I was just wondering, would you consider marrying me?"

Mistake. He blinked at her. Then, thank goodness, instead of screaming in horror, he laughed. "I play that well?"

She forced herself to smile. "Yes," she said. "You do." She cleared her throat. "So you don't mind if I call you Mick? Would you call me Timona?"

"Timona? What kind of a name is that when it's at home?"

"I was named for one of Shakespeare's characters."

He rubbed his bristly chin and squinted at her as he thought for a moment. "Timon. Wasn't he the whatyemaycallit? The lad who didn't care for the company of his fellow man."

Timona gaped at him. Many well-educated people didn't know the play *Timon of Athens*—thank goodness.

"Yes, that's the one."

"Mighty peculiar name to give a baby girl," he said, and she nodded her vigorous agreement. "D'you mind if I call ye Timmy?"

If anyone else had said such a thing, she might have drawn herself up and said, yes, she did mind. But the way he said it, drawn out in his melodic, slow voice— "Temmay"—was so sweet. And intimate.

"Please. Be my guest," she said weakly.

He finished washing out his clothes and a stack of the Tucker kids' clothes. He shoved them into the pan to take out to the clothesline. She pretended to sleep and actually dozed for a while.

She woke to the soft sound of splashing water. He

had his back to her. He'd stripped to the waist and was leaning over to rinse off in the large pan.

Well. There stood a sight she would never grow tired of. She wished the board that covered most of the room's one window was gone and the window faced something other than another building's wall. Anything so there'd be more sun lighting the scene.

His shoulders and back were almost ivory colored, and smooth. His arms were golden until just above the elbows. Perhaps the tan lingered from his days at the farm, for she did not imagine he rolled up his sleeves on his policeman's beat.

His back was broad at the top and narrowed down to his hips. The muscles under his skin moved as he scrubbed at his neck and shoulders.

If she were taking a photograph of a man's back, this would be the back she'd choose. And the angle she'd want. More light was all that was needed. He'd show up massive, strong as a mountain. Yet his shoulder blades and spine added a delicacy to the lines of his back's broad planes. As marvelous as any landscape she'd attempted to capture.

He dried off with a ragged towel, then carefully balanced a small mirror on the bureau for shaving. Their eyes met in the mirror.

"Feeling better?" he asked as he swiftly reached down and snatched up an undershirt. He jammed it over his head, to Timona's regret.

"A little. But I can see you are preparing to go out. We won't have time to track down my father today, will we."

He rubbed soapy hands on his face, twisted his cheek towards the mirror and carefully scraped with the straight-edge razor.

"I've been thinking. Perhaps we can convince the widow to let you stay the night downstairs. I might be

able to take a couple hours off tomorrow, call it police
business. That is if you truly need me help. I reckon you
don't, really. If you're frightened—no, don't make a
face, makes sense you would be—I know a couple o'
street boys who'll be glad to hire out for protection til
you feel more secure. Not all of 'em are bent on de-
struction as the ones you met up with yesterday."

She'd have to continue to undermine his efficient
planning. On the other hand, she could tell him part
of the truth, the part she figured would appeal to him.

"Mr.—um, Mick. I know you are a busy man, but before I leave New York there is one thing I hope you
could help me with."

"Hmm?"

She knew she didn't imagine the wary look in the
eyes that met hers in the little mirror.

"The girl I met yesterday. I think . . . The truth is I
don't think she wants to be in that place. She struck me
as too timid to escape, though. And I think there are
other girls like her there. And boys, too."

His eyes looked pained, and she hurried on. "It's just
that I asked Jenny Tucker about it earlier, while we
started to clean up her place. She said the police are
usually no help in these matters. I know you're a policeman, so you can tell me that she is wrong and where
I should go for help. And . . ."

The wariness was even more pronounced. His hands
had stopped and she realized he had not moved. He
stood stock still. His eyes stared into hers in the small
mirror.

"Mick?" she said hesitantly.

"Aye?"

"Tell me. What shall I do?"

He seemed to wake up. He put down the razor and
rubbed his face with the towel. "Let it be. There's
naught you can do. You can't save every suffering being

in the city." Her heart twisted when she understood he probably often had to repeat those words to himself.

"Mr. McCann. I am not out to save the whole city. That is a job for the police. Not me."

Again he froze, and she knew that it wasn't just the hopelessness of sheer numbers that weighed on him.

"Mick?" she said and stopped. Ah. Now she remembered. Her brother had mentioned New York corruption. It was one of the reasons Griffin enjoyed doing business with Tammany Hall.

She spoke slowly. "The man yesterday, at that house. He must pay off someone in the police department. That's what Jenny meant. Tell me it isn't you. Oh, no, Mick."

"Not me, exactly," he said slowly as if he talked to himself. "But close enough."

He turned around and looked at her, as if trying to take her measure. Then he turned his back again. He thumped the bureau violently. She wondered if he was taking his aggression out on the furniture, until she realized the drawers were just sticky.

When he faced her again, he showed her a fist full of disorganized bills. Money. "This is what I get. It's what all us coppers get, even an unambitious man like myself."

"Payoff for protection?"

"And for turning our backs," he said, and with a bark of unamused laughter he added, "You are a smart woman. I was going to give you some, anyway. Go ahead and steal all the money if you need to, Timmy. Just wait until I'm out of here. And whatever you take, leave the flute, if you please."

She sighed with relief. He wasn't corrupt, only caught up in a corrupt system. "This job is not for you, Michael McCann. You are too honest and you care. It'll either kill you or kill the honesty and I don't know which would be worse."

He raised his eyebrows. "And in less than one day you know so much about me? No. I don't think so, Miss Timmy. I like getting money, you know."

She snickered. "That's why you're spending it on a fancy place to live and new clothes."

The clock outside struck one o'clock.

"Oh blast!" he said. "Would you mind stepping outside? I must get ready. I'm going to be late to see Daisy."

"Will she raise a fuss?" asked Timona hopefully.

"No, not Daisy. She's a good-natured girl."

Hell's bells.

Chapter 5

Mick left, looking uncomfortable in a stiff collar, a bowler hat and a lounging jacket with a matching waistcoat that was too tight across the chest, though perhaps that was in style. His trousers, hemmed too short, showed off his obviously new, buttoned boots with cloth tops. He'd made an attempt to tame and straighten his unruly copper hair. Definitely a mistake, thought Timona, who much preferred the curls.

She'd been visiting the Tuckers, and came down to say good bye. She watched him go, thinking how much better he looked in his more simple clothing. Timona did not think much of uncomfortable clothing and usually disdained fashion when it came to bulky pinching corsets, thick padding, or huge bustles. At least Mick didn't appear to have a fondness for extremely loud checked trousers, a strange favorite of many young men she'd seen in New York.

"No," said Mick sternly when Botty tried to follow him down the steps. The dog turned and slunk back up the stairs.

Timona tried to comfort Botty, but he ignored her and slipped back under the bureau.

After Mick left, Timona knew she had to stay busy, or her mind would dwell on the most unpleasant moments of the day before.

After bidding good-bye to the growling Botty, she walked down the four flights of stairs to knock on the widow's door.

The frowning woman did not look interested in any more visitors, Timona was glad to see. Chances were Timona would be sleeping in Mick's flat again. She grinned, delighted at the idea. The widow glared back at her smile, so instead of harassing the woman with a plea for help, Timona asked to see Henry Tucker.

She had only intended to get directions to the business district from Henry, but he offered to come along with her.

She hesitated, then agreed. "Yes please, Henry. You can be my guide."

As they made their way down the street, he asked, "What does a guide do, miss?"

She thought for a moment. "When my papa and I go to other countries we hire native guides. They translate for us and help us get along with the people of the country. Sometimes they warn us about the dangerous animals in the area. Tell me, Guide Henry, what sort of wild creatures should I avoid in this country?"

Henry giggled, and she laughed along with him. She said, "Perhaps you can bring along a machete, and we can slice our way through the vines that overrun the deep jungle, where the sun never shines."

They drew a few amused looks as they glided down the sidewalk, glancing all around and on the alert for lions and panthers and cobras. Henry warned they had a long trek, because Timona had no money for transportation.

"If we are successful in our journeys," said Timona, "we shall be able to make a triumphant return home in high style."

"Streetcar?" breathed Henry. He thin freckled face

glowed. "We don't have the money, but Ma won't let me hold on to the sides. That's to keep away from the conductors so's you don't have to pay. I love those streetcars, miss."

"A streetcar at the very least," she promised. "I have hopes for a hansom cab."

"Oh." Henry was speechless for two long blocks. His hands jammed into his britches' pockets, he whistled softly to himself and critically examined every horse that passed them.

They waited on a corner for a few carriages and a horse-drawn streetcar to clop by. Timona turned to Henry and leaning down, said in a solemn voice. "Henry, are you good at keeping secrets?"

"Cross my heart and hope to die," he said at once.

"My last name is actually Calverson." She watched him, but he simply looked at her enquiringly.

"So does it mean you're kind of an outlaw? 'Cause you have an alias?" he said, his face full of hope.

"No, no. It's nothing so interesting. There are some people who might pester me if they find me. Please call me Cooper at home, all right?"

He nodded.

"I told you now only because I will have to use Calverson when we get to the bank. But you must not tell anyone, understand? You must promise."

He nodded again. "I promise." He spat on his hand and held it out. She shook it after only a second's hesitation.

The bank had replaced the old manager since her last visit, so she had a small amount of trouble. But since she recalled all the correct account numbers, and even in the purple dress could assume the air of a woman of distinction, she at last got in to see the new manager.

Mr. Antonin, a round man with thickly pomaded

and blackened hair and a tiny, waxed mustache, bowed over her hand and showed her to a comfortable chair in his office. She briefly explained her situation, leaving out the more lurid episodes of her adventure.

"It will take a day or so," he explained apologetically. "We do need to verify your identity."

She groaned. "All I truly need today is enough money to send a few wires."

Outside the manager's plush office, a few voices could be heard shouting. Some heavy object clattered on the marble floor of the lobby. The bellows grew sharper and closer. The manager looked over Timona's shoulder, distracted.

She gave a sharp cough and he looked back at her. "Oh, yes, Miss Calverson, we would be delighted to send the telegram to your father for you. But I imagine you need funds for a hotel."

"No, I am currently staying with friends. Yet I admit I would appreciate more money, if only to purchase a few necessities. Such as clothing."

The door burst open. Henry panted in the doorway. Several puffing and red-faced tellers stood behind him.

"They're trying to give me the boot, Miss, um . . ." Henry said breathlessly.

"Ah," she said and rose from her chair, forcing the bank manager to stand as well. "And here is one of my hosts. Mr. Tucker, this is Mr. Antonin, my bank's manager."

The manager frowned, obviously not wanting to be introduced to a skinny little urchin, but Timona was pleased to see he did not express his displeasure. Good. He must be nearly convinced of her identity.

She had an idea. "Dr. Dennis, the museum director, works only a few blocks from here, yes?"

The manager nodded, still speechless, possibly at the sight of Henry, who now sauntered around his office.

"If you could send a messenger to the museum, and ask him to meet us here, he could vouch for my identity. We met two years ago in England."

A half-hour later, Timona was shaking hands with Dr. Dennis, the famous explorer turned museum director. He expressed himself delighted to walk the short distance to the bank for a chance to meet up with so charming an old friend as Miss Calverson.

After meeting with the bank manager, Dr. Dennis waited for Timona to collect her cash, and then he escorted the travelers out to the street.

"And let me take you and your young friend out for a spot of lunch, hey, Miss Calverson? Perhaps we can discuss funding for my latest project. Your family has been very generous in the past, and I would be honored to give you a tour of our new facility."

Timona smiled. "I would be much obliged if you would give Henry a tour of your museum, Dr. Dennis. The problem is I don't think I could go to lunch dressed as I am."

His tobacco-stained fingers combed his unruly white beard as he stepped back to look her over. "Your gown seems a trifle large for your figure, but otherwise fine. Very colorful, in fact."

She gave him a smacking kiss on the cheek. "Thank you, Dr. Dennis, you are a dear. But if you would watch out for my friend for about an hour. I am a swift shopper. Then I—"

"Delighted, delighted." Dr. Dennis said, obviously dubious. "My assistant will be most happy to offer your young friend a tour. And when you have purchased whatever female fripperies you require, meet me at the museum. Then we shall dine, hey?"

It was almost six when Dr. Dennis handed Miss Calverson and an ecstatic Henry into a hansom cab.

Timona bought only a few things for herself, enough to fit in a small valise. The owner of the dress shop remembered her well and was happy to accommodate the strange requirements of the wealthy young woman. The modiste did not raise a fuss at her requests, not even when she asked for clothes that were "less than completely stylish."

"Whatever you wish, naturally. And the extra pockets will take two days to complete, Miss Calverson. Where shall we deliver the rest of your order?"

"I'll pick up it up myself," said Timona, firmly. She had given an address to the bank out of necessity. She knew better than to tell the whole world where she was. Solly Lothman, her favorite reporter, would probably track her down, but people far less desirable than Sticking Plaster Solly might come looking for her.

She was accustomed to traveling light, and usually her photographic equipment took up more room than her clothes. But once she met up with Henry again, she couldn't resist purchasing a few more things for him, his siblings and his mother. She forced herself not to buy anything for Mick.

The small passenger compartment of the cab was loaded down with packages and boxes, but not so many that Henry couldn't shove them aside to stare out the window.

He perched on his knees, occasionally slipping off the leather seat when they turned corners. "I'm dying to pass someone we know. Me, riding in a shiny new hansom cab."

They were within five blocks of home, when at last he had some luck. He almost launched himself out the window when he saw his old friend, promenading down the sidewalk arm-in-arm with a well dressed woman.

"Mr. Mick! Hey! Lookee at us!"

Henry stood on the seat and slid back the little hatchway so he could bellow up through the roof. "Hey, you, stop, driver!"

Timona groaned.

Chapter 6

Mick had stopped at the station house to file his report of Miss T. C.'s complaint and to argue that the police must take action.

"Sergeant. She was grabbed off the street. Surely it don't matter who she is. They can't be snatching women. Of any sort."

The sergeant finally agreed to "have someone talk to the gentlemen," which meant the pimps would get some grief. More than Mick had hoped for.

On his way out the door, Mick stopped to make smart retorts to other coppers' smart remarks about his snappy appearance.

He ended up late meeting Daisy and her giggling friend Lizbet, who acted as Daisy's chaperone.

Mick didn't have to wait long in the Graves' foyer, but Daisy had not been in her sunniest mood as she walked down the wide front stairs of her family's brownstone. Lizbet, a friendly, dark haired, and slightly bucktoothed girl, hurriedly greeted Mick then scurried a few paces ahead.

Mick understood that Daisy wanted a few words alone with him, probably to gently chide him for being late. Sure enough, she reminded him that though her father, a prominent businessman—he was in ladies' fine footwear, Mick had been told—had agreed she might see a policeman, she had the hardest time assuring him that Mick was different. "Honestly, Mick, you don't want him to think you're a mutt just off the boat."

Mick waited until Lizbet stopped to gaze at a flower garden through some iron bars to answer. "But I am, Daisy. Or as near as you can get. You know that."

Always quick to cheer up, Daisy dimpled at him. "Michael, you are too modest. I mean you're not a man who can't rub two pennies together, someone who lives day-to-day. I know you're a good steady gentleman and have real plans. A policeman makes some very good money. Didn't you say you made almost a thousand dollars a year?"

Mick had not discussed the subject with her. Had Daisy's father been asking around about that? "Daisy, I'm not sure I'm cut out for the work."

Daisy interrupted. "It's just that Daddy is convinced you don't make the most of your time . . . well, he called you a sap."

He looked at her with raised brows. She sniffed and laughed. "I declare, your scent doesn't help, Michael."

They'd caught up with Lizbet by then. "Don't you think Michael smells of a fire, Lizbet?"

Her friend giggled and blushed. Mick deduced that Daisy had been very daring to mention such a thing. Girls in this city could be so prudish. He sometimes longed for the simpler and less refined manners of his village.

Daisy went on, "Daddy said something to me as we left. He wondered if you're working as a fireman as well as a policeman."

"Oh, that." Mick sighed. "Yes, there was a bit of a blaze."

"That woman with all the children again?"

Mick wished once more he had not introduced Daisy to Jenny when they chanced to meet in the park. He certainly wished he hadn't mentioned the way Tucker occasionally set his bedclothes on fire.

"'Twas early this morning," Mick said. "I tried to clean up, but I've told you my apartment is not luxurious. I-I save my pennies for the future. Always a good plan, eh, Miss Lizbet?"

That was the right tactic. Daisy loved to talk about her ideal future. Lizbet occasionally joined in with her own hopes and dreams. Usually Mick enjoyed hearing the girls describe life in a small house with a rose garden and with real paintings on the walls.

"Long Island," Lizbet said. "Lovely to be in the country." She giggled for a full minute.

Daisy countered with a description of a good city neighborhood.

Today their words failed to penetrate the fog of Mick's mind. He was still tired and distracted by the thought of Miss Calverson.

He hoped she be gone when he returned. Why had she insisted on staying with him that morning? She had said she did not feel well, but he'd bet his last penny she felt fine.

He should have sternly informed her he would give her money, and help her find her way back to her father at once. And no more.

God above, what had possessed him to play the damned music for her? Mick never played for an audience. The vision of her stretched out on his bed as he washed up had affected him strongly. Something about her reminded him of the best places back home, the silent ancient woods, perhaps, or the cliffs near the sea. The smell of her, maybe. She seemed gloriously natural and unaffected, lighting up his room with her presence, making him homesick for love and . . .

He broke off his musing, shocked at his sentimental

rubbish. A woman like that, with her experienced body and sly smile—she wasn't a bit like the girls at home.

No doubt about it, he should have taken care of the matter of Miss Calverson before coming out to meet Daisy and Lizbet. Especially after that morning. Saints. That morning he'd been on the edge of losing control of himself in a way he hadn't since he was a lad.

Miss Calverson seemed to want something from him and he didn't know what it could be. Other than what he'd wanted from her, of course, the thought of which caused an alarming spasm of desire and answering twinge of shame as he walked with Daisy and Lizbet.

He wondered if should he mention the existence of the woman to Daisy, who was still talking in her sweet, high voice. Now Daisy was mentioning how much she enjoyed their time together.

"But the thing is, dear Michael, Daddy says I should see other gentlemen. Just so you know. Didn't he say so, Lizbet?"

"Oh yes," said Lizbet, too enthusiastically.

That cut through his distraction. "Daisy." He stopped and turned to her. "Daisy, do you want to?"

She looked at him from under her lashes. "I am very fond of you, Michael. Very." Her darling little dimple appeared in her right cheek. "You are so sweet." She darted a glance over at Lizbet who had walked a few steps ahead. Daisy's small gloved hand briefly caressed his arm.

Cool and dainty Daisy in her white dress, her curls neatly pinned up, was a sight for his rather sore eyes. She always looked so clean and bright, even on the darkest days. Nothing mysterious or peculiar about Daisy, not like the Calverson woman.

He grasped her hand. She giggled and so did Lizbet, of course. "Michael! On the street? Let us walk on to the park."

As they strolled under the trees in the park she protested when he again attempted to take her arm.

She giggled again, but her voice was irritated when she reprimanded him. "Michael, you do seem friskier than usual."

That was damn certain, he thought, again remembering how he'd awakened that morning. It was very wrong of him to take out his thwarted desire on an innocent like Daisy.

He apologized to Daisy. She allowed him to buy her and Lizbet ices.

They spoke of their favorite ways to spend a lazy day. Daisy liked to shop and read. Lizbet loved to visit the roller rink. Mick mentioned listening to music and going for walks.

Daisy smiled and briefly took his arm, pretending she needed help over a rocky part of the path. "Like this?"

"Just like this."

It turned into a fairly agreeable afternoon. Lizbet, giggling and blushing, mentioned that her mama would be worried so she'd have to leave them early. Mick gallantly escorted her up the stairs and they left Lizbet at her house. Mick looked forward to five whole minutes walking alone with Daisy.

And then Henry Tucker's yelps shattered his peace. "Mr. Mick!"

"Goodness, Michael," Daisy said. One of her lilac-gloved hands shaded her eyes as her other clutched his arm. "Do you know those people?"

Henry's yells were so loud even a few passersby stopped to see the cause of the hullabaloo.

The sleek black cab drew to a halt, and Henry bounded to the curb, followed by a stylish young woman who stepped out of the cab. "Hey Mr. Mick! Look at us," Henry said, for the thousandth time. "Miss Timona and I are going home in style."

Timona? Timmy?

Even Mick, no expert at women's clothing, could see that the smart gray velvet dress was elegant. It was fairly plain and tight in the front—though plain was not the right word for her front—and rucked up in all the correct places with a train at the back. A dashing hat with a feather perched on the side of her head, atop an arrangement of braids and curls at the nape of her neck that cunningly hid the cut he had stitched. The gray showed off her light eyes and dark hair. Mick couldn't help gawking at her until an elbow dug into his side.

"Who is this person?" Daisy hissed. Mick's mouth shut, but before he could speak, the very grand young lady stepped forward, and held out her hand encased in a dove-gray glove.

"How do you do? You must be Mick, ah, Mr. Mc-Cann's charming Miss Graves. I am delighted to meet you. I am Timona Calverson."

Daisy shook the hand enthusiastically, and squeaked, "*The* Timona Calverson?"

They stood in a small circle on the sidewalk. Mick looked sharply from one woman to the other. Daisy was now beaming, her eyes and mouth open wide.

"Yes," Timmy said, and hurriedly added, "I haven't had a chance to explain a few things to Mr. McCann."

She twiddled with the button at the wrist of one of the gray gloves and seemed to be trying to catch his eye.

This Timmy looked thoroughly at home in the stylish gray dress. His theory of the morning, that she might be upper class, hit the target dead center. More than that, he did not need to know. Mick suddenly felt a thunderous headache coming on.

Daisy poked him with her elbow again. "Michael, I know you are busy, but surely you have time to mention

Miss Calverson to me. Don't you read the *Town Crier*?
Or the *Time*'s society column? My goodness! Now I recall reading that Miss Calverson recently arrived here
in New York."

Daisy clasped her hands together beneath her chin
and twisted toward Timmy. "You and your father are
traveling somewhere for his latest work, am I right?"

She turned back to Mick. "Her father is a very dis-
tinguished explorer. How terribly exciting, Michael. To
think, you never even told me you know Miss Calverson."

"We only met yesterday," said Timmy. "He saved my
life."

Daisy laughed lightly. "Yes, he is quite a hero."

"Indeed he is." Timmy had that smile on her lips, the
one that made Mick's blood run cold. "Mr. McCann is
perhaps the most wonderful man I've ever met."

Daisy's smile showed a hesitant dimple, clearly unsure about how she was supposed to react. Mick
couldn't blame her. He had no idea what anyone could
say to Timmy's palaver. Daisy's answer seemed good
enough. "Oh yes, Michael is my favorite admirer."

The smile grew much wider, but Timmy was silent.

Mick wished he could tip his hat at these two women
and his confusion, bid them goodbye forever and stride
on home to his apartment. The torture wasn't over yet.

"Where are you and your illustrious father staying in
New York, Miss Calverson?"

"I hope that my father is on his way to Minnesota. He
should be in Ohio, or at least I pray he is."

"With his bloody secretary," Mick grumbled, but Timona did not appear to hear. And, except for a sweet
little frown at him, Daisy ignored the remark.

Timona went on. "I have been staying in the same
building as Mr. McCann, who will help me track my father down."

Though Daisy must wonder why *the* Timona was in such a poor part of the city, that answer seemed to work.

Until Henry, wandering back from admiring the black horse felt he add his little mite to the conversation

"She's staying with Mr. Mick. All dressed up like a boy, until Ma lent her some decent clothes. She was a trouper with cleaning up after the fire, too. Ma said so. So is that why you want to be called Miss Cooper? Because you're famous?"

"Staying with Michael?" Daisy did not open her mouth. The words had to squeeze their way out between her teeth. Her little frown grew dark.

Timmy gave Mick a sympathetic look but didn't say anything. So he had to answer. "Daisy, there's a good explanation—"

"Yes?" Daisy interrupted, her head tilted to the side, like a bird's.

Timmy must have at last taken pity on him. "I was one of his strays, Miss Graves. Like Botty. He found me unconscious in the street, dressed, in, er, a disguise. He took me in, thinking I was a boy. At the time he had no idea I was a female. I was too battered to be moved last night, so he kindly lent me a bed."

Daisy looked less put out. Thank goodness she had never seen his flat, and so didn't know how small it was. Or that it had only one bed.

"One of Michael's strays? Who is Botty?" she murmured puzzled. She laughed and her brow smoothed. "Mercy me! Miss Calverson, I recall reading about how you stayed with the Africans. The reporter with you said you dressed like the natives, wrapped up in big pieces of cloth. And you stayed with them and ate with them. The same food, even."

"Mr. Carter, the reporter in Africa, was a nincompoop," Timmy said decisively. "So you haven't met Botty—" she began.

"You are on a lark here in New York!" Daisy interrupted with a crow of delight. "How exciting. An adventure!" She glanced all around the street at the people bustling past. "Is there a reporter with you?"

"Not just now."

"Hoy, lady," the cabbie shouted down from his perch at the back of the cab. "Want to keep on? My horse'll get too cooled."

"May I walk with you?" Timmy addressed Daisy. She was smart enough not to ask Mick. "The evening air is so pleasant and I would like to get to know you. Might I be so bold as to call you Daisy?"

"Of course!" said a thrilled Daisy before Mick could get a word in. He'd have to wait until later to tell Timmy what he thought of her current exploits. Staying with the natives, indeed.

Good God. And he'd thought the creature was a common whore. No, not entirely. He'd never thought of her as common.

Timmy touched Henry's shoulder as he stood watching the cab with sad longing. "Henry, would you be good enough to see our purchases home? I believe you know which parcel goes to whom."

She dug into a shiny little blue bag. New, of course. And pulled out some coins, shiny and new. "This will pay for the cab and the cabby's tip. Be sure to get him to help you carry in everything."

"Got it, Miss Timona. See you, Mr. Mick. Good-bye, Miss . . . um." Henry dashed back to the cab.

According to convention, Mick was supposed to walk along with a woman on each side, but the way Daisy chattered across him as if he was some kind of post, he soon dropped back so Daisy could get better access to Miss Calverson.

He shoved his hands in his pockets and walked along behind, catching what he could of the women's talk. Most of the conversation consisted of Daisy recalling facts she had read about Miss Calverson and her famous father, and her terribly fascinating, mysterious older brother who ran the business side of things and spent a great deal of time in New York. The one who taught Timmy to knee a man in the ballocks, Mick recalled.

Occasionally, Timmy corrected a "fact." More often she tried to steer the conversation towards other topics. Mick plodded behind them as they made their way back to Daisy's house, lost in his own confused gloom. Bad enough that Timmy had been conducting some kind of masquerade with him. Worse that he'd babbled to the woman about his life and his job. Now he saw Daisy, who'd always been so cool with him, was near to drooling all over the Timona creature. Daisy repeatedly jabbered about the honor of meeting such an illustrious traveler.

He managed to pick up one fact. Daisy had invited Miss Calverson to dinner. She seemed about to invite Miss Calverson to stay the night. Timmy interrupted to say she was all set for a place to stay, but dinner sounded divine.

"And what time would you like us to arrive for dinner tomorrow?"

"Do you mean you will bring your father?" Daisy said eagerly. "I thought you said that he was on his way to Chicago?"

"Yes, and you wouldn't want him just now, at any rate. He is in a dreadful state about his projects. I meant only Mr. McCann and myself."

Daisy's adorable lips parted for a second as if she were about to speak. Then she giggled. "Michael often works so late. I suppose he could join us later."

"I'm off at five," he grunted. "But if you'd rather have just Miss Cooper. Er, Calverson."

Daisy swung around and shook a playful finger at him. "Don't be silly, Michael. I'm sure Daddy and Mother will be delighted to have you. I know we've been meaning to ask you for the longest time. Why don't we say seven?"

"This would be Mr. McCann's first meal in your home?" Timmy asked casually.

"Yes, we usually like to spend our free time away from my parents, you see," said Daisy, with a giggle.

Timmy nodded, a slight frown on her face.

"*The* Timona Calverson?" he asked, as soon as they had waved good-bye to Daisy and Timona again refused her invitation for a quick stop in for refreshment. Fifty times Daisy must have asked, thought Mick grimly.

"You needn't sound so unpleasant about it."

"You're rich."

"My father is. And I repeat, you needn't sound so unpleasant. I have lied to you about nothing. Not a single lie."

He managed to dredge one up without much trouble. "Your father's keeper?"

"If you spent an hour in my father's company when he was traveling, you would see how accurate that description is. Mr. Blenheim is very patient with Papa."

He wasn't sure why he felt so annoyed, other than his disquiet about Daisy's eager behavior. He felt like a fool, but it would be unfair to blame Timmy because he hadn't known who she was. Nevertheless, he made no effort to hide his annoyance.

"How in hell did your father get his money?" After the words came out, he realized he was unforgivably blunt with her. He'd never use the word "hell" with any other woman.

"He was born into wealth," she said at last. "And he buys land all over the world for some of his digs. He's remarkably unlucky with the fossils, but his workers seem to discover, um, other things. Father is always disappointed, but at least he ends up with money to buy more land and conduct more searches."

Mick at last recalled reading something about the eccentric millionaire with the digging habit.

"Some sort of minerals or gems?" he said dully. Among other things.

"Yes."

For the first time Mick lost his temper. He turned to face her. "What are you doing now, here, walking with me?"

Now he understood his annoyance. She was using him and his life as a diversion. He knew all about bored rich girls hunting for amusement in the slums. Some of the men on the force made good money on those rich thrill seekers. The cops led tours through bad neighborhoods for debutantes and their foolish friends itching for a taste of safe danger.

"Go on back to where you belong, girl. Leave me be."

Timona turned pale and put a hand to her throat. His voice was low, and biting cold. He sounded as if he hated her. She had to take two full breaths before she could speak. "I don't know exactly where it is I belong, Mr. McCann. Right now my bag is at your building."

"You'll collect your bag, and we'll get your famous bloody self to a decent hotel."

"No."

"What do you mean 'no'?"

"I can't. No, please, I mean I don't want to." She knew she prattled like an idiot but didn't know how to stop herself. "Why do you want me to? What does it

matter to you? I know all about you from Jenny Tucker
and Henry. You always are kind, and always kind to people who need help. I mean, you are used to people
bothering you, what difference does one more make?"

"You don't need help from me, and I am not used to
people like you. I don't care to be. You're playing with
the natives, Miss Calverson."

She gave a tiny shriek of frustration. "That nonsense.
That was some nitwit reporter's idiotic interpretation of
our visits to our friends. He didn't respect the people
who lived in the countries we were visiting. I did. I do,
always. I care about my friends. Just the way you do."

She must have said the right thing, for the pinched,
tense look vanished from the corners of his eyes. He
even smiled. But then he said, "Even if I grant you good
intentions, you can't be friends with the likes of me and
Jenny. You didn't so much as tell her your real name.
You can't be a friend with a lie like that between you."

"Who says that? Where have you seen that written
down, Mr. McCann?"

He only shook his head. "All right then. I suppose I
cannot force you back to your proper place, Miss
Calverson." She felt encouraged until he added, "I
don't have the money to pay your damn passage."

"Mick," she pleaded. "Oh, please don't talk to me in
such a cold manner."

He stopped and looked over at her. "I'm sorry, Miss
Calverson. I don't mean to hurt your feelings but . . ."

"Call me 'Temmy.' Please."

"Don't you mock me accent," he said curtly, and
strode on ahead. The misery returned but she was determined not to let it swamp her.

She picked up her skirts and trotted down the sidewalk after him. "I'm not making fun of you. I'm saying
my name the way it sounds best to me."

He stopped short. "Jesus," he muttered. "I think I get

it now." He took a step away from her and gazed down at her with a horrified stare, as if she'd grown another set of eyes. "You believe you've, er, developed a care for me."

She wouldn't have put it exactly like that way, but she wasn't going to argue about that subject. "Yes. I have."

"No, oh, no. You only think you have, Miss Calverson. I've heard of such things, and seen them in my work, you know. A man is right horrible to a woman and the next man who so much as smiles at her becomes her dream rabbit."

She laughed and put her gloved hand over her mouth. "Dream rabbit?"

He wouldn't be distracted. "That's what happened to you yesterday, innit? Those brutes had you, and then I picked you up, and was human to you."

She shrugged. "Perhaps that explains why I am in love with you—it certainly sounds plausible. You are human to me."

"Love?" He snorted the word. "People don't truly fall in love in one day. 'Tis nothing but gratitude. I take it as an honor and a thank you. I say you are most welcome. Glad to have been of service. Now. You go to a hotel, I get back me life." He started to walk away again.

She had to run to keep up with him. "No. Not yet."

"What will it take to get you gone?"

"One of us must be convinced. I must believe you, or I must convince you that we belong together."

"Together? You and me?" He made an extremely rude sound. "Impossible."

"I don't think so," she said.

He stopped again, and swung around to look at her. He put his hands on his hips. He squinted at her. She could see a spark of a challenge in his blue eyes, but thank heavens, none of the frightening and cold anger.

"And if I did let you stay, Miss High-and-Mighty

Calverson? What do you suppose Daisy will say to this arrangement? And how long before I can be rid of you?"

She tried not to smirk when she saw he was curious. "If it comes to that, I shall be the one to appease Daisy. How long . . . er, I think one week is not too much to ask?"

He muttered something under his breath and took off walking again, faster than before.

She rushed to catch up and stumbled as she jogged along the uneven sidewalk. He put out a hand automatically to steady her.

The moment she had her balance, he yanked his hand away and said, "What if I tell you to go to the devil?"

"Would you do that, Mick? Aren't you the slightest bit interested in me? You were this morning."

He blushed, but firmly replied, "That was before I knew what, er, who you are. 'Twas sex. Just sex. I made that clear."

She frowned, confused. "Yes, maybe that can be true for you. Maybe men are different after all. I don't know. I had never in my life felt anything resembling that. Jaysus," she whispered, and was horrified to feel tears in her eyes.

"No. Ah no, don't. No. I'm not agreeing to any of your daft schemes," he yelped. "But tonight and tomorrow you can stay. And, mind you, it's because Daisy expects you."

She realized he had probably given in temporarily because she had grown upset. She barely cared why. As long as he agreed.

Chapter 7

Mick was too wily for her. He agreed that Timona could stay at his place, but he'd borrowed a straw mattress from the Kelly family next door.

He'd sleep on the floor.

Good. She would not sleep with him unless the Daisy question was settled. She knew that Daisy did not have a serious attachment to Mick yet, but she was not sure how he felt about the girl. In the meantime she wanted to stay as near him as possible. She could not recall wanting anything more.

She sank down on his bed and groaned with pleasure at the chance to rest. The day had seemed endless. Her shoulder and head throbbed.

Soon after their return, Mick silently grabbed some clothes from the bureau and disappeared for a long while. While he was gone, Timona got up. She looked and Botty sniffed through the parcels that Henry had brought up to Mick's flat. Every time she reached out to pat Botty, he slipped away from her fingers. Not far, just out of reach. Henry had told her that only Mick could touch the dog.

Timona sat back on her heels to examine the clothing and objects she had bought. She wished she could throw them somewhere. They took up too much room.

She was just shoving the last parcel under the bed next to his medical kit, when there was a knock at the door.

"You don't have to knock at your own door," she told him.

"I do indeed if I'm sharing the one room with someone, especially a female," he said grimly.

Timona decided to let it go. She said, "I bought some tea. And some pastries."

He slammed the door shut. The latch was broken and the door only closed properly if it was thrown shut. Still she thought he slammed it harder than need be.

"You eat 'em." He threw himself down on the straw pallet and pulled off his unlaced boots. He was wearing loose gray trousers and a simple farmer's smock now. Much better, Timona decided. She liked the look of the strong column of his neck against the vee of the rough-woven white shirt. And she caught sight of his clavicle and below that an interesting swirl of hair. So his front was not as smooth as his back then.

"If I made tea, would you drink it?" she asked.

"I only have the one mug."

"I bought another cup." She stood and inched past his pallet over to the small cookstove.

He looked up at the pretty floral teacup with its matching saucer and announced flatly, "Tonight. That is it. After tonight you can stay elsewhere."

"Do you want tea, or not?" she asked as she fumbled with the tin of matches.

He stood up, impressively tall, even in his stocking feet. "Move over. I'll do the tea."

"Thank you." She scurried back to the bed.

She watched him light the stove and set the water to boil. He peered into the parcel that held the pastries.

"Lord, woman. How many did you buy?"

"Several. For breakfast, too."

He pulled one out and got a dollop of cream on his

finger. Timona felt her stomach twist over as he gave his finger a lick. His tongue. The kisses this morning. Other men had tried to kiss her like that and she had thought it disgusting. What a fool she had been.

"You may change your mind about the pastries after that taste," she said. "In fact I hope you will. That cream-filled sort won't last."

He grinned at her, sheepish. "Thank you."

She couldn't help grinning back, and the smile vanished from his face at once.

In silence, he found the new sack of tea. He set one of the new teacups and his old chipped mug onto the chair which he shoved between the pallet and the bed, to act as a table.

Botty stood alert at Mick's side, ready to grab anything that fell to the ground.

Mick's tension seemed to lighten as he made the tea; his hunched shoulders eased. Timona thought she might safely ask him a few questions.

"How many McCanns are there in your family?" She watched him. What a lovely straight back the man had. Strong.

"Six of us kids. There were seven, but a middle boy died."

"I am sorry."

"Ma and others said it was a blessing."

"How could that be?" She waited for him to be offended by her unguardedly astonished tone, but he wasn't.

"Donncha was what we called a *duine le Dia*. A child of God. Backwards, I think they say here. Oh, he was a sweet little baby though. None sweeter."

He opened the tea pot and poured in water to warm it. After he dumped it out into the big pan, he measured tea into the pot. She was glad to see Mick knew how to make tea properly.

"You didn't think it was a blessing when he died, did you."

"Ah, well, I cared for him."

"You said he was sweet—didn't anyone else like him?"

"No, I mean I took care of him. When he was born he couldn't properly nurse. Ma said it was God's will the baby should die."

Timmy wasn't sure she was going to like this mother of his. "Did you believe that?"

"No, can't say I believe God wants babies to die of starvation."

"How did you take care of him?"

He poured in the water as he spoke. "Ma's milk dried because he couldn't nurse right, so I used the goat our neighbor had then. Cow's milk didn't stay in Donncha's gut. I dribbled it into his mouth. Feeding time took hours, til he got the hang of the bottle Da and I rigged up. His cry was too quiet, so I strapped him to me when I went about the place. That way I could tell when he was hungry. Kept him warm that way, too. Da wanted to help, but he was too weak by then. Still, he could tell me what was needed."

"How old were you when Donncha was born?"

He turned to look at her with his light ginger eyebrows raised. "You are one for questions, aren't you?"

She blushed. "Am I bothering you? With the questions I mean." She knew she seemed to annoy him in other ways.

"Suppose no," he grunted.

"So, er, how old were you?"

He stopped to think. "Da was that sick. Ah, I'd say about eleven."

An eleven-year-old fighting to save a new baby's life. Oh, poor Mick when he lost the fight.

"Mick, I am sorry. How long did Donncha live?"

"Seven years. Influenza killed him off. He always was a delicate lad."

Timmy almost laughed aloud. Of course Mick kept the baby alive.

The tea was ready, and he handed her the plate of pastries.

"No, Botty. You sit down, you miserable mongrel. This food is far too good for the likes of you," he said as he broke off an end of an eclair and fed it to the dog.

She pulled out one of her new embroidered handkerchief and used it as a serviette as they ate.

She watched him eat and drink. He seemed to be avoiding looking at her. That made it easier for her to greedily admire him and manage her food at the same time. The times his eyes met hers, she found it more difficult to swallow or breathe.

His mouth was wide, his face broad but carved with signs of character. When he smiled, lines framed his eyes. She guessed he was perhaps twenty-eight, but the marks of laughter were already permanent.

He finished the eclair and leaned over. His skillful fingers slowly caressed the enthralled Botty, rubbing circles on his fur. Her stomach flip-flopped pleasurably at the thought of those hands touching her. Her gaze traveled up his arms to the strong broad shoulders. Even in the dim candlelight she could see the definition of the muscles in his shoulders and arms. But he wasn't fat. Brawny. Wasn't that an Irish word?

"How do you say a big brawny man in Irish?" she asked.

He gave her a disgusted look.

"Well, go on. Tell me," she said.

"*Fear leathan laidir,*" he mumbled through a mouth full of eclair. "The word for you is *óinseach*—foolish woman."

She grinned. "Now why are you acting so cantankerous, I wonder? Did you think I meant you when I asked for the definition of big brawny man?"

He laughed. "You been gawking at me. I thought there might be a connection."

She laughed too. "I'll never admit it now."

He looked at her, serious again, forehead furrowed. "You are the strangest woman, Miss Calverson. Don't you have any shame? No, don't look aggrieved. I just mean, eh, don't you even care that you seem," He paused and picked up his mug. "Just that, you show no pride in yourself. Hell, I don't know what I mean."

She sighed and reached for her teacup. "So which is it, Mick? I show no shame or I show no pride?"

He shrugged. "I can't explain."

"I wish I was more what you want," she said.

He put down his mug so hard it rattled the other dishes on the chair. "See now. That's just what I mean. The nonsense you come up with, Timmy. You are a pretty woman. Smart and friendly too, from what I seen. Rich. I don't see why on earth you'd want to change."

"I am satisfied enough," she said. "But you are not."

"Timmy! You—you *óinseach*. You can't go wishing to change yourself to fit some other person's whims."

"Of course I can't change, not for whims. Oh, probably not at all." She put down her cup and swiped at the mess on her hands with the handkerchief. She should brush her teeth but she was too tired. "I wish you wanted to be with me. That's not a bad thing, is it?"

He just looked at her for a minute, then shook his head.

After a while he said, "Er. The food is wonderful. Thank you for it."

"You're welcome."

She pulled off her new half boots and Mick made a grunt of protest.

"Here, now. You can't get undressed with me just sitting here."

"Turn your back then," said Timona and sniffed fiercely. Oh, how she hated wishing she were sweet and innocent like Daisy Graves. A regular girl. Heavens, she hadn't felt that way since she was seventeen and enraged with the world because, after her stay with Aunt Winifred, she understood she would never be normal.

She stripped down quickly, and pulled her white cotton nightgown over her head. She had spent almost five whole minutes picking out the gown at the shop—a long decision about clothing for her.

She found her new hair brush. "You can turn around now."

He thoughtfully eyed the folded pile of clothes on the bed next to her.

She pulled out all of the pins in her hair and began to attack her hair with her brush, until she hit a bruise near her cut.

"Ow." She tossed the brush onto the pile of clothes. Then she flopped down on the bed and pulled a blanket over her head. The blanket was worn, but not as filthy as she had first imagined. It was faintly redolent of Mick, which comforted her.

"Miss Calverson. Timmy."

"Yes?"

"I am sorry if I hurt your feelings." She heard a rustle and clink as he stood up, collected the plates and put them on the small table that held the stove and pan.

She poked her head out from under the blanket, and gazed at him in astonishment. "Mick, you have nothing to apologize for."

"You are angry with me." He poured the rest of the hot water into the large pan.

"I am sad, I would say, and certainly not angry at you. You have been nothing but generous to me."

He was shaking his head. "I was right. You are the strangest wom—"

"No. Don't start that again or I shall grow angry. Mick. Leave the dishes in the pan and I will clean them up tomorrow." He opened his mouth to protest, but she added, "I promise not to make a habit of acting as if I live here, but I know you must leave early in the morning. It makes more sense to leave them."

They settled on their beds, and Mick blew out the candle. Timona heard him restlessly throwing the covers about, as he tried to find a comfortable place on the bed on the floor

"Will you kiss me goodnight?" she whispered.

He groaned as if in pain. "I am not going to risk such a thing as that."

She smiled into the dark. He still wanted her. Good to start somewhere.

"Botty, will you at least give me a kiss?"

Mick snorted. *"Óinseach,"* he said without heat.

Timona yawned. It felt wonderful to be lying down, even on this bed. She pushed her head back and forth to find a comfortable place for her bruises and cut, then heaved a great sigh. She was asleep within five minutes.

Mick lay curled on his side. He listened to every squeak, rustle, and breath coming from his bed. He wondered if the Calverson creature took up with a man in every city she visited. Who would she pick out? Working men, rich men, street car conductors—the first man she met, maybe.

She had met him. And no one appeared at his doorstep to prevent her from sleeping with him. From a few things she said in passing, he wondered if her father even cared.

For a moment he felt sorry for her, but then remembered she had money, fine looks, and the bravery of a tiger. Daisy had said Timmy went by the treacly title of Our Traveling Sweetheart. No need to waste pity on the likes of her.

She must have some practice with attracting men, for she knew how to make a man want her—beyond the bewitching body and enticing smile.

The gift of charm came naturally to her. And she behaved rather like himself with one of the youngsters, he reflected wryly: She coaxed him with sweet food, listened intently to his words, and asked questions about himself—made him feel he mattered.

But then there was the sweetest of all enticements for a grown man, her body.

Why not? He thought, two seconds, less than three steps across to his bed, and he'd have her in his arms. Just the thought of her made him hard as a damn billy club. Which meant he'd had hours of her painful and annoying presence.

She as much said she would yield to him. Who would know?

He would know, that's who. It was plain wrong. And if this worldly woman managed to get some kind of hold on him—he supposed he couldn't bear that. Though at the moment he couldn't quite recall why the idea was so unbearable.

He switched to his back, and tried going over the manual of police procedures in his mind. That had always been a good way to put himself straight to sleep. A soft sigh came from the bed and interrupted his mental review of Section One, "The Uniform."

Was she awake and waiting for him? A kiss good night, she had said. Ha. If he so much as touched her full lips, or possibly even just her cheek with his mouth, that would spell the end for McCann.

He'd seen her chemise and other undergarments. And he knew what he suspected was true: She had no proper corset, the jade.

And what's more painful, he knew what was under that nightgown. Nothing other than her body. He'd be damned if he'd think about it. Especially not her breasts or that flat silken belly or her bottom that fit his hands so perfectly . . .

He heard her breathing was regular and heavy, and he wasn't sure if he was disappointed or relieved. Both, he decided.

For the first time in his life, he got all the way to Section Ten before finally drifting off to sleep. The church clock had struck midnight. He'd have less than five hours sleep. Again.

Chapter 8

When Timona woke, Mick had gone to work and Botty had disappeared. Mick had left behind a note, written on the back of a picture card that looked as if it had spent several days stuffed in someone's pocket. She looked at the picture of the Iron Pier at Coney Island, then flipped it over to examine his painstaking scrawl.

"Back at 6. Wait for me. We go together." Not the most romantic note she had ever received but she tried to convince herself she was glad he wanted to go with her.

After she ran some errands, she decided that if she only had one week for her campaign, she'd best seek out Mick even during his work hours.

She found Henry again, pitching pennies in the alley behind the apartment.

"Do you know where Mr. McCann walks when he is on duty?"

Henry stood up and dusted off his hands on the backs of his new britches. "Oh yeah. He tells Rob about his beat in case we need him back for Pa. This month he's not around here. He told his friend Mr. Bairre— he's the officer on our route now—to keep an eye on us. I think they got Mr. Mick on a bad route lately, though. Not the worst but pretty tough, he says."

After some persuasion, and a bribe of a sumptuous lunch, Henry and his friend Matt agreed to show Timona the route Mick was walking.

"Not a good place for ladies, iffen you know what I mean."

Timona understood. She picked out her least attractive new gown. Too bad, since she did want to impress her future husband. But a quiet blue dress without a single bow and with a high collar was probably best.

"We'll come too," said Henry.

"No, I thank you, Henry, but it is not necessary," said Timona. "I will manage."

"No, see, I got to, Miss Cal—Miss Cooper. Mr. Mick asked Rob and Sarey and me to keep an eye on you if we could."

Timona wondered what Mick wanted to protect her from—or protect from her.

The exhausted Mick had to drag himself over his beat that morning. He had to stay on schedule. Doherty, the roundsman, was still out to get him.

The blasted coot seemed to resent the way Mick did not socialize often with the lads or attend church.

Doherty made a point of checking on Mick nearly every shift, popping up in front of him, hoping to be able to write him up. Other cops had warned Mick that Doherty wanted to nab him—he had claimed as much to them.

Two other officers went so far as to deliver a complaint to the sergeant that Doherty was harassing Mick.

The sergeant, a fair man, had asked the reluctant Mick to confirm the story.

"Wouldn't have listened to you alone, naturally," said the sergeant to Mick, "but if these boys say it's true, well then. I'll have a word with him."

"You're not a partying man, is all," one of Mick's comrades had told him as they walked away from the sergeant's desk. "I won't forget how you come running and swinging when those drunks jumped me. As long as you're there with your club out when I need help, you're my idea of a fine officer."

After that, the pressure from Doherty eased somewhat, but Mick was conscientious about staying on his beat. He wasn't one to take long breaks at the taverns, like some that walked that busy route. He usually bought or took his lunch from street vendors and ate as he walked.

He'd just stopped to reprimand a man pissing against a lamppost, when he caught sight of the little group making their way down the street towards him. The street was crowded, yet he recognized her from a block away.

The dress was not so tight-fitting, thank God. But her figure wasn't as well hidden as it should have been. Hadn't she already learnt a lesson about lone women wandering these streets? Hell. Two half-grown boys were not escort enough.

She strode along confidently, as if walking a path through rowdy drunks and other rough customers was customary for her. She laughed at something Henry's friend said, and several of the men outside the tavern stopped to watch, and loudly admire her. She ignored them as if she heard lewd comments every day of her life.

Mick held back his urge to apply his club to the louts gawking at her and tell them to move along. Of course, the strongest urge was to say the same to the blasted woman.

It wasn't enough that she keep him awake all night long with her soft sighing and rustling presence on his own bed. Now she had to come bother him during the day, too.

She walked towards him now like a woman comfortable in her own skin. Did she know she was pretty? She didn't have the fetching little ways of Daisy—ways that Mick, traitorously, once or twice, had wondered if Daisy practiced in a mirror. This Calverson woman didn't seem to care what appearance she presented to the world.

From the corner, she caught sight of him watching. She gestured and talked to the boys and all three waved happily. No, thought Mick, it wasn't that she didn't care how about what other people thought, it was more she acted like she had nothing to prove to anyone.

That wasn't true, of course. She had to explain to him why she was here.

"I think there is no emergency back home. So what the devil are you thinking coming here?" he growled at Henry when they drew near. The boy's happy smile vanished, and Mick at once felt like an ogre. He grunted and put a hand on Henry's capped head. "Nah, Henry. I know it was Miss . . ." He glanced at Henry's friend and continued, "Miss Cooper here that talked you into it. She presses a person to do what she bids, don't she?"

"Well," said Henry reluctantly.

"Of course I take blame," Timmy interrupted. "But I fail to see why blame needs to be assigned."

He pulled her slightly away from the boys and was curt with her and, as usual, far blunter than he would be with any other woman. "This isn't a safe area, miss. I told you before, in much of the city after dark, any woman would be taken for a whore. Here that's true during the day, too. You of all people should know the danger of this area."

Interested but unafraid, she looked around at the motley collection of buildings and a garbage-filled empty lot near the sidewalk where they stood. About a third of the buildings had broken windows; some boarded up, most just showing gaping holes. Loitering men stood in the open doorway of a saloon, marked only with a dirty awning. A man leaning against the basement entrance to a stale-beer dive tipped his bowler to Miss Calverson and showed a near-toothless grin. He gave Mick the thumbs-up.

In a low voice she said, "So this is near where you suspect I was grabbed? I wish I could remember more clearly. I do detect the scent of beer and burning scrap heap, which seems familiar. But if you worry about my safety, I should tell you that at the time I was ill prepared, Mr. McCann. Now I am not."

She reached to her hip, and when she raised her gloved hand, Mick realized she held a blade. Her loose grip showed she was a woman who'd been properly trained to use a knife as a weapon. She had a good fighting stance, legs apart for balance, low center. For the first time he noticed her dress was loose about the legs, and not in the current tighter fashion and he wondered if she had it made specifically so she could hunker down and balance better. Funny to see an apparent gentlewoman crouched in such a manner.

The brother's instruction, no doubt.

Mick couldn't help laughing. "Ah, no, I should not be surprised that you can handle a shiv," he muttered to her. "And I will not fuss at you for I am not responsible for the safety of such a noted traveler as yourself, Timmy. Thank the good Lord. Might I see it?"

She handed him the sheath knife, a sleek, modern French dagger that opened with the press of a button.

He gave a low whistle and shook his head. "Ever used it?"

"No," she said cheerfully. "Not this one, anyway. I just purchased it this morning."

He didn't have a chance to ask about past knives. Henry, behind them, held up a basket he'd been lugging.

"We have brought you lunch, Mr. Mick. Miss Cooper thought you might like to join our picnic, since the day's so clement and all."

"I'll not stop for a break for nearly another half hour," he said.

"May we walk with you?" Timmy asked. And before he could open his mouth to answer, she added, "I know the boys and I shall be perfectly safe. Come on, Henry and Matt. We'll stay within Officer McCann's view now."

They strolled down the sidewalk like they were taking air in the park. Or were part of a damned circus parade with him as the last elephant in line.

At least with Timmy ahead of him she wouldn't try to slip her arm into his.

Mick gave up grouching to himself about his uninvited company, and decided to be entertained by them instead. He walked behind, keeping watch for trouble, half-listening to their conversation.

She spoke to the boys as she had to Rob, as seriously as if they were adults. They discussed baseball and Henry declared that cricket could not hold a candle to such a wonderful game. Timmy confessed she did not know either game well.

"How can you not know cricket?" demanded Matt. "You're a Brit, ain't you?"

"I may sound English," she said, "but that is likely due to my brother's and father's influence. Since I turned five, I have spent perhaps five years total in Britain."

The boys and Timmy debated whether ice cream tasted better when the weather was too hot or just warm enough.

They were moving on to the engrossing subject of popcorn—did it taste better with sugar or salt?—when

Doherty came round the corner right in front of them. Probably to see if Mick was trying to go off to his break early.

Doherty eyed the boys and then Mick, as if Mick wasn't doing his job moving ragged urchins along. Though come to think of it, Mick reflected, as he looked young Tucker up and down, Henry looked less ragged today than he ever had. Timmy's doing, of course.

But Doherty's real interest, of course, was almost immediately caught by Timmy.

Flirting with pretty women did not come under the heading of police work. Doherty was probably just about to launch into "what's all this, then," when Timmy held out her hand.

No knife this time, Mick was glad to see.

Still, Doherty looked down at Timmy's hand with a suspicious look, then up at her face. The wide smile she wore must have given him a clue.

"I am pleased to meet you," she said, heartily shaking the hand he finally put out to her. "I am a friend of Officer McCann's."

That tears it, thought Mick gloomily, though he was amused to note something like a beam of admiration on the stone-faced Doherty.

Timmy had a contagious smile.

"We were just discussing buying tickets to your next police event." Timmy turned to Mick. "What did you say it was, Mr. McCann?"

He didn't. He knew he was supposed to be selling tickets, as usual, but he'd lost track of which sort of ordeal it was for. Had Timmy found the tickets jammed into his bureau?

Snooping female.

"A ball to be held at Mulberry Street," Doherty announced. "Were you interested in going then, Miss . . . er?"

"Miss Cooper."

"Delighted, Miss Cooper. I'm Doherty, Daniel Doherty. So you're going to buy tickets, then? It so happens I have a few available."

"Splendid," said Timmy. She left Mick and their little group, strolled over to Doherty and took the astonished, but obviously pleased, man's arm. The way she pulled Doherty ahead caused Mick to squint after them thoughtfully. He had not known the woman long, but already understood she had conniving ways about her.

He realized, to his dismay, he was smiling at the thought. He felt actually interested in whatever the hell kind of nonsense she was up to.

The boys chattered happily, as they trailed after the slowly strolling Doherty and Timmy. Mick, behind the boys, twirled his club by its leather strap, watched the back of Timmy. He mused on why he put up with her.

With a stab of disgust at himself, he realized he felt flattered by the attention of the famous girl. *The* Timona Calverson, wanting a man like him.

Mick knew he had physical appeal. He liked women and they liked him. He'd noticed the way they sometimes looked at him—the widow, for instance. Some women he had met on his beat had gone out of their way to bring him food or to linger, talking. But no woman had ever openly pursued him before.

It was shameless of the girl, the way she refused to budge from his room.

Her behavior, and even her conversation, was not that of a lady's. Last night, for instance, she had collapsed on his bed and mentioned that her *legs* were tired. Mick understood that a real lady did not mention her lower extremities by name. Limbs, she might call them. And then there were those undergarments of hers . . .

The way Daisy had talked yesterday, this Calverson female was some kind of exotic creature, nothing like a regular girl.

Mick watched Timmy pat Doherty's arm as if they were old friends. Exotic? He figured that out soon after she opened her mouth. No, her scent alone could have told him.

She did not seem to operate with the same rules other people did. Perhaps all of her money and all of her fame let her get away with her nonsense.

Mick sighed and twirled his stick the other way. He knew he was thoroughly unfair. Timmy had been more than friendly to his neighbors; she had gone out of her way to help Jenny. Clearly the hoyden had some set of rules. Truth was, he was curious about them.

Doherty was taking his leave of Timmy. The old blister smiled, showing his teeth. He stopped to tip his helmet to Timmy. Well. Who would have guessed?

"*As ucht de,*" Mick murmured. For heaven's sake.

Doherty actually took the helmet off. And he bowed.

And then, wonder of wonders, he smiled in Mick's direction. Doherty whistled as he took off to find another copper to harass.

"How many hundreds of tickets did you buy?" Mick asked when he caught up with Timmy.

She frowned at him. "Nonsense. I only bought a few. I doubt I'll use them, for I dislike balls enormously."

"How's that?" asked Mick.

"I do not know how to behave at very formal events, so I keep my mouth shut tight and smile and nod. Mr. Blenheim taught me to dance, and he has kindly offered to teach me deportment and the fine points of etiquette, but my aunt had already tried for a solid year. I fear I cannot get the knack of it."

"I find that right hard to believe," said Mick dryly.

"I suppose I do well enough to go on," she admitted. "But I would rather face an enraged, spitting camel than such a crowd. Surprising, rather, since I have been dragged to the wretched events much of my life."

"The policeman's ball is no grand formal thing. And what about tonight at the Graves's house then?"

"Oh, that's just dinner."

"A spitting camel?" Matt asked, suddenly interested.

"Just an expression," Mick put in, before Timmy could talk about the thousands of camels she had likely met. Probably rode on as well. "Isn't it, Miss Cooper?"

"Absolutely, Mr. McCann," she said.

She managed to slip her hand through his arm and held on as if they were on a promenade.

At last he gave in and ordered a halt for lunch.

They ate their lunch sitting on empty crates in a quiet back alley. Their luncheon spot did not stink as horribly as most alleys in the district, though a nearby stable lent a horsey air to the meal.

Henry acted as host of the feast. He dramatically flung open the basket, and gave each of them a thick sandwich wrapped in paper. Matt gave a gasp of delight as Henry pulled out bottles of ginger beer and slices of cake.

Mick expertly flicked back the wires, yanked the corks, and handed round the bottles.

"Oh bother. The man forgot to pack such niceties as napkins," grumbled Timmy.

Mick looked over at her. She was eating an enormous pickle, and using her sleeve to wipe at the juice running down her chin.

He choked on a mouthful of ginger beer.

She looked at him enquiringly. "Are you all right, Mr. McCann?"

He got back his breath, and nodded. Five more minutes, he thought. They shall leave in five more minutes. After that, he might be able to concentrate on his job. He'd welcome breaking up a good brawl. Anything to keep from thinking about this damn Timmy creature. Especially thoughts about her in his bed.

Chapter 9

Mick was moody when he came in that evening. The circles under his eyes made Timmy wonder if he had slept badly the night before. She would insist on taking the straw mattress tonight.

After a terse greeting, he tossed his helmet onto the chair and hung up his coat on a hook on the back of the door. She watched him empty his pockets. The occurrence book—no, he called it a memo book—came first, then an amazing pile of junk.

"Where'd the slingshot come from?" She picked it up.

"Took it off a boy what was killing birds and cats."

"The corks? Aren't they from lunch?"

"Eddy collects 'em."

She picked something up and stared at it. "Is that a sock filled with sand?"

"Ah, damn. Forgot to drop that at the station. A man was beating his best friend with it. Mighty effective thing, a cosh."

"And the marbles?" Timona reached out and covered the five marbles lying on his palm with her hand. The glass was cold, his large palm, warm and hard.

He snatched his hand away and took a deep breath. Ha. The contact must have washed through him, too.

She wondered if he was about to do something decisive, like tell her to get the hell out. She had so hoped her one week challenge intrigued him. She bit the inside of her lower lip, waiting for him to announce that the week had ended early.

He didn't say anything. Instead he dropped the marbles into his trousers pocket. He exhaled and shoved his fingers through his thick tawny hair.

"Ah. The marbles are Petey's." Without looking at her, he said, "I promised to give them to Petey yesterday. So. If you will excuse me. We have time yet, and I should like to catch Dr. O'Toole. He said he'd stop by at the end of my shift about now."

He started up the stairs to the Tuckers, and Timona trailed up behind him, hoping he didn't mind. She wanted to say hello to the Tuckers, too, and she carried Jenny's freshly brushed purple dress over her arm.

The doctor was putting his tools back in the bag as they came in to the small cluttered Tucker apartment. The sharp stench of smoke from the fire still hung in the air.

Mick shook hands with Dr. O'Toole, and greeted him in Gaelic. The doctor pulled on his jacket and Mick walked him to the door.

"*Tá sé ag seargadh,*" Dr. O'Toole said quietly, just before he left. He turned to Jenny and said in a louder voice, "Good night Mrs. Tucker. I will call tomorrow."

Tucker lay in the corner, asleep. Jenny asked Mick to look him over too. "I trust you as much as any doctor," she said.

"No Jenny, I'm no doctor. And Dr. O'Toole's bothered Tucker enough already. I'll just say good night to you. After I deliver these." He dropped the marbles into Petey's hand and said, "Mind you keep them away from Meggie and Quinton."

As Mick and Timona headed back down the stairs, Timona said, "I hope you don't mind if I ask, what did the doctor just say?"

Mick frowned. "He told me Tucker is wasting away. Ah, poor old Tuck."

They walked to Daisy's again, side by side. Timmy waited in vain for Mick to offer his arm. She considered putting her arm uninvited through his again. She loved the solid feel of his arm and substantial warmth of the man. But he seemed to have erected an invisible wall around himself. Composed of tension, she thought.

Was he thinking of his sick friend, Tucker? Or was he fretting about her presence?

For the first time, Timona felt conscience-stricken about imposing on the poor man. Perhaps he needed time alone in his flat.

She wanted to ask him, but wasn't sure she wanted to hear his answer.

"Are you well, Mick?" she asked timidly.

He looked over at her, and their eyes met for the first time that evening. "I am. But I do wonder if this dinner is a good plan. Perhaps I should have not come with you."

Timona felt her shoulders relax with relief. She had forgotten he might worry about the silly dinner. "Nonsense. Miss Graves, I mean Daisy, is your friend."

"You won't do anything to hurt that friendship, will you, Miss Calverson?" he asked dryly.

"Such as what?"

"Such as announce to all and sundry that you are sleeping in my one-room flat."

Earlier that day she had considered saying something along these lines. She had at once felt ashamed of the idea. Publishing the fact that she, an unmarried woman, shared his flat did not disturb her in the least.

It was the cheating half-lie of such an announcement that she could not like. And it would reflect badly on Mick, who seemed to care deeply about such matters.

Guilt made her voice sharp with indignation. "Mick McCann, what kind of a person do you think I am?"

He looked over at her again, and grinned for the first time in a while. "I have no idea, Timmy Calverson. None at all."

Dinner was a triumph for everyone. Except Mick.

Daisy's mother was happy because the food she had ordered for the big occasion was delicious and the family managed to find a large contingent of neighbors to show off their famous guest of honor. The neighbors were pleased because they were present at a private exposition of the famous Miss Calverson's adventures and Timona showed herself willing to tell stories to the friendly audience.

"Did you really say that famous line? The one about 'I do not turn from adventure, I embrace it'?" asked Daisy's younger brother.

Timona wrinkled her nose. "I was a silly girl. My father had gotten lost in the desert and I was so relieved when they found him. I was positively giddy. I never thought anyone would take me seriously—I recall I said that line about embracing adventure and the next bit was 'but I much prefer a cup of tea.' No one wrote that part down. I actually am not that fond of adventure."

Mick must have overheard. He made a muffled snort of a noise, loud enough to cause Daisy to turn and frown at him. It was one of the few times all evening she deigned to pay attention to him.

Daisy did not appear to notice Mick. She had her eye on Richard Shea, a slender man with bristling muttonchop sideburns. She giggled or rolled her eyes at nearly everything Shea said.

"Mr. Shea," she had told Timona as she introduced them, "has risen from sales clerk to general manager of Howitt's Dry Goods. He will be responsible for opening the store's next branch. Such a terrible lot of work, just getting ready to open, he tells us."

Richard Shea had chiseled features, pomaded hair and soulful dark eyes. He sat next to Daisy and worked hard to hold Daisy's attention. He succeeded. It was clear Mr. Shea had eaten at Daisy's house before. And Mr. Shea was on a first name basis with Daisy's father.

Throughout dinner, Timona saw the storm rising in Mick's blue eyes. Timona noticed with some indignation that he seemed to be watching her even more than Daisy. Did he blame her for the unpleasant fact that his Daisy was flirtatious?

Timona picked at her meat and potatoes. She chatted with the people on either side of her, a fruit merchant and Daisy's mother. Timona thought them delightful people, especially Daisy's mother, who had an amazing store of information about the history of clothes' fastenings—Timona said truthfully that she felt sure her father, Sir Kenneth, would be fascinated by Mrs. Graves's knowledge. He loved minutiae.

Timona listened to Mrs. Graves, but still managed to watch Daisy and Mick.

Despite her intentions, she liked Mick's Daisy. The girl was as pristine and fresh as the flower for which she'd been named. Daisy was an adorable girl. Sex was probably nothing that had crossed her mind. Neither the word nor the act.

Timona, on the other hand, felt she had always known about sex and its command over humans. Before he left his father's retinue, Griffin made sure she knew about all of the weapons that might be used against her, including subjects usually never mentioned to females.

Timona had soon found she had to be careful when she spoke to girls—even married women she met sometimes knew almost nothing of sexuality.

WhenTimona looked at over at Daisy, the girl was wide-eyed and smiling as she listened to Richard Shea. Timona felt another frisson of envy for Daisy's sweet air of naiveté.

She looked at Mick, and wished she hadn't. Cold blue eyes glared back.

During this dinner, Daisy had revealed her flirtatious nature didn't bloom solely for Mick.

Mick probably hadn't even understood he had serious rivals for Daisy's attention. Timona had assumed as much after she met Daisy and the girl made the casual remark about other admirers.

Silly of Mick, really, if he thought he was the only one to flock around the adorable girl with the rosebud lips and enchanting dimples and the thoroughly coquettish manner.

Timona watched, sad for Mick, but certain she no longer needed to think of Daisy as competition. He was too proud a man to pursue a woman who was foolish enough to pit her suitors against one another.

They made their farewells in the foyer, surrounded by the other guests. Timona graciously signed autograph books and shook hands. She promised Daisy's brother to mention him the next time she talked to a reporter.

"I shall be meeting with one soon, I am sure," she reassured him. "I shall tell Mr. Tothman all about you."

Mick, impatient to be gone, walked down the stairs to wait at the bottom for Timona, and tried not to show a hint of his gloom. But as they walked down the street, he could feel Timona watching him, her eyes just about boring into the side of his head.

About two blocks from his apartment, she broke the silence. "Mr. Shea and Dai—"

"Don't say a thing," Mick interrupted. He expelled a deep breath. "I thought I cared for the girl. I do not want to hear that I am a blind fool."

But Timmy apparently never learned the art of staying quiet. "No you aren't. Daisy is a darling. She is charming and lively. She is, er, young."

"She is twenty-two. Isn't that about your age, Miss Calverson?"

"I'm almost twenty-four. Anyway, age has nothing to do with it."

He shot her an exasperated glance.

She must not have understood how fed up he was with her and her chatter.

"She is a lovely, spoiled, happy girl. Her parents adore her. I imagine she must look like paradise to you," Timona spoke thoughtfully.

"Stop it. Stop trying to make me feel better or feel worse or trying to understand me—or whatever you're about. Just hush up."

She nodded.

He opened his mouth to say he needed to be alone for a time.

Before he could get the words out, she spoke again. "For what it's worth, I am sorry, Mick."

"Just leave it be, will you, please?"

"I understand. Please tell me if there is anything I can do."

Damn the woman to the devil. She obviously had to have the last word. Oh, she seemed to him to continually mock him. Not to mention drive him over the edge day and night with useless, brain-numbing desire.

Mick suddenly wanted to make the too-complacent

woman next to him as angry as he was. He wanted her to feel as empty and foolish as he did.

And he wanted to have the last damn word.

He wheeled and started to grab her shoulders, then remembered her wound. So he grabbed the tops of her arms instead, none too gently. "So you think you want to be with me?"

"Yes." She tilted her head and watched him with a surprised, but unafraid, expression. "I do."

"Well, then. You come right on in to my bed then. I badly want a woman just now. I want a fuck and don't care to pay for it. So if you want to play whore, I'll give it to you. Just don't tell me or yourself it's anything more than that."

Mick had never in his life spoken to a woman in such a dreadful manner. He wondered if she would pull out the knife, or take off running.

She gasped. And looked him straight in the eye.

And began to laugh. "Mick, you silver-tongued devil."

He blushed. The boiling anger had flown, probably with his terrible words. But he couldn't afford to take back what he'd said, not with her. He dropped his hands and took a step backward. "I- I don't want to fool you, Timmy. So. You understand? I won't give you anything else."

She was still laughing, a hand at her throat. "My word. With that elegant approach of yours," she gasped, "I wonder why the women are not lining up for a chance to—um—to fook ye."

He rubbed his chin, still thoroughly abashed by his own outburst. But really. What an outlandish woman. At the very least, she should be screaming in outrage, not laughter.

He caught her eye. He felt himself grinning, shame-faced, at her. Suddenly, he was laughing, too. They laughed so hard they had to collapse onto a stoop together, startling a woman on her way out the door. The woman picked her way down the stairs and rushed off, glancing over her shoulder back at them.

Naturally, that only made them laugh harder.

Mick started to regain his composure, when Timmy, still roaring, eyes filled with tears, wheezed, "Fooking Don Juan McCann."

Five full minutes later, when he could breathe again, Mick gasped, "Timmy, you are thoroughly daft. Did you know?"

Exhilaration poured through him as he spoke. He hadn't succeeded in driving her off. It was not just that he was dead certain he would bed the most desirable female he'd ever encountered, though God knew that was no small matter to him just now. She was like nothing or no one he'd ever stumbled across. He suddenly knew he would miss the crazy woman when she moved along to her next adventure, her next man. Despite all the considerable discomfort she caused him.

They walked the rest of the way back to his building in silence, again not touching. He wasn't sure he could bear her touch. And he wasn't sure if he could bear to be near her without it.

They started climbing the stairs slowly. At a landing they paused and Mick looked over at Timona and attempted a leer. "Still time to turn back, you know. Before you start playing with this native."

He grew serious and bent down to her, almost touching her forehead with his. He breathed, "If you come in my flat, I'll be in that bed with you, Timmy. I expect the Tuckers could make a space for you if you'd rather not stay with me."

Chapter 10

Timona was gripped with dizzying excitement. Even if Mick thought it would be passion without a soul, she knew him better. He was incapable of operating without love of some kind.

But a small twinge of fear made her stop and look up at him. "If I come with you, will I be able to change my mind? And say no?"

He stroked her cheek with a forefinger. "I'd never force a woman, Timmy. And I won't be angry if you change your mind."

"Well, then." With one hand on her heart and the other pointing in the air, she declaimed in her best overwrought manner, "I do not turn from adventure, I embrace it."

Mick snickered. "An' I'll even give you a cuppa tea after."

They raced up the stairs, hand gripped tightly in hand, laughing breathlessly and tripping over the rubbish strewn in the hall.

Botty was waiting and slipped past them to crawl under the bureau. They managed to get the door closed before launching at each other, but only just. The room was dark and Mick didn't have the time to waste lighting the kerosene lantern or a candle. Between their impatient scrabbling and tearing at one another's clothing, they ripped a collar, the placket of a new dress, the side seam of a chemise.

They stood near the door kissing. The feel and taste of her went straight to Mick's head, his heart, and his crotch. Her breasts and other curves were even more blissfully delicious than he remembered. If he didn't have her soon, he'd be driven to screaming madness.

Still standing by the door, Mick slipped his hand between her legs. She moaned. He felt that she was already damp and slick. Now. He pushed her against the wall and hitched up the last piece of clothing between them as he rubbed and thrust against her. He shoved his thigh between her legs and started to reach around her to cup her bottom to hoist her up, when he remembered her injured head and shoulder.

Saints, he was a rutting beast.

He pulled his mouth from hers and, panting, leaned his forehead against the door. "No, no. I'm no animal."

Timona gave a breathless laugh; the soft shush of her breath touched his throat. "Oh, my. I think I might be."

"Nay, what I'm feeling is all woman." He gently ran the tips of his fingers over her sides, the edge of her breasts, and up to her face. In the dark, the texture of cloth, the brush of hair and skin, seemed even more intoxicating. He leaned in to savor her lips again.

"Mick," she whispered. The sound and feel of her voice uttering his name against his mouth drove him back to brainless desire.

The bed, he thought hazily, and made his way across the floor, clutching her hand and pulling her after him.

More kisses, more satin skin.

"Timmy. I can stop. But soon . . . I don't know. Is it what you want?"

She was silent for a moment. He didn't know what

he'd do if she said no. Perhaps howl loud enough to wake the dead.

"Yes," she said at last. If he weren't so completely on fire, he might have stopped to ask why she hesitated.

He'd grown more accustomed to the dark but it required some fumbling and feeling about under the bed.

"What are you doing?" she whispered.

"Medical kit." He got back on the bed and groaned as he slid a hand down the insides of her smooth thighs.

"Why?"

He kissed her jaw. "*Coiscin.*"

"Koshkeen?"

He kissed her throat. "No babies. Condom."

"Ahhh." Her word turned into a long sigh as his mouth found her breast and his fingers probed between her legs.

He moved up to kiss her mouth again.

Timona gave a cry when he at last pushed into her. He could not tell if it was a pleased or frightened sound. She seemed so entirely tight around him. So he gritted his teeth and forced himself to stay still, buried in the heat of her. He slid his hands under her bottom. What a perfect body.

"Thank you," she whispered, and he took it as an invitation to move.

"Oh," she breathed into his ear as he tried to move slow and careful. He wanted it to last at long as possible, for he would not feel the like of her again. But he'd been craving her too long. Too many long hours.

She arched her back and tentatively squirmed when he stopped for a moment in a last desperate attempt to hold back.

"Ah, no, Timmy, God, don't," he groaned into her

fragrant hair, and he nearly blacked out with the pleasure.

When he could think again, he felt ashamed. Not his
most inspired lovemaking. Maire, his first woman from
home, would have been disgusted. A well-off widow,
Maire occasionally introduced some local boys to lovemaking. She would have scolded him, one of her
"pupils," as a brute.

"Vigor is all very well, but a woman appreciates tech-
nique," she had said.

Thoughts of any other woman vanished when Timmy
stirred in his arms. He rolled away from her and fumbled around for the candle.

"Mick," she said, and he could feel her skin as she
moved close and brushed against him. "I don't think
you have kissed me enough. I do like your kisses." Her
soft hands lightly stroked up his belly and across his
shoulders.

In the dark, Mick found her mouth and he kissed
her. His tongue traced her lips. The tender kiss deepened and bloomed into something demanding and
rich. He ripped aside the last scrap of linen that was
once a lacy petticoat he'd caught glimpses of, and there
was nothing but sweet bare skin between them. He forgot about light.

Timona ached with simple pain in her head, her
shoulder, between her legs. Another, more complex
ache haunted her body that she knew was unfulfilled
lust. Odd that she should know it, when she had never
experienced it. To such a degree, at any rate.

The sensation of Mick as he had touched her and
pushed against her at the door had been astonishing.

She had never in her life felt such heated sensual eagerness. Good that he pressed against her and held her up, for the backs of her knees had felt too rubbery to stay straight.

But then on the bed, before she even could catch her breath at the contact—all of the skin, the solid bulk, and the immediate warmth and weight of his body—he'd plunged inside her. The shock of the size of him—what did he have down there, a telegraph pole?—gave way to pain. Almost at once the pain gave way to the awareness that if he kept thrusting in that manner, he would go right through her to the other side. Which actually she identified as pleasure about the moment he stopped for a few seconds. And when he started again, he finished far too quickly.

She gave up worrying when she remembered that she was now allowed to indulge in something she'd longed to do. She could touch his skin. Everywhere. And she could have kisses at any time and those were without a doubt the best thing her mouth had ever experienced. Whether they were delicate teasing nibbles or sloppily passionate, Mick's kisses were sweeter than any food.

As they kissed in the dark, Mick's hand smoothed over her and she reveled in the feel of his calloused fingers as they skimmed her breasts. His delicate touch caressed her nipples, relieved and incited an ache in her breasts and her belly. When she moaned, his touch grew more urgent and his fingers dipped down between her legs. She pressed her legs together automatically, but he caressed the inside of her thighs gently until she opened them again.

"Lie still for a minute," he whispered in her ear.

Oh good. Or was it bad. He would climb on top of her again. She wasn't sure which of the two aches inside her would win over her body. But she could not help trembling with excitement.

He didn't move on top of her. Instead he kissed her and licked and touched her body. Everywhere. His skin and hair rubbed her. He used his hands, and the damp warmth and pressure of his tongue, breath, and even his teeth on her breasts and then down her belly to the sensitive flesh of her inner thighs and then, oh my, between her legs until she writhed, agitated beyond thought.

His touch grew less delicate. And his mouth when he moved back to hers plunged in, tasting of her own salt and demanding more from her.

"Oh, yes, please," she managed to say and when she thought she was going to have to take matters into her own hands and climb on top of him, he was there, ready for her to wrap her arms and legs around his body and pull him in. The unpleasant pain was long forgotten. And now he fit into her just a little too perfectly large, instead of uncomfortable. She moved around him and pushed and forgot that anything existed beyond their two bodies. He whispered soft, guttural words in her ear.

And then at the very second she nearly screamed aloud with frustrated need, the rush of relief crashed through her.

"Oh! That's it," she gasped.

Mick cried out as he drove into her.

Timona lay stunned and limp beneath him until he began lift himself away from her. She did not want the touch of air on her skin. She would much rather have the feel of warm Mick everywhere.

"Timmy, hush, I am not going anywhere," he whispered in her ear as she scrabbled to pull him close again. "I just don't want to crush you to death."

"The most perfect way to go," she murmured. "Oh, Mick, Mick. Thank you."

"It is I who should thank you."

She twined her legs around his, yawned, and pushed her face against his shoulder to cover her open mouth. He gave a low laugh. "How polite we are with our thanks and graceful manners."

"Hmmm," she agreed. For a long while, she let her hands explore him, lightly stroking him to memorize the shape of his shoulders, back, and bottom. All long smooth flats and hard curves, she thought drowsily. His hair was softer than she expected.

At last he pulled out and away from her and lit the candle. He lay down on his back and turned his head to smile over at her. He stretched, pushing his hands high over his head.

The chance to look at his naked body woke her up. Looking was not nearly enough, and her hands and mouth explored the silk skin of his body. Odd that such soft skin covered the hardness of his belly and the tender inside of his powerful arms.

She put her tongue against his chest, lapped the nipple and enjoyed his hiss of pleasure. He tasted slightly salty. His skin still smelled faintly of smoke but she detected a subtle musky flavor on his skin she knew must be pure Mick. The soft hair on his chest was damp with sweat. The hair swirled down, over his belly to the thick hair around his member.

She sat back on her heels to examine him again. She wondered if he was ticklish. When she moved to find out, he quickly seized her hands and easily held her wrists with one hand and with the other discovered that she, too, was very ticklish—though he quickly rolled away from her. "No, not time yet to pull out them shoulder stitches of yours."

From under the bureau, Botty occasionally growled at their horseplay.

"Don't fret, Botty," Mick would say and the dog would sigh.

Timona had not known making love could be . . . so pleasurable. Occasionally a romp, too. The whole experience had sounded like so much work when Griffin had described it, a solemn, serious business. But then, of course, he had been talking to his sister.

She wriggled away from Mick and climbed onto the sweat- and sex-slicked skin of his hips to straddle him. He fought off her attempts to attack him again by gently grabbing the sides of her head, avoiding her cut, and pulling her down to him for a kiss. A few minutes later, still crouching above him, she observed that this might be another position in which to make love.

"Perhaps 'tisn't a good idea," he murmured doubtfully. "Don't want you to get sore there too."

"Excuse me, but I believe it could be a very good idea," she whispered.

A little later, he whispered back, "Slow and careful, then."

She was already sore, but oh, it was worth it. The delicious ache won out again. His large hands clutched her hips as she squirmed tentatively on him. They both soon forgot about the slow and careful.

Mick had never been so entirely and happily exhausted in his life.

Timona lay next to him, one arm crooked behind her head. In a sleepy voice she remarked, "I think this is wonderful. Why do you suppose women are told they shouldn't enjoy it?"

The woman obviously was not mortified by her wanton ways—but Mick realized he didn't want either of them to be ashamed. Especially not Timmy with her enthusiasm for life and . . . other matters.

"I do not know why females are told such a thing. But I am surely glad you do not believe it." He spoke firmly but was annoyed to feel himself blush.

She must have been watching him for she said, "I do like the way you blush. It turns your face and neck a rather reddish gold."

He snorted. "And I suppose you never blush, shameless one?"

"Often. But I go bright red."

She lay on her back. Mick stretched out next to her, propped up on one elbow. He admired her body in the soft light of one candle. Mick's finger slowly traced her thigh. She was a small woman, but she was graced with such good, long curving lines. He stopped at a large bloody smear that stretched across the smooth skin of her thigh, and he peered at her shoulder. "Ah no. Did one of your cuts open? Or are you having your monthlies?"

He lightly kissed her injured shoulder above the cut, and, as an afterthought, tasted the side of her elegant neck with the tip of his tongue.

She looked down at her leg unconcerned, and rubbed at the smear. With a musing air, she said, "Now that is interesting. I'd assumed with all the hard travel and some of the wretched horses and pack animals I've ridden there wouldn't be a hymen left to rupture. I must have been wrong."

He shoved himself bolt upright and stared down at her, horrified. "You- you are . . . a virgin?"

"Not any more." And she showed him the sleek, sly smile.

He reached down and gathered her up, as she squawked with protests. He pulled her onto his lap and rocked her and rested his cheek on her hair. "Oh,

Jesus, I didn't know, Timmy. I'm sorry. I'm so very sorry."

None of her encounters with other men on her strange journeys, nor even the brutes from the whorehouse had stolen her virtue.

He had.

She squirmed backwards in his arms. The wide green-gray eyes searched his face. "Why? I'm not at all sorry. It all has been far more pleasurable than I ever imagined."

"I do not see how you could do such a thing," he said sadly. "To give up something like that, something so precious, casually to a man you've known less than a week."

"It was not casual," she said. "You know it wasn't. And you cannot—you will not—make me feel bad about this, Mr. Mick McCann. It is too wonderful." She shoved away and rolled off his lap and lay on her side away from him, sulky for the first time since he'd met her. "So don't start in with your this-is-only-sex talk again."

"No. I know I was insulting before. I was trying to be a bastard. Turns out I pretty well succeeded, eh?" he muttered. He knew he shouldn't grab at her again, so he pushed up his knees and rested his arms on them.

With a soft exhalation of breath, he laid his head on his folded arms and examined her stiff, offended back, wondering what he was supposed to do or say.

What the hell did this mean, he thought, lost in strange confusion of annoyance, fear, and anticipation. What in God's name were the rules?

She was natural in her body, happy with play, and he had never felt so in tune with a woman during intimacy. Not that he'd had legions of females. He believed he knew her because he had discovered how to please her. Saints above, how shockingly wrong he had been.

He mumbled, "Strikes me as beyond strange that we

could be so close here in my bed and I understand you not at all."

She didn't answer.

"Please do not grow angry. But tell me how could you give up your honor so easily?"

She did not answer immediately. "I am not sure how I knew it was right. Except that I knew I gave it to an honorable man."

Oh. Blast. He could guess what that meant. If she was anything like the women he did understand, she would expect him to make amends.

He felt a flash of resentment. She should have said she was an innocent.

But even as the bitterness filled him, he knew he was unfair. She never mentioned the matter, he recalled. She was an experienced woman of the world and Mick chose to believe that was true in all matters.

He'd had a choice. No one held a gun to his head and demanded he push his cock into this woman.

Oh Lord. If she said yes to him, he would be in for more than he ever bargained for. Trapped forever.A gorgeous body, the loveliest he had ever beheld, but what a strange, outlandish person inside.

He gathered the courage he needed and after a long silence he whispered rather unsteadily, "Shall I marry you then?"

A longer silence.

She rolled onto her back and looked up at him, intently. "Do you love me?"

He spoke louder, in a firm voice. "Timmy. I took your virtue. It is right and proper I offer you marriage."

"What would you do if I hadn't been a virgin? Would you have mentioned marriage to me? Would you have even thought of marrying me?"

He didn't answer for several long moments. Thought had little or nothing to do with the last few hours.

Should he be honest and say "no"? And was the honest reply "no"?

He'd always understood marriage equaled a quiet life with a woman you cherished and respected. A woman you had known and admired for a long while before you took that big step.

Taking a woman from outside your own walk of life. Taking her with crazy—no, brainless—animal lust. That had naught to do with the word marriage.

And she had been as much of an animal, too. She had allowed him to do whatever he wanted and did some shocking things in return. Did he want to wed any woman who would use her mouth in such scandalous and interesting ways? Well, as it happens, he might reply "yes" to that particular question.

Before he could figure out an answer to the larger question, honest or otherwise, Timmy groaned. "Oh, bother. No, I won't marry you, Mick."

"Timmy, think now, becau—"

She interrupted. "I wish I hadn't told you I was a virgin. Or you weren't quite so bloody honorable."

He gave a startled laugh. "I don't understand, Timona."

"It makes perfect sense. I hate men who think to compromise women in order to force them into marriage. I, ah, have had some brushes with men like that. I despise coercion."

He thought she would elaborate. Instead she said, "But tell me. Why did you couple with me, Mick? And, pray, do not tell me again about men with their needs."

He thumped down onto the bed next to her again, and took a deep breath. The inhalation carried the scent of sex, sweat and pure Timmy. A fragrance that brought back echoes of his fearful craving for her.

"What else was it then? Pure hellish need. The smell of you makes me dead faint with hunger. Watching you walk, laugh, even sit at the Graves damn dinner table about drove me out of my wits. Even while I was fuming about Daisy's sparking another lad, there I sat, panting after you."

"Last night I could barely keep myself planted on that floor. The whole damn night I lay awake, half a minute from crawling across to get into my bed with you. See? It's easy to explain. Even if I had gained relief on me own . . ."

He paused to look at her, not sure if she took his meaning and fairly sure he didn't want to explain self abuse or self pollution, as Father Connor called it.

But she nodded her understanding, so he went on. "Well. The point is, I would have shattered if you'd stayed here another night and I hadn't had you."

He held his fists above them, and opened his fingers to demonstrate an explosion. "Boom. The very first man in history to have died of lust."

She giggled. "That's easy enough to understand."

"Ah, sure. I'm easy. You, though—ach, I wish I could fathom you. And your world."

"That's a start," she said cheerfully and turned onto her side to face him again. "You don't have me pigeonholed anymore do you?"

"Do you mean do I begin to understand you at all? Not bloody likely."

"Very good," she said and moved close to lightly kiss his neck. He moved onto his side toward her. She ran her hands lightly over and over his shoulders, then down his spine. Incredible. He felt the hint of lust stir again.

"And are you at all curious about me?" she whispered.

Mick laughed. "Mostly terrified. But, aye, I am a bit curious about what makes you tick."

She inched away from him. Then she blushed. A soft

pink he noted, not bright red. She toyed with a lock of her hair that lay across her charming breast. He wondered if she were about to reveal some horrible secret, like she was engaged to a lad with Othello-like tendencies.

"You were kind enough to play for me on your, ah, flute. So . . . did I mention I like to take pictures? Lately I've taken pictures of buildings. Man-made structures. Do you know how photography works?"

"No, but I'm willin' to learn, Timona. Though I'm not sure a bed is the best place to teach a man—"

She pulled him down to her and kissed him.

Chapter 11

Blenheim found the latest telegram waiting for him in Chicago. "AM DETAINED IN NEW YORK STOP WILL MEET YOU IN MINNESOTA STOP PLEASE RESPOND SO I KNOW YOU ARE WITH FATHER STOP APOLOGIES FOR DELAY BUT NOT TO WORRY STOP TIMONA C."

He sent his response to the New York bank right away, and made his note as terse as hers. She'd see how it felt to get so little information. "RECEIVED YOUR MESSAGE IN CHICAGO STOP YES I AM WITH SIR KENNETH STOP BLENHEIM."

But he felt he should do more. He nervously rubbed the solid chain of his watch between two fingers as he reread the short note. She never worried about saving money on her telegrams. Usually telegrams from Timona were as long as letters.

Something was wrong with the blasted girl. He would bet his last shilling that his beloved had perhaps somehow gotten thrown into a predicament—of her own making, no doubt. He sighed. If he set Taylor or Benhurst from the New York office on her trail, they might elbow their way into her attentions, particularly if they came to her rescue.

The last time they came through New York, Taylor had made it clear he liked Miss Calverson's looks. Very clear. Blenheim saw Taylor's interest, but Miss Calverson who never appeared to pay attention to such things, did not.

The first time she'd noticed Blenheim was when he fetched back her father from a Hindu temple the old man had wandered to. Her grateful hug on that occasion still formed a role in some of his fantasies.

On the other hand, if he left either Taylor or Benhurst or anyone in the smaller Chicago office in charge of Sir Kenneth, the old son of a bachelor might take a liking to one of those chaps. Blenheim might find himself back in an office somewhere in the Calverson organization. He'd lose his plum job and constant access to the woman he loved.

What to do, what to do.

Only one man had the connections in New York to deal with the problem and not threaten Blenheim's ultimate plan for Timona. Blenheim pulled out a telegram form and started a carefully worded note to Mr. Griffin Calverson. A splendid chap, Griffin, splendid. But it did not do to rile him unnecessarily.

Blenheim had heard from the New York office that Griffin was actually in New York State, too. Albany or somewhere. Good, Taylor could track him down if the bank couldn't.

"CONCERNED TIMONA C IN SOME SORT OF TROUBLE STOP BANK MANAGER SHOULD KNOW HER WHEREABOUTS STOP BLENHEIM." He crossed out "trouble" and wrote in "situation." And then he crossed out his name. If the bank manager didn't, in fact, know where Timona was, then he'd be the one to get the blame. Blenheim addressed it to the Calverson office in New York City and handed it to the Western Union operator.

For a moment he leaned against a wall of the station

to finger his watch chain and worry about Timona. But then he heard Sir Kenneth's happy chatter.

From the sound of it, the blighter had found a railroad enthusiast and was eagerly listening to some nonsense about steam engines. It wasn't dinosaurs for a nice change.

Nevertheless Blenheim would have to interrupt and drag him along to the hotel before Sir Kenneth wandered off with the railroad man. Sir Kenneth often appreciated fellow fanatics no matter what their interests. At least in Chicago the dreadful nuisance of a man wouldn't go off with cannibals to observe their rituals.

After their night of making love, Mick woke first. Afraid to move, he watched Timona sleep. What if she woke and finally fathomed the serious mistake she'd made? Would she bemoan her lost virtue? What would he do, how could he comfort her, if she felt shame and shrank away from him?

Eventually Botty, and his own body, demanded they go outside.

He quietly pulled on trousers and a shirt and went out back.

When he returned to the apartment, Timona still slept. Mick hesitated, and then peeled back the covers to get back in bed. He stopped. She lay on her stomach and the sight of her naked back in the dim daylight that filtered through the half-boarded window enthralled him.

He pulled the covers down further to admire her mesmerizing body. Her long hair fanned across her back and onto the bed.

The place where her rear met her legs had a curve that made him wish he could draw. He stood by the bed and bent to trace the line of her with his hand.

The moment his fingers lightly stroked the curve of her bottom, she woke. Almost at once she rolled onto her back and held open her arms. The welcoming arms and her sleepy smile made Mick release a breath he hadn't known he was holding.

Again! He thought, and his heart beat very fast with anticipation and something he dimly recognized as relief. He shucked his shirt and trousers and crawled back into bed with her.

After they made love, they talked. Or rather, Timona continued asking questions.

She leaned on her elbow and stroked her other hand across his chin. The bristles on his face were pleasantly scratchy on her fingertips. "Tell me more. Tell me why you are in this country," she demanded.

"Money, of course."

"How on earth did you end up as a policeman?"

"I made the crossing from Ireland with the second cousin of Kelly, who's a Tammany boss. That and me size gave me the excellent job."

"Excellent?" She tried not to sound snide.

"Oh, now, a copper's pay is mighty fine for a man like me. Even without . . . that." He waved a hand at his drawer full of cash. "And back home Mam and the kids required money as soon as I could lay my hands on some. I did not have the time to wander out to a farm or ranch in search of work."

Mick mentioned his mother's propensity to sit back and wait for heaven to take care of matters. But he didn't condemn the woman. "After all," he pointed out, "after Da died, all she had was bills and hungry children. 'Tis no wonder she turned to prayer."

Timona, hesitant, asked, "Do you wish to go back to live with your mother some day?"

He laughed. "Nay, never. She is too sad around me. I am too like Da to make her comfortable and too unlike him to make her happy."

"Unlike? How?"

"Da wanted to be a doctor, but spent his life scrabbling for food. His dreams were big, but he lacked the wherewithal or drive to make them real and he didn't get anywhere. I loved and respected the man, but he was something of a failure, you see," he said, bitterly. "I shan't fall into that trap."

"What do you mean?"

"I keep my ambitions small, Timmy Calverson. I won't hanker after the impossible. I watched him lose his joy in life because he longed for something he could never afford to be or do."

He looked at her, troubled. And seemed about to speak, but then clamped his lips tight.

"Go on," she urged. "What were you going to say? I know you were about to—"

But he had inched close to her and now leaned over her and stopped her mouth with his.

She dissolved into his warm kiss, all the while thinking, damn the man: Perhaps he was going to tell her he didn't want anything to do with her. She imagined he would come up with some dreadful nonsense, like she drew too much attention for a humble man like himself. Or something horrid about money again.

Fine. Timona would never pressure him. She made that decision the night before, after she saw the look of horror enter his eyes, just before he asked her to marry him in a French-nobleman-facing-the-guillotine voice.

She would wait for a very specific, clear signal before she again broached the subject of their future together.

When they stopped kissing to breathe, she opened her mouth to speak. But Mick's lips and tongue swooped in again. He clutched her hungrily, as if he'd never so much as touched her before. The fire was not banked far down in her, either.

Much later, she lay with her head resting on his chest, and the hair tickled her ear as she listened to the deep rhythm of his breath and heartbeat. She said, "Tell me how else you are different from your father."

"You are the most persistent little pest," he said mildly.

"Yes. You will be astonished to hear that you are not the first to mention it. Go on, please tell me, Mick."

"Yes, yer royal highness. Well, hmm. Da was a far gentler man than me. He would never have been able to use the club on his worst enemy. And he kissed Bottom's arse."

Timona understood he meant the landlord, Botham, not the hideous mutt.

"Go on," she reminded him as she ran a hand over his chest, memorizing the feel of the skin and muscles under her fingers.

"I was not so obliging. When Da died, we were in arrears with our rent, tithes, grocers, oh, any debt you could mention. I worked me tail off, and so did Dee, my sister, but we could not get ahead of the bills. So a few years ago, I wrote to Bottom, asking for help finding a solution."

"Did he help?"

Mick shook his head. "Bottom summoned me and Mam. And he offered me a job in his filthy stables and with his mangy hounds. But a whole day's work, every day, for no pay—only to make up the family's rent which we hadn't paid in full for almost a year. And as the deal stood, t'would have taken a good many years to pay that off. Mam wanted me to oblige the man. Da would have done it and been happy about it."

Timona shifted her head so that she could hear his

slow, steady heartbeat again. "And what about you?" she asked.

"At the interview I didn't even stop to think it over, the way he and Mam asked me to. I told the man to kiss my arse for a change."

He laughed. She loved the way the low-pitched velvety sound of it filled her body. "Bottom might have gotten over it by now, but me poor Mam never will."

He touched the tip of her nose with his forefinger. "Now tis my turn to be inquisitor. I know something of your father and brother from all yesterday's talk of your adventures, but what of your mother and any others in your family?"

"Oh, I can barely recall my mother."

"I am sorry."

"She's not dead, just no longer a part of our family."

Mick appeared to be waiting for an explanation, but Timona was entirely uninterested in discussing herself. At the moment she was tired of being one of the famous Calversons. Besides she was ravenous.

"Wait here." She hopped out of bed, grabbed the parcel of pastries and two plates, and her handkerchief.

She carefully lowered herself onto the edge of the bed next to him. "Breakfast is served. I consider it the height of luxury to eat breakfast in bed. Even this bed."

She doled out the last of the stale pastries and started to wipe a bit of jam off her finger with her handkerchief.

"Here, wait," protested Mick. He grabbed her hand and gently and thoroughly sucked the jam off her forefinger. "Now that is the way to eat a good breakfast."

Timona breathlessly agreed.

Mick lay, one hand cupped behind his head, the other balancing the plate on his bare chest. His clear blue gaze steadily regarded her. He had a wide grin on his face. "Hey, girl, I hope you notice I allowed you to

change the subject? When you would dodge away, I let
you go. And wasn't merely because I was famished meself. I'm what they call polite. Not pushy, like some I
could mention."

She grinned back. And here she thought he simply
wasn't paying attention. "Perhaps someday I might
learn from your improving example, but I would not
hold my breath if I were you, Mick McCann. So now,
tell me about your village."

The next day, Mick went back to work, and he took
a long break to go into the library. He asked for articles
that mentioned Timona Calverson.

The head librarian certainly had heard of Timmy.

"We had a librarian who collected all the columns
that mentioned the crazy Calversons."

The woman found the thick, leather-bound scrap-
book and handed it to Mick, warning him to return it
to the desk when he was finished.

What he found in the book entirely stole his peace.

Timona had indeed ridden camels. And led llamas
through the high mountains in South America. And
fled a man-eating tiger in India. The next day her
brother joined a hunt that went out and brought the
tiger down.

She had been captured, kidnapped, escaped fires,
climbed mountains no white woman had ever even
seen before and gone deep into jungles few had even
heard of. She had visited kings and princes and sheiks
and rajahs. As a young girl, she had lived for months
with a tribe of South American Indians. And the mate-
rial pasted into the book ended two years earlier. Who
knew what she'd been up to since then?

Mick looked up to see a man with yellow hair walk
past. There was something familiar about him . . . but

Mick soon forgot everything else as he read about Timona Calverson, visitor to the court of the Russian Czar.

Mick wandered out of the library in a daze. He'd hoped to understand her better after reading the stories of Timmy, but the outlandish woman seemed more alien than ever.

She must get struck with travel lust every few weeks. She would never stay put when adventure beckoned— no matter that she claimed she'd rather have a cup of tea. And what on earth did she want with him? Other than the obvious, of course.

He did not dare to ask.

Instead he waited.

Chapter 12

One week passed.

Caught up in a delirious passion of laughter and sex, the likes of which he had never in his life imagined, Mick did not dare mention that deadline Timona had given herself.

Now Mick feared what he'd thought he wanted: Timona vanishing from his world.

They had quickly fallen into something like a routine. When Mick worked the day shift, Timmy walked out with him, even at dawn.

Then she turned toward the part of New York he didn't enter. She talked to other photographers, met up with old friends, and was delighted to finally meet a famous photographer she'd been corresponding with, a Mr. Jackson.

She mentioned her days' activities to him when they shared the evening meal she bought or he made. They ate and talked like friends, though sometimes they were naked in bed as they shared the meal. They seemed unable to keep from touching one another. And rarely waited till proper bedtime to make love.

She talked of pictures, she described her friends, she even talked of her past, but she never spoke of the future.

Every moment he expected Timmy to lean towards

him and announce, "This is my last kiss for you, Mick McCann. We did have a boatload of fun, didn't we?"

When he walked home from work at the end of the day, he wondered if he would find her or her note saying good-bye for she was off to Turkey or Brazil or Minnesota.

She was so thoroughly out of place in his humdrum, tatty existence he had trouble thinking of her as one of his own kind. Even if he hadn't known of her travels, she appeared to him a wondrous, bright-colored bird of paradise come to perch among a bunch of sparrows. Amazing that no one else in his life seemed to see that Miss Cooper did not fit.

The neighbors obviously must talk about the delicious scandal of her: the unmarried woman in Mr. McCann's bed. Yet Mick came home from work one afternoon and was amused to find Timmy earnestly talking with Mrs. O'Neal, the most easily scandalized woman in the neighborhood. Even that judgmental woman could not hold out against Timmy's charm.

She eventually won over the two unbendingly shy creatures in his life, a dog and a boy.

Every couple of days Mick fed some of the kids from the alley. They went out to dinner at Miggie's diner, a cheaper and more dubious establishment than Colsun's. Timmy agreed to go there only because Eddy, the boy from the alley, felt comfortable at Miggie's. Tonight only Eddy lingered near the front stoop waiting for an invitation for food.

Timmy pushed the gray, nameless "Meat Special" around on her plate. Mick remembered some of the meals she'd described eating in South America.

"Strikes me as odd you don't like old Miggie's fare, but you've munched down bugs."

She put down her fork with the bent tines. "Ah, but

the bugs were fresh and had been prepared by a woman who knew what she was doing."

Mick chuckled. "So tell me, what amazing things happened today?"

"I think Botty almost let me pat him today."

Shy Eddy opened his mouth in her presence for the first time. "I bet ya you can't. Botty only lets Mr. Mick touch him." He murmured the words, probably figuring she wasn't listening. She was, though.

"You're on," Timmy said at once. "How about I get one week to try?" She flashed a brief, wicked smile at Mick.

Abashed that an adult other than Mick actually talked to him, Eddy shrank down in his chair. He turned pale and whispered, "No, ma'am, I'm sorry. I was just fooling and didn't mean a real bet you see—"

Timmy calmly continued, "If I win the bet, you must either go to school for three mornings or let me play teacher for that long. I dearly enjoy playing teacher, as poor Henry and Sarey Tucker can tell you."

"An' if I win?" said Eddy at last.

"A whole pie. Any flavor. And for you alone to eat."

Less than two days later, as she read and Mick quietly played music, she looked up from her book to give him a triumphant smile and said, "Look."

She appeared ridiculously proud of herself and directed her gaze down to show him why she looked like the cat that swallowed the canary.

Her hand rested on Botty's head.

"Ah, poor Eddy," said Mick. "No pie for him."

Within two days, the dog even glumly allowed her to pull him onto her lap.

Another week passed.

Mick still waited for her to take flight, but neither of them brought up the subject. She never mentioned leaving his flat. And she didn't ask him to follow her to better apartment.

Sometimes when they lay together or he kissed her, or she smiled at him, or she said something outrageous, he imagined never enjoying that particular pleasure again. At those moments he believed he would follow her wherever she asked him to go. India, Australia, Fifth Avenue—he'd trail right along after her.

Other times, usually as he walked the quiet part of his beat, he wondered if he'd lost all sense of pride to imagine himself happily reduced to nothing more than a rich girl's playmate.

The worst moments came when he understood what he'd done—turned her sense of indebtedness to his own advantage. Eventually she'd wake up and see that she'd fallen into that old trap. He almost squirmed with shame when he imagined the moment the scales fell from her eyes and she realized her "rescuer" had used her gratitude for his own selfish desire.

But she did not go, or even talk about leaving. Mick managed to forget she would eventually move on. He even began to think of her as his own.

Until part of her real life barged into his flat, uninvited.

Chapter 13

When Mick worked the night shift for the first time after Timmy came into his life, he collapsed into bed at five in the morning next to the sleeping Timmy, who was delighted to wake up and greet him properly.

He fell asleep. When he woke up in the afternoon, Timmy was gone. He remembered she said was going to see someone off on a train to Colorado. Mick yawned, rolled over and nearly suffered a heart attack. He looked up into the face of a well dressed stranger who stood close to the bed, watching him.

The brown-haired man was about thirty-five. He had a slender, well-proportioned figure of middle height, and wore the dark suit, gold watch chain and fob, and full but neatly trimmed mustache of a businessman. The handsome, though expressionless, face stared down at Mick. There was nothing startling or threatening about the man, until Mick looked into his eyes, and saw they were pure emerald green and as cold as a day in February.

Between one breath and the next, something shifted in the stranger's face, and the peculiar notion Mick had that the man had no soul seemed daft. Yet Mick had seen those eyes, and understood he beheld a dangerous human. He'd met others like him, and knew enough to be apprehensive. He squinted at the card the man handed him. And then back at the man.

Lord God.

"So you are Timona's Griffin, then?"

"And you are Michael McCann. Mick to your friends."

Mick nodded and waited.

Calverson walked to the only chair in the room and sat down. He glanced around. Mick waited for a remark, but Griffin Calverson showed no reaction to the shabbiness.

The man must be a marvelous poker player.

Mick glanced to where Botty slept peacefully under the bureau. Some watchdog.

Calverson said, "I hear from impeccable sources that my sister cares about you, Officer McCann."

"She believes she has a care, but I am not of—" Mick began.

"Timona, unlike myself, is quite passionate. She is loyal to a fault. If she thinks she cares about you, I believe her." The voice was smooth, cultured, and held only a small promise of violence that lay not far from the surface.

Jesus, this one might be a right lunatic. Didn't do to show hesitation with that sort of man.

Mick frowned. "I asked her, and she said 'no' to marriage with me. I will not be intimidated into marrying anyone, Mr. Calverson, if that is what you are about."

If Mick were Timona's brother, naturally that's exactly what he'd be doing. Marriage is what any normal brother would demand. But he suspected all bets were off with this lot.

He was right.

"Good, I am glad to know you're not easily intimidated," said Griffin heartily, and his eyes looked almost human. "I don't care what you do as long as you are honest. Or as honest as you coppers can be. Leave Timona if you feel you must. She is old enough and I daresay tough enough to take care of her own emotional claptrap.

"But if I find out you leave her pregnant, or you are in it for her money, or you are involved in some other dishonest scheme that will affect my sister, I will hunt you down. I will cut off your testicles and force you to eat them."

Mick did not doubt it.

Griffin got up, walked over to him, bent down and stared into Mick's face. "I may not be a daily presence in her life, but I care deeply about my sister's welfare. I beg of you, for your own sake, do not forget that."

Mick flinched away from him and gave a groan of disgust. "Christ, what a clan you must be. How did so sweet a woman as Timmy end up with a brother like you?"

Griffin Calverson straightened up and actually laughed, an unexpectedly merry, infectious sound. At least he shared that trait with his sister. "You'll do, Mr. McCann. I have not seen her for some time and I forgot what a good judge of character my sister usually is. I think I'll trust you. For now."

Well, at least the man with the cold eyes didn't say anything obnoxious about Mick's nationality or his pitiful room.

And standing in the middle of the room, Calverson actually went so far as to explain his presence.

"I don't usually meddle in her affairs but I received a telegram saying she was in a 'situation.' I am relieved to find that it is merely that she's wandered away and found herself a lover."

Calverson pulled the gold watch from his waistcoat. He appeared to be finished with his strange interview.

Mick said, "Timona didn't wander. She was kidnapped, Calverson. She managed to escape on her own."

The watch snapped shut. The eyes instantly went hard again. "Tell me about it."

"No. I think it better if I let her tell you."

Griffin nodded his approval. "You'll do indeed."

He walked to the door. "My address is on the card. I shall be in New York for about two weeks. You or Timona may call on me at any time. Goodbye, Mick McCann." He paused. "One more thing. Please do not tell her about this conversation."

Mick grunted. "Why ever not?"

The edges of Calverson's mouth almost quirked into a smile. The green eyes were nearly warm. "She'll give me holy hell."

After Calverson left, Mick sat on his bed and rubbed his face with both hands. He felt ill. Kind Timona, who had a care for all she met, had that man as a brother? There were advantages, he supposed—for instance, now he fully understood how she'd gotten out of the bordello intact.

Feet stamping on the stairs woke him from his reverie.

The door burst open. She ought to learn to knock, he thought, fretting over what he could say to her about her brother. But it was Henry who stood there.

"I think Pa is gone, Mr. Mick. I- I think he's dead." Henry burst into tears and flung himself at Mick. After a few minutes of rocking and soothing Henry, Mick walked upstairs holding the big ten-year-old on his hip as if the boy were a toddler.

Jenny sat in a corner, white as paper. Poor Tucker's eyes stared at nothing. Mick put down Henry and crossed over to close the man's eyes. He drew a blanket over Tuck's head.

"No!" shrieked Jenny, and Mick knew he had a job on his hands. He sent Henry and Petey for Rob and Sarey to go after Dr. O'Toole. Too bad he couldn't shove them all out of the room.

Jenny looked up. "Mick, you're getting the doctor? You think he can help?"

Mick crouched by the woman and took both her hands in his. Slowly and distinctly he said, "I'm fetching the doctor for a death certificate, Jenny. Tucker is gone."

She shrieked and shrieked again. The baby started wailing too.

So Mick grabbed the baby and Meggie, the three-year-old. He shouted over his shoulder, though he doubted she heard him. "We will be downstairs, Jenny. I will come up when the doctor gets here."

No need for the kids to see their Mam like this. He hauled them down to his room. They played a game which featured Mick the bear trying to eat Meggie. The baby watched and gurgled his approval. The sweet sound blended with Botty's growl.

Mick heard the clock toll and realized he was supposed to be at work again within the hour. Mrs. Kelly next door would be home soon enough to care for the small kids.

The light, quick step and rustle of a woman's dress wasn't Mrs. Kelly. Timona spoke quietly from the open door. "The children out front are wildly excited because someone has died. Tucker?"

Mick met her worried gaze and nodded.

"Oh, no. Poor Jenny."

His heart yearned toward Timona.

He stood up, with Meggie still clutching him around the neck, and pulled Timmy into his arms and held her tight. Meggie swung around Mick's neck and thrust herself between them with a happy shout. The baby on the bed began to cry.

* * *

Jenny refused to prepare Tucker for burial, so Mick and Rob did the job rather than pay the undertaker's assistant. While they worked on Tucker, Timona took Jenny out to buy food for a wake to be held in Colsun's restaurant. Colsun said he was willing to hold a wake, but he would not supply the food.

"Thank goodness for that. It's rotten food." Timona said. Mick didn't argue, though he thought the food was not so bad. Price was good, anyway.

"I imagine Jenny will agree to take part if we simply call it a party," Timona went on.

Mick and she sat side by side on the bed. He picked up her hand and absently played with it. Such elegant little fingers, even when stained dark with strange photographic chemicals.

"Whatever the wake is called, I don't like you paying for it," he grumbled.

"Mick, pray do not start with that now. It is for the Tuckers."

"I don't like it." He drew her pinkie to his mouth and kissed it.

She pushed her head against him. "Would you rather use your money? From the drawer?"

"I don't like that, either." He smiled down at her wryly. "Seems I don't like much of anything don't it? But I do damn-all to stop any of it. I don't like the way you will sleep with me, but you don't see me kicking your sweet body out of the bed."

She grinned back at him, unoffended as always. "Buck up laddie. We'll get through this and then you can be as miserable and cantankerous as you like later on."

He blinked and laughed. "Do you know, I believe that sounds like the sort of malarkey I'd offer up."

"Where do you suppose I learned it?"

* * *

The wake, held two days later, was well attended by the neighborhood. Lester Tucker wasn't Irish, but his neighbors decided he deserved a proper wake. The promise of free drink and food brought out a number of people Mick rarely saw, but he spent the wake watching Timmy.

He drank a mug of beer and watched her hand out ham sandwiches. She grew solemn and nodded thoughtfully, as someone recalled a story about the late Les Tucker.

Mick leaned against a wall, Tuck and Jenny's sleeping baby a sweet weight on his shoulder. He watched Timmy throw back her head and laugh as a drunken man told her a meandering story about the time Lester insisted on balancing a broom on his nose while standing in the middle of the street.

Timmy got on with them all like a house on fire.

The baby woke, and Mick handed him off to Jenny.

A few minutes later, Mick spotted Timmy hugging Rob. In the safety of her arms, the boy broke down and cried for his father.

Eventually Timmy looked over at Mick. She smiled and he felt his usual response. His groin grew heavy, his heart grew light—torn in half. Poleaxed with lust.

She turned towards him, watched him watch her for a moment, and her eyes suddenly narrowed, speculative. She strolled over to him and leaned her head against his chest for a moment.

He slid his hands around her waist. Oh, he was so glad she didn't lace up those perfect curves with a heavy corset. He buried his face in her hair. She usually used a fancy French bar of soap, but she'd grabbed his soap that evening. He felt another wave of lust when he caught a whiff of her spice under his own boringly familiar scent—as if she'd purposefully marked herself as his. Just to be saying something, he mumbled, "You lied to me, Timmy."

She pulled away to look into his eyes, a mix of apprehension and puzzlement in her. His heart lurched. Had he been so condemning of her early on that she might still worry he would hurt her?

He tried to reassure her with a grin and said, "You said this was your first. But how many Irish wakes have you been to?"

Timmy's eyes lost the fearful look, and she even laughed. "None, truly. But this is the sort of party I understand. No need to memorize how to properly address people."

Across the room, Colsun waved a hand at her.

"He wants to break open another keg, I suppose," Timmy said. "I'd best go speak to him."

She skirted her graceful way through the crowded room. Mick watched her. What a lovely neat back she had, and under the silly bustle such a rear end and legs as he previously could only dreamed of. The sight of her attracted his gaze like the sun drew a sunflower.

At the wake of his good friend, the late Lester Tucker, all Mick could think about was getting Timona into his room and into his bed and himself into her. He tried to conjure up Daisy for a moment, just to test out the idea. Had he ever felt anything like passionate need for Daisy?

Never for her, or any other woman. Not the way he had from the first morning Timona lay in his bed with him. Before then. From the moment she lay across his lap to get her poor head stitched up.

His craving for her didn't abate after they made love; the hunger increased. For the whole of her. He was that greedy for her laugh, her silliness, and her cheery, calm self.

Mick recalled two nights earlier, when he was on patrol on a quiet gas-lit street at two in the morning. He had covered his mouth as he yawned and had caught a whiff of her on his fingertips. He'd nearly forgotten what he was about as he fought off the urge to run back to his bed to make sure she was still there.

He couldn't find Timmy in the crowd for a few minutes, then spotted her listening gravely to the widow from the first floor, who'd drunk enough to be maudlin about her dead husband, whom everyone knew she hated. Timmy listened and nodded.

Maybe Miss Calverson, that rare—no, unique—woman, was on to it days ago, something he was only now understanding because he was too stuck in the rut of what people should or should not be.

He wanted to explain it to her, tell her how right she was, but he couldn't find the correct words. A few minutes later, she walked past him. "Timmy!" he called to her. "Oh, Timmy, I want you."

"What can I do for you, Mick? I'm busy carting out this box of rubbish. Unless you want the job?"

She looked into his face and he held his breath. He might as well have been hit on the back of the head with a blackjack, for all the dizzying power of her.

He'd never thought of himself as a slow learner, but how long had it taken him to figure this out?

He'd long known he was a besotted fool for her, but this was something more. Perhaps he hadn't caught on because he'd fought hard against it from the start. With no luck, because he had been changed forever. "Sure an' I'll take out the rubbish. But what I mean is I want you. In general," he added lamely.

The words, pathetic though they sounded to him, must have been right, for she dropped the wooden box with a clatter. Her face bloomed with the sweetest smile he had yet seen on it. He lost track of where they stood as she looked at him and he watched her face.

She walked straight into his arms.

The box of garbage stood in the middle of the floor for the rest of the night.

They went back to his flat and made love against the wall, then on the chair, then in the horrible bed.

Jim thumped on the wall. "Mick, I'm glad you're getting some. It's about bloody time," came his weary shout. "But could you two pipe down a bit?"

Timmy got the fit of the giggles and had to stuff a blanket into her mouth. Botty growled.

Mick could barely drag himself to work before dawn the next morning. Timmy didn't even stir as he made ready and left.

On patrol, Mick caught a glimpse the man with yellow hair again, this time in a large crowd waiting at the corner for traffic to pass. His beat had changed, yet there was the man. Once again, Mick didn't bother to show he'd spotted him. No point in putting the man on his guard; by now Mick assumed he was only paid to watch and not take action.

It was a long, hard day. Pay packet day in the neighborhoods usually were: The bars were full. He came back that evening with a sore nose acquired when he didn't duck fast enough breaking up a pool hall fight. At least his nose wasn't broken again.

He found a note from Timmy.

Mick, you forgot to inform me that my brother visited you. I hope he was not unpleasant. I found his card whilst straightening up, and am going to visit him today. I would have cooked something for you like a proper housewife, but I am a terrible cook. Did I ever mention that failing? One more thing: I hope it does not make you nervous to read this, but I truly do care for you. T.

He stared down at her handwriting, the neat sloping script of a well educated woman. It had been a while since he remembered she was *the* Timona, but the spiking, elegant handwriting brought it back.

She'd left her brother's calling card on top of the note. Mick fingered the card for a moment, wondering if she wanted him to follow her. He decided he was too tired and collapsed across the bed without even taking his uniform off.

When he woke the next morning, his head in a fog, she still wasn't back. The bed felt far too empty. He looked out the window at the church tower clock. Hell, only half an hour until he was supposed to report at the station.

Someone thumped at the door. "Mr. Mick?" It was Eddy, the neglected kid that Mick, and now Timona, fed most often. "My kitten is sick."

The sick tabby probably had worms. Mick suspected the pale and peaky Ed did too, and made a note to himself to stop by the druggist's.

By the time he looked up at the clock again, he knew he'd be late for roll call.

The buzz around the station house was a murder discovered at five that morning. Double-Punch Jack of the Lucky Flower was found beaten to death outside his own whorehouse.

"Coroner's office says the man was beaten, but might have been a heart attack. Whatever it was, one of the girls finally got her own back," Bairre said as he tucked his day-stick into his belt. "He paid a fearful lot to stay in business, but I say thank heaven. That place was too dreadful, eh? Remember the naked boy we found dead outside there, three years ago?"

Mick smothered a yawn. "No, wasn't on the force then, but I'm not surprised to hear about the boy."

A boy. Hell.

He sat down heavily on a chair by the door and rubbed his forehead with his palm.

"You all right then, Mick?" Bairre asked.

"I'm well. See you later."

Mick sat and his fingers drummed the helmet on his lap for a minute or two. Then Mick stood up and found a superior officer.

"Sergeant, with your permission," he said, "I'll be checking on a tip someone gave me about the shop thefts on Lexington. I'll be back on beat soon."

The sergeant would have been surprised to see Mick swing himself onto the horse-drawn streetcar going the opposite direction.

It took a minute or two to gather the courage he needed to push past the two brass-buttoned, stern doormen standing guard at the entrance to the Fifth Avenue Hotel who stepped in front of the wide glass door to stop him going in.

"Police business," he growled and gave them a bit of a shove as he went past. Huh. Their polished boots and the silver braid festooning their uniforms could blind a person, but the men themselves were purely decorative. The fact should have fortified Mick. It didn't, of course.

Mick could face a crowd of drunken rowdies without fear. This world of opulence, however, was beyond his ken and gave him a dire attack of nerves. It didn't help him much when he fetched up the memory of hearing the mirrors alone had cost $60,000 when the place was built a couple of decades earlier.

A clerk with slicked-back hair, wearing what Mick suspected was full formal evening wear stood behind the gleaming front desk. He obviously also did not like the sight of a cop in the lobby. The clerk scowled hurried out to waylay Mick.

"Excuse me, officer," he hissed. "We prefer the police use the side or back entrance. We do not want our guests to be disturbed unnecessarily."

The spectacle of all the shining marble floors, thick carpets, chandeliers, and huge potted palm trees had already pushed Mick far into what he thought of as his Irish galoot-just-off-the-farm state of mind. Saints, he hated being reminded he was a inferior rustic. He took off his helmet and scowled right back at the over-dressed hotelier.

"Need to see Griffin Calverson."

The clerk looked shocked. "Mr. Calverson? The gentleman is too . . ."

A shriek of joy interrupted the polished clerk's indignant answer.

"Mick! Oh, Mick! I saw the uniform and hoped it was you." Timona Calverson breezed in through the front door, and then rushed across the wide lobby and threw herself into his arms. Despite Mick's gloom, he couldn't help appreciating the moment.

Over her shoulder his eyes met those of the dumbstruck clerk.

Mick gave him a wink.

After planting a long, obviously lustful kiss right on his mouth, Timmy tucked her arm into Mick's and, ignoring the discreetly goggling crowd and the flabbergasted clerk, walked him towards the elevator.

"Oh, I'm delighted to see you, Mick. I want to tell you that Griffin was actually impressed by you. He never likes my friends. Poor Blenheim is positively afraid of him."

"I need to talk to him," said Mick, still unsettled by the hotel's opulence and now, on top of that, her apparent ease with it. "Is that where we're headed?"

"Yes, we'll take the lift." She strolled into the strange

gilded boxy cage of an elevator. He gingerly stepped in after her.

She inched close to him. "I wanted to get back to you last night, but I grew so tired, I fell asleep here in Griff's suite." She grinned. "Can't imagine why I was so tired."

She looked at him so outrageously Mick wanted to haul her into his arms at the same time he wanted to apologize to the back of the elevator operator. He jumped when the elevator shuddered to a stop.

A maid opened the door to the suite and led them into another room where Griffin sat on a wide, over-stuffed couch, drinking coffee and reading the paper. He appeared unsurprised to see Mick.

Mick wished he could adopt that blank face, but his own jaw had dropped. Perhaps permanently.

In his time as a policeman, he had seen the scenes of murder. He had witnessed mothers trying to sell their babies. He had seen—and stopped—men from beating each other or their own families to pulp. But nothing he had witnessed in his wide experience in the stews had prepared him for this display of a place in which a single person slept and ate and lived. Not even the lobby downstairs hinted at it.

He'd seen plenty of public majesty in this city. Anyone walking past Grand Central Depot would feel awe at the huge brick building. But, saints, Mick had never seen such a place for a man, just one man, to inhabit.

Even Botham's house, that huge old stone pile in Ireland, did not come close to this magnificence.

The elegant, wide open rooms of the hotel shocked him to his core. Thick Turkish carpets were arranged on polished marble or wooden parquet floors. Huge arched windows framed views of the city and were in turn framed by yards of brocade cloth.

Mountains of fresh flowers in displays larger than a man, carved wood panels polished so bright he could see his face reflected in the walls, a piano, rooms large enough to fit his entire floor of four flats, tall enough to house a double-decker bus. Mick stood near a wall and, mesmerized, ran a finger over the richly colored wallpaper only to discover it was actually silk cloth covering the walls. The rooms' fresh scent of flowers and lemon and beeswax polish held no stale trace of previous meals or unwashed tenants.

Mick had stumbled into a private luxury he had never in his life seen nor yet even imagined.

And Mick had to turn himself into a police officer because Mick the man swooned inside him, passed out in a state of shock. Maybe a chunk of him had died when he walked into the rooms.

"Mr. Calverson," he said stiffly. "Might I have a word?" He turned wretched eyes to Timmy who watched him, puzzled. "Excuse me, I need to talk to Mr. Calverson alone."

She helped him regain some of himself by being entirely herself. Instead of gasping and demanding to know what was wrong, she merely rolled her eyes. "Mick, you silly," she said cheerfully. "Of course you can. I'll skip along to the other room where I stashed my new camera. I can't wait to show it you."

Griffin waited until the maid closed the double doors behind Timona.

"Sit down," he said to Mick, and nodded to the maid who poured out a cup of coffee and silently set the bone china cup and saucer on the table beside Mick.

"Something to eat, Mick?"

Mick perched on the edge of the gilded chair.

"No. No food. Thanks."

Calverson nodded, and the maid silently left the room. Mick didn't want the coffee, but took a sip anyway. Jesus. No wonder Timmy made faces at the coffee at Colsun's. This tasted of heaven. He put the cup down and cleared his throat. "So. Sir. The Lucky Flower. That's the house where Timmy—Miss Calverson—was taken. Am I right?"

Griffin fingered his mustache for a moment before answering.

"Yes."

"God above. Ah, you work fast, Mr. Calverson. She probably gave you a description of the man and the place, what? Yesterday, midday?"

Griffin drained his coffee. He put down the cup and slowly, deliberately folded up the newspaper that lay next to him. He leaned back into the sofa. The hard green eyes in the bland face examined Mick, who refused to look away or flinch.

"I must say I am surprised that you didn't check into it yourself, Mick," he said at last, very softly.

"No, you are not. You know all about the damned Lucky Flower and the damned police department."

"I did not mean as a policeman. I meant as my sister's . . . friend."

"I couldn't at that." he said bluntly. "I wasn't entirely certain where she had been taken. Mind you, I suspected. But even had I known for sure, I don't know what I coulda done. I'm right sure I don't have what it takes to march in and kill even that lowlife in cold blood. And unless I had killed Mr. Two-Punch Jack, once I messed with him, I'd be dead meself. And the department wouldn't lift a finger to keep me alive."

Griffin's eyebrows raised. "I like your candor. You impress me, Mick."

"I wish I could say the feeling was mutual."

There was nothing more to be said. Mick stood up.

"I should tell you that I was surprised Mr. Jack died of his wounds." Griffin paused. "I am not displeased, you understand."

Mick sighed. "I won't mourn the rotter. For what it's

worth, I'll go further than you, and say I am right glad he is dead." His mouth quirked into an ironic smile. "And I am sure you pay even more than he did, so I know it's no use telling my superiors what I know. But . . . ah, hell. I don't even know why I am here."

"To see my sister's new camera?"

"No. I'm on duty. Give her my regrets." He looked at Griffin closely, not that the man's face revealed a thought or emotion. "Does she know what you've done?"

"Of course not. I summoned an associate about the job while she was out hunting for a camera. I would appreciate it if you didn't say anything to her."

Mick snorted. "She's no idiot, Calverson."

"No, she is not, but I don't think she's as clear-headed about her brother as you are."

"Aye, Calverson. Yes, it would break her heart if she knew what a wicked devil you are."

"So we won't tell her, will we?"

Mick was about to leave when he remembered something else.

"Mr. Calverson. About the man with yellow hair, brown eyes. Maybe six two, with a scar on his neck, usually wears dark clothes?"

Calverson's eyebrows moved up a whole quarter of an inch. On another man, it would have been an open-mouthed gawk. "Again, you impress me. He is the best in his business."

"Call him off me, aye? I'd never harm your sister. You know that by now."

Calverson stood. He held out his hand and then surprised the hell out of Mick by saying, "Mr. McCann, I rather wish you liked me as much as I like you."

Mick shook his hand in a daze. He clapped his helmet onto his head and walked out without looking back.

* * *

When Timmy reappeared in his life that night, he held her tight and made feverish love to her. But he no longer thought of her as his own. She might be too earnest and infatuated with him to know they did not fit, but he knew. He had seen her real world and knew she was a princess romping with peasants. Her true home was back in that marble palace of a hotel. Good God almighty, Mick was afraid to even consider what the bloody king was like.

In the middle of the night she nudged him awake.

"Aw sweet, I am too blasted tired," he moaned.

She was sitting up. He blinked at the pale shape of her face, all he could make out of her in the dark room. Wide awake, she bent over him, and he saw her teeth flash into a brief smile. "Not that, Mick, you filthy-minded beast." The smile was gone. "I- I just need to ask you. To tell you, actually. Please don't inform my brother . . . about things. He wormed the story of the kidnapping out of me yesterday morning, and I am afraid he might do something. I so wanted to take care of it myself."

He pulled her down on top of him and wrapped his arms around her small frame. "Yes, I understand," he whispered into her hair. "Your brother is a strong-willed man and he cares for you something fierce."

"He does. Truly." Her voice sounded thick and Mick wondered if this woman whom he'd never seen shed tears, not even after being kidnapped and nearly raped, was crying. He gently touched her cheek. It was wet—she'd likely been crying for a long while.

"Hush, hush, a Timmy, a chrói," he crooned, but she was still talking.

"Griffin did something already. That's why you

showed up to talk to him. The man is dead." It wasn't a question.

"Your brother came right out and said he did not mean for the bastard to die. No one is crying for the villain."

A small squeak sounded from his arms. "I am. And for Griffin, too, I suppose."

"Timmy." He found her mouth and gave her warm kiss. After a few more kisses, it turned out he wasn't too blasted tired after all.

Afterwards, she settled on her side, tucked to fit perfectly into his arms, and was soon asleep. But he stared into the darkness, contemplating what he would do with himself when the time came for her to leave. He found no answers other than the same old dreary understanding that he would have a great chunk ripped from his soul.

Ah well. He would discover a new meaning of the old saying. "*Go milis an fion, tá é searbh ri dhiol.*" The wine is sweet, the paying bitter.

He woke in the gray dawn and watched her sleep until he heard the clock toll the half hour before he had to report to the precinct house. Shaving and breakfast be damned. He wanted to stay for every moment she lit in his life.

He dressed as quickly and quietly as possible. For a long minute before he left, Mick stared down at her high cheekbones, her slender neck, the great cloud of hair pulled carelessly back with a ribbon. If a man wanted to pick the most appealing sight in the world, this would be a likely winner.

With a sigh, he snapped his fingers for Botty and they left while she still slept.

Chapter 14

Another dutiful message from Miss Calverson arrived. And like the others, it told Blenheim nothing. Sir Kenneth sat at his desk reading an article and occasionally burbling on about jawbones and femurs. Blenheim ignored him and reread the stack of telegrams.

The only clear signal Timona gave in her messages was that she had no intention of immediately returning to her father's retinue.

And Griffin obviously had taken no action or the girl would have changed her tune. She'd be back where she belonged.

Blenheim paced the downstairs of the Minnesota farm house and looked out the window. During the last several years, he'd grown familiar with this vision. In the unusually warm weather, a few dozen men worked in pits, digging between the strings that Sir Kenneth used to measure off possible sites.

Over time, he'd seen different countries, different collections of laborers but they were the same everywhere. Peasants.

These grime-covered men talked to one another, bellowed with laughter, almost all speaking with the broad and atrociously crude accent of the Irish. Oh, for pity's sake, one of them was dressed in nothing but a grimy breechclout and boots.

Blenheim turned in disgust from the window.

He needed help.

There was the little matter of requiring more money, but Blenheim refused to explore that thought. No need to panic, yet. Mr. Taylor in New York had mentioned he was exploring "possibilities."

Timona had done worse than not coming to heel fast enough. Not only had she failed in her duty to him and her father, his beloved had shown she had feet of clay, no, mud. From consorting with a man like those workers.

Taylor had sent an outraged message to Blenheim, as if it were somehow Blenheim's fault.

The harlot, wrote Taylor, was openly living in sin with a man who could barely sign his name.

Timona Calverson, the famous Traveling Sweetheart, was trying as hard as she possibly could to turn her name, and thus her family's name, into excrement. Taylor would do what he could, but Blenheim had better contact him as soon as possible.

Blenheim planned to eventually forgive his beloved. In the meantime, Griffin was obviously not going to be of any aid in his reclamation of the lost female. So Blenheim would have to use another, more dependable Johnny-on-the-spot.

He'd have a ten-mile ride to the station. But he wasn't about to trust his messages to anyone else.

"No, I am sorry. I cannot go. I must work." Of course Mick was anything but sorry. He'd rather face a group of drunken rowdies than a gala ball. Two groups of rowdies. Armed with clubs.

"I'd rather not go myself. There will be a reception

and a cartload of dignitaries. Dr. Dennis insists I'm some sort of guest of honor. It's supposed to raise money for the museum. Otherwise I'd cry off, too," Timona admitted.

"I'm not crying off," said Mick with an attempt at dignity. "I shall be at work until eleven o'clock."

Timona brightened. "Oh, you can come after that, then. Please, please. Mick. You come extricate me. Dr. Dennis swears he will be my escort but I know he will stay until the bitter end. And then I will end up having to stay at the hotel."

"So you're saying that unless I get you, you'll be staying away from home."

"Home," she said, and her face grew bright. "Yes, that is just what I'm saying. Away from you."

He rubbed his chin. "After work. I'll come to fetch you. I'll not stay for a moment, Timmy. I have seen those parties from afar and I'd fit there as well as a- a sheep might."

"I know precisely what you mean." she said, nodding. "B-a-a."

"Nonsense, Timmy. You grew up with such a life."

She shook her head. "I've been to formal events. But I haven't had instruction on how to be a proper young lady."

He gave a disbelieving sniff.

She ignored it. "My impression is that New York parties are not so plagued with pomp and ceremony, but I still will be glad to leave early." She handed him a large, gilt-edged invitation that bore his name, written in a gorgeous curling script. The thing smelled like an upper-class whorehouse.

"Here's your card. You'll need it to set me free."

Mick walked his beat that afternoon and evening and when he thought of the ball, a sense of morose amusement filled him. He did not want to be reminded of her real life so soon again. He enjoyed pretending she belonged with him.

The entrance to the pale mansion was well lit and well guarded. The warm night meant the guests lingered near doors and on the patio and balconies of the place. Bare arms and necks glittered with jewels. Large feathers in elaborate coiffures. Men in white tie and tails. Jeroboams of champagne, a full orchestra at the back of the cavernous room. He'd had glimpses of this scene before. Mick had gotten an extra couple of dollars working a few gala events.

At least he didn't recognize the men hauled in to guard the doors. They were pulled from the Broadway division, the tall, good-looking officers hired with an eye to impress the public.

He pulled off his helmet and tucked it under his arm. Christ, hadn't he just lived through this? The Fifth Avenue Hotel all over again. This time, however, he had a ticket allowing him to temporarily enter the forbidden kingdom of the rich.

The room was crowded, but he spotted Timmy almost at once. The largest circle of men and women surrounded her. They talked animatedly to one another, but glanced at her, the colorful and illustrious Miss Calverson, as if she were their touchstone.

For a long moment, he simply watched and admired her. Her dark hair was piled high, flowers artfully arranged in the curls. The gown shimmered on her shapely body, with the barest wisps of sleeves cleverly designed to cover the red mark of her still-healing shoulder injury.

Her clothing was no surprise. Though she had not shown him this gorgeous overdone dress before, he'd easily imagined her dressed as royalty. But the look on her face gave him pause, a haunted look that reminded him of the first days after he had met her.

Skittish, that was how she seemed. She smiled, nodded, answered questions, but anyone could see she was preoccupied. He could, at any rate.

And then she caught sight of him. Her expression changed so completely into delight that he wondered that the people around her didn't notice. Perhaps they did, for a few in her circle looked over at him as he gently shoved his way through the crowd, murmuring apologies. She might have shouted his name, her message was so clear to him.

Don't grab at her, he warned himself.

He reached the group that contained Timmy. To get through, he laid a hand on a gentleman's shoulder. The man gave him a scared, startled look, then scuttled backward to let Mick into the circle.

For lack of knowing what he was supposed to do, he sketched a rough bow to Timona. She showed a graceful treat of a curtsy in return. As if she'd been practicing the move for years. She probably had been, come to that.

"Will you excuse me, Dr. Dennis?" she said to the white haired gentleman at her side. "I am afraid I am expected elsewhere."

The man merely harumphed and plucked at his disheveled beard with his fingers. He didn't look remotely surprised. Well, so Timmy had told this man about her policeman companion.

Getting away took some doing.

"No, I am not under arrest," Timona said again and again, always with a laugh, as they made their slow way towards the door.

Mick wondered if he'd imagined that look of discomfort on Timona's face. She seemed perfectly able to talk with these people. To him, the women decked out in jewels and elaborate gowns and the men in their black-and-white getups all might have been speaking a foreign language.

They didn't even smell like regular people. Their breath was sweet or laden with sweet wine or brandy, rather than raw whiskey or bad ale or rotting teeth. Even the hint of their perspiration was neither rank nor stale. They'd bathed recently, not just splashed in a shallow pan of cold water.

Mick knew people's sweat often stank of what they ate. He could tell no one in this lot consumed garlic or cabbage in the quantities like most of the crowds he'd barged through.

He stood, attending Timmy, fidgeting with the leather strap of his helmet, waiting an interminable age, while people touched Timmy and kissed or shook her gloved hand—or, even worse—insisted on shaking his hand. The worst were the people who asked for introductions to the officer. Mick must have mumbled a "how-do-ye-do" several hundred times.

But oh, it was worth every mildly embarrassing moment when he followed her out of the stuffy room into the cool night air. She peeled off one of her long white gloves, he yanked off his own glove, so their skin could touch.

Astonishing that he could walk off hand-in-hand with this vision of beauty and no one would yell at him to take his squalid self away.

"Let's not take a cab," Timmy pleaded.

"'Tis fifteen blocks back to my flat."

"But the night feels so soft and wonderful."

He smiled. "It does at that."

Timmy's long and elaborate lace train dragged on the dirty sidewalk. She could not gather it up properly without exposing her legs.

Mick had the idea of using his badge. He squatted

behind her and pinned up as much of the gossamer lace and the underdress of silk as he could.

She giggled and said, "Do I look very silly?"

He tilted back his head to examine her. The flickering gas-light caught the shimmer of her dress, the curve of her long neck and turned her gold. Hardly mattered to him what she wore. The haphazard bundle he'd created below her bustled backside looked nice, actually, something like a waterfall. "Nah. Could be the start of a new fashion, I'd say."

He stood up.

As he took her hand again, he blurted, "You don't enjoy that kind of thing much, do you. You weren't just saying it to . . . to make me feel better."

She squeezed his hand. "I haven't lied to you, Mick. Ever," she said cheerfully.

"No," he said at last. "I see that."

It hurt his heart to understand how open she was to him.

So maybe he didn't want to fool himself about her place in his world, after all.

Ah well. If he did need to be reminded, it was easy enough to give himself a jolt back to reality. He only had to pull up that picture of Griffin sitting in that hotel room.

She looped her arm through his. "You have tomorrow off?"

"Aye."

"Come play with me. I want to take a few pictures of you."

"Timona. You like to take pictures of buildings and I am not a building."

"It won't take long, I promise. And you have said you wanted to see my equipment."

Determined to shake his strange despondency, he

gave a playful growl. "And what made you think I was speaking of photographic equipment?"

She laughed. "You undress for me and I'll show you any kind of equipment you want."

He stopped dead and frowned at her. "Undress? Unless you're speaking of undressing for your eyes only, it's a no, Timmy."

Mick glared from the dais built into the studio Timmy borrowed. He folded his arms across his chest. "I'm telling you, not the trousers, woman. And I'm not showing the world my chest, neither."

Timmy hummed as she checked the glass plate holder. Getting a picture of his back was more than she'd hoped for. She looked up and smiled. "Fine. Would you like to take a look through my camera? I have the ground glass in now."

Mick hauled on his sleeveless undershirt and jumped off the stage. She showed him the bellows and the lens and how the shutter opened up with a pull of the string.

She lovingly touched the mahogany frame of the camera. "This Scoville weighs only twenty pounds. My last one was heavier. Oh, but my best new purchases are the dry-gelatin plates. My assistant, Mr. Kendall, and I always have had to work with so much equipment. We even have a special wagon to carry it all. Because you see, with the wet sort of plate, any time I wanted to use the camera I had to prepare the film before and after right away and . . ."

She clamped her lips together. She could almost hear Mr. Blenheim's mild reprimand. She was doing it again; talking too much about her picture taking.

Mick gave her a nudge. "Go on, then. What's different about the film now?"

She shook her head. "Photography is dull stuff."

He clamped his hand on her arm and gave a tiny shake. "Nonsense, Timmy. I want to hear. You know I like your pictures. They steal my breath away, they're so wonderful."

She knew she was a good photographer but still, her chest throbbed with delight at his words. She felt as if she'd just won a prize. "Do you really think I'm good?"

He grimaced. "Why else would I agree to strip off me clothes?"

"Oh, poor Mick. Let's hurry, shall we?"

The sunlight was strong and she found a special flood lamp in the studio. No need to use the dangerous flash powder.

She directed him to the back of the stage, not too close to the ornate sofa. "If you wouldn't mind standing up for this one. Find a position you can hold for at least two minutes."

Grumbling under his breath, he dropped his shirt, and then leaned his forearms against the wall and rested his head on them.

She took a step back. "I'd like to try a couple of exposures of you lying down. But I don't think we'll use the sofa, it will detract from what . . ." Her words died in her throat. She had seen him naked, but not from any distance or outside the dim light of his flat. The solid muscles of his shoulders, the tapering waist dipping into the rough trousers, oh, she had forgotten the sheer magnificence of the man.

She also forgot to walk to the camera.

In the silence he twisted around and looked at her. "Not good?"

"No. Very good."

Mick squinted. "Your face is pink. You feeling well?" A second later, the squint melted into a grin. "Could the lady be embarrassed?"

She shook her head. "Turn around."

"Timmy. I told you. Not the front."

"Just for me."

The grin grew wider and wicked. "Oho. That's the way of it, then?" He pushed away from the wall and put his hands on his hips. Unashamed, swaggering, he held even more power.

She swallowed.

"C'mere," he murmured. "Did I mention there'd be a fee for my service as a model?"

They ended up using the sofa after all.

Later on, Timona took what was to become one of her favorite photos. The picture of Mick's back seen twisting from the side, rising from the bottom of the picture, like a powerful force of nature was unusual and rather nice. She knew many would consider it the best of the lot. Yet the one she loved most was a portrait of his face staring at the camera, his mouth and eyes set in serious lines but brimming with kindness.

Mick returned to work the next day. Soon after roll call, the captain summoned him to a cramped little office.

"Officer McCann," Captain Johnson boomed.

Mick didn't like the captain, who put his nose into everyone's business, and was always on the prowl for more influence and "sugar." Johnson knew a few Tammany Hall bosses, and considered himself a *boc mór*. A big shot. Mick considered him a *bromaire*. A gasbag.

The captain stood up and leaned across the desk at Mick, who wondered if he should worry, until he saw Johnson had his hand out for a shake. "I must congratulate you, officer. Someone in Tammany likes you. Very much."

Uh oh. Yes, indeed, Mick should worry.

Johnson went on, "You have skipped over the usual promotion list, McCann. You've saved yourself thousands of dollars. Just to be promoted to roundsman is nearly a thousand, you know. Your new assignment starts tomorrow. But I assume you know all about that."

"No. I do not have a clue what you're talking about, sir."

Johnson winked, clearly certain Mick played coy. "No, of course not. But I did a bit of digging for you, and I've heard your new job should bring in more than triple what you make now, man. And some nice benefits too, no doubt about that. Pays to cultivate friends in high places, McCann. You've shown some enterprise. I'm glad to count you as a pal. And I hope you won't forget your old friends here in the station?"

Mick's stomach lurched into the sinking sensation he was starting to associate with Griffin Calverson. What had the devil of a man done now? A busy man, that Griffin.

"And what if I don't want this new job, whatever it is?"

"You're an idiot, man. Of course you do. Damnation, how else are you going to keep that fancy woman I hear you're going about with?" He leered. "News travels fast round here."

Damn Doherty.

"I don't keep a fancy woman, sir."

The godawful wink again, accompanied by a leer. "Well, then maybe she is keeping you, eh? You are one smart worker then, and not just on the job, eh, Mc-Cann? Now you're getting paid for it."

Mick had heard enough. He'd had enough, too, come to think of it.

Time to leave.

He unstrapped his nightstick and tossed the stick and belt with a loud clunk onto the cluttered desk. He yanked off the eight-sided brass star, and threw it down too. Then the helmet. He considered plastering Johnson one, but decided it wasn't worth the trouble.

He walked out of the office and slammed the door behind himself hard enough to cause the glass to shake and the busy room to grow suddenly silent. The men looked up at him.

He strode from the room, and then the station, without meeting any of his former comrades' eyes. They'd have to rouse one of the lads in the barracks to do his shift, but they'd manage.

He hadn't much liked being a copper, anyway.

It was not only the corruption. The job consisted of too much bashing and not enough healing. It was a dead cinch you'd turn into a domineering tyrant when you wore the uniform.

A cop depended on that stick, the stick became an extension of his hand. He sometimes hit—he had to—without thinking where the blows might land. Sure, it could be a matter of life and death when he patrolled the streets alone. But brutality became too damn matter-of-fact. Too bloody easy.

Griffin had unwittingly done Mick a favor. This provided the excuse he had been waiting for.

He'd finally use all of the money from the drawer, a considerable sum by now, he guessed. Half of it he'd send home, along with a warning to expect a dry spell. The other half, he'd use to buy a ticket to get away from New York and to live off until he found a job. Maybe find a farm that needed a hired hand.

He missed the sea.

Some crops didn't flourish near salt water, but he'd make the trade off. Besides, he'd like to be around more beasts of the non-human variety again.

Timmy seemed to like animals, too.

A block from the station house, the thought of her stopped him in the middle of the sidewalk. He paused for a moment to catch his breath.

Timmy. No. *The* Timona Calverson.

Well. She had been the highlight of his life. The best thing that he had ever encountered or was ever likely to encounter. Hard as it was to imagine her as a policeman's wife, she was definitely not a hired farm hand's woman.

And he was not interested in being a lover, at least, not as a way to make his way in the world.

He smiled to himself as he thought about her and her pictures of him. They were fine, but best of all were her photos of buildings. She had shown him some of the pictures she created using her hulking big camera. Long streets of tall buildings stretching away. Magnificent views of the cement city.

Weren't a great number of tall buildings on a farm.

Timmy could make space seem huge and powerful on the small page. The woman could see places and things in a way he'd never imagined before. His smile grew broader, as he realized how, when he looked out at the world now, he frequently could see it through her vision of beauty.

Clotheslines.

That was one of the many good gifts she'd given him and one he could keep forever even after he let her go. Some of her other gifts, sheer joy and laughter—he wasn't sure he would be allowed to keep those when she went back to her real world.

Timmy was sitting on the stoop in front of the house, reading a Buffalo Bill adventure to a group of Tuckers, Eddy, and other children from the building. Sarey held the baby. There was no sign of Jenny. She still huddled up in the flat, hiding away even from her children.

Timmy put the book down on her lap and engaged in a passionate argument with Henry. "Yes, I am certain Buffalo Bill can read, Henry. Cowboys learn to read. African guides do, too. You will just have to buckle down, and that's that, Henry Tucker."

Then she noticed Mick.

"Mick," she said and stared at him curiously. "You look different. Oh, I think I see."

He nodded. "I'm out of a job."

She stood up, her finger wedged in the book to mark the spot she'd stopped reading. "Why?"

"They wanted me to do something I didn't want to do. Wasn't corrupt, mind you."

Or, as he didn't add, it was as corrupt a business as usual. He certainly wouldn't tell her about his suspicions of the pestilential Griffin's influence. He added, "'Twas just not to my liking."

Her face brightened. "Splendid! Now we can go, too."

"And where is it we are going?" he asked suspiciously.

"To Uncle Dave's, of course."

Of course. That very first morning, Timmy had announced she was going to help. The woman was as unrelenting as her brother. But Mick wouldn't complain. He could be with her. What the hell else was he going to do with himself?

A great cry went up down the street at the corner. It was the holler of city children spotting a hearse, an ambulance, an ice wagon, or any form of free entertainment. This entertainment proved to be a uniformed boy on a strange bicycle.

"Look, now, that's one of those funny machines," said Henry. "The wheel in the front is the same size as the one in the back. Nothing like an Ordinary."

The boy rode down the street, the bicycle's heavy tires bouncing over the cobblestones. Straight-backed and solemn, he was marvelously indifferent to the gang of ragged children racing behind him.

"Oh no," groaned Timmy. "Another one."

The boy stopped in front her and handed her a pad. "Sign here."

She tucked the book under her arm.

Then she signed the pad, took the paper, and handed him a coin as a tip.

"See ya soon," the Western Union messenger shouted over his shoulder as he pedaled away. Timmy, opening the paper in her hand didn't bother to answer, though she waved after him absently.

"That's the third in the last two days," Henry piped up.

"Fourth," Sarey corrected. "But they keep asking for Miss Cooper by a stupid name."

"Third."

"Fourth."

"Thir—"

"Hush, you." Mick watched Timmy's face as she read. "Bad news?" He'd never seen anyone get a telegram, but knew they were generally only used for huge occasions, such as death.

"No, no. Just Mr. Blenheim again. He has gotten hold of this address, and understands it is not a, uh, superior neighborhood. He wishes to understand what I am about." She sighed. "He is a helpful man, but a stickler for decorum. And now he hints that Papa is upset. I find that difficult to imagine, but I suppose I should ensure Papa is well." She crumpled up the sheet of paper and thrust it into a pocket of her gown.

Timmy held out the Buffalo Bill book and said, "Sarey, let's trade. I can take Quinton. You take a turn at reading. Show Henry what you can do."

Timona gingerly took the baby. Mick was amused to see she still held Quinton like he was going to shatter in her hands at any second. He plucked the baby from her arms.

"He's a puker, this one. He's likely to give it up any second," Mick explained. "And ruin that pretty silky thing you're wearing."

He leaned against the wall absently patting the baby. "I know you told me he's your father's keeper. But who is Blenheim to you again? Some sort of boss of ye?"

"Really, he's my father's secretary. For me he is rather more of an instructor." Timmy frowned as she considered the matter. "He is the nephew or grandson of a duke. Or is it an earl? I cannot recall. I hired him out of the London office. He had done some studies in antiquities, and when Papa's last secretary left I thought the best thing was to find a man who might be able to talk about Papa's digs. Mr. Blenheim has turned out to be good for me, as well."

Mick forgot about losing his job. He wasn't sure he liked the sound of this Blenheim. "Aye?"

"He knows about society manners and that sort of thing. He teaches me how to behave like a 'good' girl." She grinned at him, her sly look that once gave him mortal fear, and now made him wish he were in a room alone with her. "You yourself have remarked on my deficits in that regard."

"Timmy, you have no such faults," he responded firmly. "Twas me who needed to learn."

"Truly, I have great gaps in my education. I have had occasional bouts of governesses when we settled for a half a year here or there. But I preferred to be with Papa and he would not tolerate governesses—they wouldn't tolerate our life."

"I don't believe it. What's wrong with your life?" Mick

summoned up the palatial hotel and the ball and felt his usual pang of desolation.

"Oh, it can be quite primitive. We often live in tents and in spots hundreds of miles from civilization. After Griffin left I was lonely. I would hate . . ." Her voice trailed off.

She frowned and her eyes seemed unusually somber. Mick straightened up and, with one arm, pulled her against him. His hug brought her smile back and caused the kids to start wailing like a bunch of banshees. Or maybe she grinned and they screamed with delight because the baby chose that moment to puke copiously down Mick's shoulder.

They went to lunch soon after that, just the two of them, with no Tuckers, Lex, Eddy, or any other of Mick's strays tagging along. Timona thought they might venture to a better restaurant, but these days Mick refused to go anywhere he could not afford.

"Not Colsun's," begged Timona. "Nor Miggies."

So Mick led the way to a small, drab restaurant Timona hadn't visited, tucked between two storefronts.

"I'll not be reduced to being your dependent yet, Miss Calverson," he said, prickly when she suggested she pay for the meal.

She groaned. "Please. Do not sound as if you are my victim, Mr. McCann."

With obvious effort, he smiled back at her. "Aye. I'm at it again, aren't I."

"Yes. Once again you are practicing to be an irritable old curmudgeon."

Mick's smile grew more genuine. Timona loved the way he could be teased out of the sulks. Even when he was firmly determined to be grouchy or pigheaded he couldn't maintain the attitude for long. He was too prone to good humor and fairness.

The waiter strolled over and slapped Mick on the back. "In the middle of the day, lad? Off duty?"

"Off the force," said Mick. "I left. Timmy Calverson, this is Eamonn Dunellen."

The waiter, a large man with dark hair and a full beard, resembled a young Father Christmas.

He smiled and bowed to Timmy. "Call me Eamonn." He turned his attention back to Mick. "You left a marvelous job like that? You must be crazy."

"No, no. I'm heading for the country."

Eamonn looked at Mick and muttered something about how only fools leave New York.

He refused to take their order and announced sternly, "I'll bring what I think you should eat. If you don't like it, I'll eat it myself." He sauntered off the kitchen.

Timona looked at Mick, who still had that pinched and harried look he got whenever the subject of money or the future arose.

"I hope you don't mind going to Uncle David's?"

He shrugged. "Seems like a fine plan. For me, anyway. I have thought it time to leave the city for a while. Losing my job must be a sign. But what of you, Timona? What, er, what will you want to do?" He asked slowly, and shy, as if unsure of his right to pry.

She looked at him for a long minute. The man was utterly dense. Didn't he understand he would have to change into a different person or drive her away before she left him?

She considered telling him so again point-blank, but she would have to squelch the urge to punch him when he stared at her as if he did not believe her. And he already had the pained look in his eyes. Her heart

lurched when she saw that look. At last she said, "I shall
be fine."

Their food arrived. Timmy had resigned herself to
one of the dreadful-looking sandwiches she saw other
patrons eating. But she was pleasantly surprised by the
large platter of fragrant lamb stew the waiter set down
in front of them.

Eamonn said something to Mick in Gaelic.

Mick laughed and shook his head.

"What did he say?" Timona asked.

"Oh. He told me if I regained my sanity and wanted
a job I could have one. He's the owner of the place."

"How did you meet him?"

"His baby was ailing. I got Dr. O'Toole to help."

Eamonn, swooping past with a plate of insipid sandwiches, must have overheard. He dumped the
sandwiches and came back. "Dr. O'Toole did less than
you yourself, McCann."

He looked at Timmy and grinned. "When he came
banging on the door, I thought, Lord, preserve me. On
top of all my other troubles, I'm under arrest. We had
no money a couple years back and we couldn't pay for
a doctor, so my oldest boy had stopped this lad on his
beat and dragged him in. After his beat he came back
and spent two days and nights caring for that baby.
Who knew the angel of mercy would be dressed as a
copper?"

Mick said something obviously disparaging. Eamonn
laughed.

"Don't give me such nonsense, McCann. You're a
clumping big oaf, but I say you're an angel of God. Eat
your stew."

Someone yelled from the kitchen. Eamonn winked
at Timmy and sauntered away.

Mick took a bite. "We should leave the city as soon

as we possibly can, Timmy. I worry about Jenny. Maybe getting her out of that flat will help."

"Do you know you were absolutely right that first morning when you talked to Rob about Jenny? She's hopeless. Her milk has dried up, too, so poor baby Quinton is a wreck. We found someone to nurse him until we leave. And she's delighted to have a baby to hold, poor woman."

The pinched look was completely gone. Instead his wide smile glowed at her in a way that still made her insides grow warm and her heart beat almost too fast. "Timmy. You are something special. How do you do it?"

"Ho, Mick, I'm nothing special. You're just fond of me."

"You are special," he insisted. Haltingly, not quite looking at her, he added, "I do indeed like you. Timmy you're a grand woman and I, ah, am quite fond of you."

She drew a deep breath. Close enough to the signal for which she'd waited. She could bring up the subject she'd avoided. Time to try again, if she could ignore the fear gathering in her throat. If he said no . . . she spoke before trepidation made her silent. "Do you remember when you asked me to marry you? I now accept. Will you marry me?"

Mick's smile broadened, then quickly faded. His mouth opened. Then closed. At last he answered, "Timmy you must see it wouldn't be right."

She blew out her lips, impatient, but relieved. Thank goodness she had seen that first reaction, one of his lovely smiles. He might get the picture eventually.

She said, contemplatively, "So that's once you've asked, and I refused, and twice I've asked and you've refused. We'll be on the same track some day."

Mick took her hand between his, and began what Timmy suspected was a speech he'd thought up earlier. "You don't see it, but I do, clear as day. I understood it when I—that day when I went to see your brother at that hotel. It wouldn't be fair to you, chaining you forever to a man like me. Especially as I have no job just now. There is a chasm, Timmy love. You fly across it like an angel, but I can never cross it. Never in this life time . . ." He interrupted himself. "You asked me to marry you before? When?"

"Just after you first played your flute for me. That second day."

He frowned, then laughed. "I'd forgotten. I thought you were having me on."

"No, I most certainly wasn't. You know I love your playing. It reminds me of all the wild places I'd seen. The very best places."

"And here I thought you liked cities."

"Yes, I like them too."

He took the hand he still held and slowly and deliberately kissed her palm and then each of her fingers. Oh lord, she loved the way his soft strong mouth felt against her skin. "Is there anywhere you don't like?"

She was distracted by the feel of his mouth, now on the sensitive skin of her wrist. It took a moment to think of an answer. "Oh, no. Other than the sheik's harem and the bordello, I suppose. And Moscow in the winter."

"And where is your favorite place? The spot you've been happiest?"

This time, she answered without hesitation. "Your room, your bed."

He laughed, but she didn't.

He stroked her arm and hand, and then, to her regret, let go of her to pick up his fork. "What about that tribe—the Mlylans? You liked that bunch, didn't you?" he asked, startling her with the name of a group of friends she had known since she was a young child.

"Oh Mick! How do you know about them?"

He leaned back and smiled at her, she could see by the uptilt at the edge of his mouth he felt self-conscious. "I read what I can about you."

Timona grinned back at him, pleased that Mick bothered to find out about her, and happy to recall her good friends, the Mlylans.

"They are wonderful. Griffin loves them too. That first visit, Papa had to drag Griffin away before he missed two full terms of school. Griffin goes back to the tribe any time he can. He says he feels that is his home."

"The thing I read said you could never locate the village again."

She waved a dismissive hand. "Oh, we said that so no one would go larking about their jungle. And we made them sound far more dangerous than they were."

She sighed. Mick would love the Mlylans when she finally managed to lure members of her favorite foster family to visit her. He'd enjoy them far more than many members of her real family.

Someday soon, she'd have to tell him about the branch of her family that contained such specimens as Aunt Winifred, also known as the Viscountess of Windrow. She dreaded what Mick would think of Aunt Winnie. Timmy understood he was something of a snob about ranks and titles. He hated them almost as much as Mr. Blenheim adored them.

Chapter 15

Two days before they were to board the train west, two unpleasant events occurred: a heat wave gripped the city and four men in business suits showed up.

The men opened the door to their carriage and glanced around as if they were certain they would catch a disease, or worse, the moment they stepped out of the elegant carriage.

Timmy was off buying trunks and clothes and train tickets. Mick had given up trying to stop her from using her money on the Tuckers. He had to, since after sending money home he only had enough for his own travel and perhaps a month's food and board, if he ate naught but oatmeal.

No breeze stirred. The day was hot, far too hot to be indoors. The sky was the gray of a long-dead fish's belly. The air smelled about that rank, too.

Mick sat on the stoop, a small dog tucked under his arm and over his lap. He rewrapped the dog's infected foot, all the while talking to the lads, Henry, Eddy, and Tick, who stood nearby watching anxiously. Tick had found the dog and brought it to Mick. Mick didn't hold out much hope for the dog's toe, but at least Eddy and Tick looked healthier these days.

Mick's heart sank when he saw the men. No one in

the building but his Timmy would know types like these.

One of them called out to him. "Hey, you. We're looking for a man named Mr. McCann."

He wished he'd shaved that morning. And he wished he hadn't donned his old farm clothes. He looked the picture of an unemployed vagabond. At the time, it had made sense to wear the tattered linen overshirt while lancing a dog's pus-filled foot.

He finished with the dog, carefully handed it to Tick and wiped his hands off on a rag. "Mebbe I know Mc-Cann. Who're you?"

"Where is he?" Another one barked.

"Come now, Taylor, no point in being rude," the first one said and turned back to Mick. "We can offer you a reward if you tell us his whereabouts."

Henry opened his mouth, but Mick shot him a warning glance.

"Is he wanted by the police then?" Mick said mildly. "Well, well. What do you know? A criminal. Gracious!"

Eddy leaned close and whispered, "You are not, Mr. Mick. Aren't you going to tell them who you are?"

"Soon enough," Mick said. "Just having a bit of fun."

The group of men had obviously grown impatient with the loiterers hanging on the stoop. They walked away, off to Colsun's.

Their carriage was still drawn up to the curb. The sight of the fine horses and rig alone was enough to lure the bored and curious of the block. Mick considered shooing the more aggressive kids off, but decided to go wash up instead.

The men were out front again.

"McCann," one of the men said loudly as Mick returned from the outside pump where he'd cleaned himself. The group of kids around the carriage had grown larger.

"What's it gonna be? An arrest?" One of the kids yelled out, excited.

"Mr. McCann, they want you, you know. What for? Does it have to do with that Miss Cooper you've taken up with?" Mrs. Welty, the old gossip from the second floor, leaned out her window, direly interested.

Mick wished he'd acted less of a fool and gotten rid of these finely dressed dolts earlier. He didn't want to present a spectacle for the whole neighborhood.

"Aye, I'm McCann," he said. He wasn't going to let this bunch up to his flat, so he'd lead them back to Colsun's. But no, that probably wasn't quiet enough just now. He buttoned up his shirt, tucked it in, and yanked up his braces.

"There's a tavern round the corner. We'll go there," Mick said. He pushed his wet hair out of his face—he needed a hair cut as well as a shave—and rolled up his shirt sleeves in a futile attempt to cool off. He turned to the boys. "Eddy and Tick, keep your eye on the pup. Henry, please come to fetch me if I'm needed, eh?"

McFee's tavern stank of sour beer, stale smoke, and unwashed men, but at least it was dark, and cooler than the street. Botty was allowed in here, so he clicked in after Mick and the men.

Mick nodded to McFee and the men standing at the bar. The fancy gentlemen settled at a booth.

"I'll just have a word with my friend McFee," said Mick.

When he came back, the four men insisted on buying Mick a beer though he told them he didn't want a drink.

"Come on, McCann," one of them said as McFee went to fetch the beer. "Obviously you're a regular here."

Mick could hear them as if they spoke aloud. *It's morning but the Irish'll drink any time of day.*

He folded his arms across his chest and sat back in the booth and waited. And ignored the full glass sitting on the table in front of him.

The largest man with slicked-back hair, soup-strainer mustache, and a chin shadowed with stubble, leaned forward and squinted at Mick. He went straight into the attack. "We know you don't have a job to go back to. You think you don't need to work anymore, do you? Now that you've hooked up with Miss Calverson? We come from the Calverson Company, Mr. McCann. We know a great deal about you."

Mick rubbed his chin and stared back at him. "What is it you want from me then? And who sent you lot? Griffin?"

The men exchanged surprised looks. Mick wondered if he was not supposed to have heard of Griffin. Or maybe not refer to the royal prince by his first name.

The big dark-haired man with heavy sideburns leaned forward, too—even more threatening in his posture. He was the rude one called Taylor. Well. Two men taking on a posture designed to intimidate one poor unemployed dope. Mick would have been impressed, but the big shots lost some of their effectiveness the way the sweat poured down their flushed faces.

Taylor growled. "You are messing with a very powerful organization and family, McCann. I don't care to toss around threats lightly but—"

"Threats? Then it was bleeding Griffin? Funny, seemed to me that he didn't mind me so much."

The exchanged looks seemed even more surprised. "Do you mean you've actually met Mr. Calverson, Mr. McCann?" One of the other men, a skinny, graying guy with a trimmed Vandyke beard asked. He was almost polite. He must have drawn the short straw and had to play good cop to the other's bad one. "When did you meet—"

"Right," Mick interrupted. "And so at this moment I'm thinking it wasn't Griffin that put you on to me. But who else would have a say about Miss Calverson? Other than that useless da of hers, naturally."

Silence followed, broken by Taylor. "None of your goddamn business who sent us. Suffice it to say that we are here on Miss Calverson's behalf. I'll be blunt. We will offer you money. A great deal of money. More than you could earn in a decade. That is if you still had a job." Taylor sneered.

"Twenty-five thousand dollars," another man put in. This one was fat with mouse hair and a mole on his cheek. The roly-poly rodent man, Mick christened him.

"And what do I do for this money?" Mick asked. He idly watched McFee wipe down the table next to them.

"Disappear," Taylor said.

"It is not in the best interest of Miss Calverson for you to remain a part of her life," the kindly graying one said.

"Saints, I'm remembering now I saw a play on the Bowery about this once, an age ago. But the floozy they paid off was a woman. She got a cool one hundred thousand, I think. Terrible show," Mick added thoughtfully. "A sloppy piece o' writing."

The biggest one spoke up. "Mr. McCann. You will not get any more money out of us. But we can make your life awfully difficult if you do not cooperate. We know she is staying with you."

Mick sucked in a deep breath. He reflected they'd gone about this all wrong. If they'd dragged him into their territory of offices and educated wealth, he'd have been trembling in his hobnail boots. They would not have seen his fear, but he would been scared witless. On his own turf, they barely seemed worth the bother.

"You gentlemen say you want to help Miss Calverson. Shall we stroll back round the corner again? So you can have a chat with her? I expect her any minute."

They looked at one another, dubious.

Mick did his best imitation a music hall comic's Irish as he drawled, "Naow, gents, I poot it to ye thoosly. I say narry a ward. I don't tell the rich lassy about the loovly prapasition you've affared me. Crass me hea-urt. And ye'll explain to hur all aboot what a witless thing she do, keepin' company with an oaf like meself. Let her chuse. She's a groown lay-dee after awll."

"I told you it was bad idea to approach him like this," the friendly gray one said to Taylor.

Taylor shot him a glance of poison, then turned an even more hate-filled look to Mick. "Yes. We will go find her."

The carriage still waited, though the nearly spooked horses nervously twitched their ears and occasionally backed. The driver had jumped down from his seat to chase off the kids who seemed determined to startle the horses.

Mick grinned at the driver's harried attempts to grab at boys without leaving the horses' heads.

Mick called out to the largest boys in the crowd, "Lex, Tom. A dime to each of ye if you protect this poor man and his beasts."

Lex and Tom stepped forward, delighted. Tom held a makeshift club and gave it a few sharp practice swings in the air. That was enough to send the rest of the kids scurrying off a short distance.

"Thanks, boys. If you see Miss Timona, send her on over to Colsun's. And Lex, don't let them boys hurt Botty, please."

Mick pointed to Botty, then gestured to a spot near

near Lex, "You, Bot. Stay." The dog sat down and heaved a growling sigh.

Mick pointed to the men and made a similar gesture at Colsun's. "You lot. Come. I'll buy you a cup of the worst coffee you'll ever have. Or so my Timmy tells me."

Colsun's wasn't crowded. Mick strolled over to say hello to Colsun himself. Then he joined the Calverson men over at the table in the far corner near the door. He sat on the hard wooden chair, passive, but alert—an imitation of Griffin Calverson.

For a while they all sat in silence, but eventually the men began to talk. They talked about politics, the stock market, the heat spell. They even tried to engage him in the conversation. He ignored them and pulled out a pencil and his memo book, which he was still in the habit of carrying.

Timmy came through the door and stopped dead. In her pale blue muslin dress, she managed to look clean and cool, though at the sight of the men, her lips pressed tight as if she held back a cry of dismay.

She walked slowly toward them, and the men all stood with a scrape and whine of chairs.

Mick went to meet her. "These men are worried about you, Miss Calverson. I'll let them talk for themselves, shall I? If you decide to leave with them, would you be so good as to come and tell me good-bye, lass?"

"Oh no, Mick."

At once he felt ashamed. She looked so pale and distressed.

"What on earth have they been doing."

"Nay, sorry, *a ghrá*. They must tell you. I swore I would not say."

"For pity's sake." Her fingers were chilly on the skin of his forearm as she grabbed at him. "Sit down, too. Don't go, please, Mick."

He nodded. After fetching a chair for her, he sat

down again. He sprawled, hands behind his head, elbows out, legs stretched long, a working man settled in for a dull sermon.

In stark contrast, she sat straight-backed at the edge of a chair, as nervous as a defendant in a murder trial. She nodded to each of the men in turn. "Good morning, gentlemen. Mr. Taylor, good to see you again."

They stared at her.

"Well, go on, lads. Speak your piece." Mick said heartily. He wondered how they'd react if he pulled Timmy onto his lap to comfort her. Timmy clutched the strap of the purse in her lap till her knuckles turned white. He had never seen brave Timmy so fearful before and he wished he could drive off these dragons of hers.

Silence.

"Is there a more private place we can talk?" one of them finally asked.

"No," said Timmy.

"Miss Calverson, I do not wish to embarrass you and I feel that—" another began.

"Then don't. Embarrass me, I mean."

"Christ," exploded Taylor. "It's—it's this Irish fancy man. Are you aware that soon after he found you, Miss Calverson, he quit his job? Don't you think that was more than a coincidence?"

Miss Calverson graceful, regal, stood up, the tension gone. "I thank you for your interest, but I believe you have said enough." Her voice was calm but stern. A princess addressing minions.

Mick should have known she could take care of her own dragons.

"Miss Calverson, you must listen." Taylor's bellow was loud. "We are authorized to take you back to your father. There has been enough talk and we're trying to stop more."

"Good way to do it too," said Mick approvingly. "Shouting your fool head off in a crowded restaurant." He winked at the man watching at the next table.

Taylor ignored Mick. He pulled several hand-written sheets of paper from his pocket, unfolded them and tossed them onto the table.

The title caught Mick's eye. "Traveling Heiress's Love Nest."

Mick dropped the indifferent act. He sat up straight and picked up the paper. "Hell," he muttered as he read about the scandalous Miss Calverson's shameless antics with an illiterate Irish immigrant bum, fired from the NYPD for corruption. Now where'd they get that last little tidbit of misinformation?

Mick felt as if the bottom of his heart had given way. Poor Timmy didn't deserve this sneering piece of filth written about her. For himself, well, there must be dozens of Michael McCanns in New York City. And, come to that, he was not going to be one of them for long.

"We have paid substantial amounts to keep this from being published, Miss Calverson. The best thing we can do is get you out of here as soon as possible. And Mr. McCann, do not even consider selling your story to the paper."

He sighed, handed her the story, and watched her attentively as she read.

Her shoulders relaxed. And she giggled. "'Luxurious love nest.' Ha! They haven't seen where you live, Mick."

Mick gave an inward sigh of relief. *A Dhia*, how wonderful Timmy was.

He took the papers from her, folded most of them meticulously into an even smaller rectangle, and handed the rectangle back to Taylor.

"Miss Calverson. You mean you don't care?" The kindly gray one sounded truly shocked and distressed.

"Your reputation. It will be in tatters. You will go from being an adored celebrity to something . . ." his voice died away.

"A wanton laughingstock," snarled Taylor. "A harlot who ruined her reputation and exposed her family's business to the worst sort of ridicule for the sake of a roll in the h—"

Mick blew on his already reddening knuckles and watched Taylor's co-workers heave the man to his feet and pick up the chair that had fallen when he'd gone over backwards. He wasn't sure Taylor was listening, but thought he'd offer the man some advice anyway.

"Mr. Taylor, if you're going to go about picking fights with people, you're better off sticking to gentlemen like yourself. I suggest you avoid Irish fancy men even if they are ex-cops. We aren't civilized enough to slap you with a glove, or what have you. Well then, sir, if you wish to press charges, you know where to find me."

A few minutes later, Mick and Timmy watched the four men leave in silence. The rest of Colsun's patrons weren't so quiet. All around them, people expressed sorrow that the other man didn't punch back.

"I was hoping for better than that," the man at the next table complained to his companion. "I want to see McCann in more of a real brawl."

"Thanks for that, Padriag," Mick muttered.

"Slap him with a glove?" Timmy asked Mick.

"Whatever is the proper way to challenge a man to a duel. I took Mr. Taylor out with no warning. Not sportsmanlike. Mind you, if he shows up again, I'll let him know that I intend to beat the living crap out of him before I start."

She sighed. "And I think of you as such a gentle man."

Mick waved good-bye to Colsun, and escorted Timmy

from the restaurant. He pulled her close as they walked down the street. "Timmy. You have to go away from me. Or . . ."

"Or what?"

"Marry me."

"Oh, I'd pick that one. But no, I will not allow some dreadful stranger to dictate to you or me how we will lead our lives."

"Jesus. You're the one who asked me to marry you last, Timmy, wasn't it? I'm saying yes. Let's get married. Now. At once."

"Yes, as I recall it, it was your turn to ask, and my turn to say no. And now I am saying I would rather wait and marry at our convenience, when we choose. Not because someone is holding some kind of newspaper gun to your head. Do you care that they wrote that garbage about you, though, Mick? It was awful, but I was so afraid they'd do worse."

He shook his head. "No one knows me from Adam. 'Tis you that gets the worst *cac capaill.*"

"Cock . . . ?"

"Er, horse manure."

"I like that. You are using such interesting language today. Well. If you don't mind, then I shall be like Wellington and say publish and be damned. And I shan't marry you. Yet."

He gave a yowl of despair. "Miss Calverson. For a little while I thought I understood you. A very few days, I admit. Now I can't imagine what you're about."

"Good. Perhaps you were already becoming complacent. We have only known each other thirty days. I hope you have many years yet to figure me out. I don't think this is so very complicated, though. It is simply that I do not want you to hurriedly marry me either out of a sense of guilt or fear of the penny press. Horrible yellow papers."

"I say I will marry you. Isn't that enough?"

She spoke almost as if to herself. "Oh Mick, I wish I believe you're truly willing. If only those silly men hadn't showed up. That article would haunt me forever if you gave in now. I find I am superstitious about this wedding business."

"Crazy woman," he grumbled.

One of the things she'd said stuck in Mick's mind as they went up the stairs to his flat followed by a puffing Botty.

"Only thirty days together?" he asked.

She nodded and beamed at him, the other smile he liked—the one filled with glee.

"Amazing," he breathed so softly she could not have heard. "Thirty days of heaven."

As Mick closed the door, Timmy turned to him. "Do you suppose Mr. Taylor was about to say *roll in the hay*? I have heard that expression before. I imagine hay would be rather prickly and uncomfortable. Is that where you farm boys traditionally meet your farm girls for trysts?"

"Of course. And a roll in the hay with a good blanket underneath isn't so bad, you know. I hope I can show you some day."

Timmy laughed. "Bother. I can no longer make you blush, Mr. McCann. What a pity."

He leered at her. "How 'bout you try something other than words to embarrass me, aye? Actions might do the trick."

He was delighted to see her turn pink.

Chapter 16

Mick lay naked on the bed, happy, hot, and sticky. The unusually hot, thick air did not stir. It weighed down on them and dried their throats.

"I shall be glad to flee the city," Mick said. "Too bad we don't head for the open sea."

Timmy seemed suddenly to grow still and Mick waited, but she didn't speak.

"Come now, Timmy. I know there's something on your mind. Spill it, *a ghrá*."

"Oh. Several things really. That story Taylor showed us, it occurs to me that it's not with a publisher yet. The blackmailer going for large amounts usually shows a typeset story. More impressive than hand-written. I wonder where it came from?"

Mick yawned and stretched. "The same thought occurred to me. And how did those blessed Calverson types get hold of it?"

"I suppose it doesn't matter. But I think I'll talk to my pet reporter and see what I can do about my own version."

"Your pet reporter?"

"Solly Lothman. Good old Solly. I'm quite fond of the rascal." She stretched, then looked over at him. "Solly isn't the only thing, I, ah, should mention. I bought a couple of extra tickets today . . ."

He pushed himself onto an elbow and looked down at her.

"And who are the tickets for?"

"The Tuckers, of course. But I thought perhaps your friends Eddy and Lex."

"They are just boys."

"Yes, but I have checked and they have no immediate family and their extended families seem utterly indifferent to them. I think we can find something for them in Minnesota. If they hate wide open spaces, I have other ideas."

"Timmy, you might have said you were going to do this." He snorted. "Runnin' your own version of an orphan train."

She looked surprised. "Do you mind?"

"No, no. 'Tis your money. But. I- I suppose I feel like a kept man after all. Along for the ride."

She was silent for a moment. "I am used to making decisions on my own. I rather think the situation similar to the fire. You sometimes act without consulting me."

"That sort of thing is an emergency, Tim-girl. If I were going to do so much as invite a friend to dinner I would let you know."

She frowned. "Of course. You make perfect sense, as usual. You are absolutely right and I am sorry."

"Well, now. If that is not the grandest apology I ever heard." He moved towards her. With his knuckle, he caught a droplet of perspiration that rolled down the valley between her breasts. "I may even forgive you if—" A sudden hullabaloo started up outside. Joyous and astonished cries filled the street.

Mick looked up from Timmy's sweet round breasts into her face. She looked suspiciously innocent. "Now what is it you have done?"

She smiled sheepishly. "I suspect it is the ice wagon. I purchased a few blocks to be delivered here and there. When I was sitting on the front stoop with Sarey and Henry, I heard the woman next door complaining that because ice was too expensive, the milk was going bad and her children were often sick."

"So you bought her some ice. Does everyone know by now you're the big benefactor of the block, Timmy?"

"No, I have a helper. Henry is very good at keeping secrets, you know. Henry walked with me to the iceman's, and he suggested perhaps I could get some delivered to the front stoops."

The yelps of delight increased. "I hope you haven't caused a riot, love."

"No, of course not. The iceman swore his assistant would help divide up the blocks. He was most obliging because I've put in the same order every week for the rest of the summer."

The shouts, and the clop of the iceman's horse's hooves sounded very near. Timmy stretched her arms over her head. "Maybe we can get a few shards. Poor old Botty's tongue is going to fall out of his head with all the panting he's doing. And I would love to run an ice chip up and down my body about now."

Mick jumped out of bed and yanked on his trousers. "Do not move. I'll go fetch a few chips. I'll do for you, if you do for me."

They said their good-byes at Colsun's and left the street before dawn in the middle of a downpour that broke the hot spell. Timona had bought a collar and leash for Botty, who hated the things, but suffered nobly after Mick ordered him to "stop that nonsense."

Mick felt nothing but a light heart for himself, though he worried about the street creatures, human and otherwise, left behind. He made sure that the widow downstairs wrote down the name and direction of Dr. O'Toole so if any of his "patients" showed up, she could send them somewhere. She frowned and complained about the extra work, but he noticed she carefully pinned the directions to the inside of her door.

He was surprised at how many people seemed upset at their leaving. The street had many who came and went.

Mrs. Kelly wept as she hugged Timmy.

And Jim, Mick's neighbor, actually admitted he'd miss Mick. "You're the closest thing we have to a leader in this neighborhood, McCann." Jim put a meaty hand on Mick's shoulder. "And I'd say you've been our fire department, police department, and hospital. Can you blame us for getting all choked up?"

Jim looked around the crowded restaurant and then nudged Mick in the ribs. "And not least, you finally added a bit of class and beauty to the place with that Cooper woman of yours. You sure you don't want to bequeath her to me? Is it true she's all that and plenty of money too?"

"Jim, I thought I would miss you but I have just this moment changed my mind."

The Tuckers and Eddy settled into the train carriage's red velvet seats giggling with excitement. Even Jenny managed a ghost of a smile at her children's joy. Lex, whom Mick guessed was fifteen or sixteen, tried to act nonchalant. But he couldn't stop himself from looking around with avid interest. Everyone jumped and laughed when the train let off a howling shriek and jerked to life.

Mick followed Timona to their seats. She shook her head.

"We can't settle here yet. Solly'll go up in the next

car, a Pullman Palace car. He was so pitiful I bought him a ticket too, and he talked me into first class, as usual. You can help us work out a story. It might counter the nonsense Taylor showed us, that is, in the event the—oh, what is it you called it?—*cac capaill* shows up in our lives again."

She pulled the leash out of her pocket and Botty growled. But he sat down at once, so she could attach it. He already seemed to understand that if he didn't wear the leash, he got left behind or stuffed into a basket.

They made their way to the front of their own car. An angular young man with wiry black hair sprawled on a seat, one leg lolling over the polished wooden arm rest. He jabbered at a pretty young blonde.

The man got to his feet and bade the woman a reluctant goodbye.

Timona introduced Solly to Mick. Solly stuck out a boney hand. "S'apleasureameetcha." He spoke faster than anyone Mick had ever met.

As they moved toward, Solly chattered. "Now I wish I could remain back here with you hoi polloi. Isn't that blonde tasty? Hey, food. I'm hungry, Timona! Feed me!" The man made every statement sound stop-the-presses important, Mick noticed. A hazard of his work, perhaps.

Solly caught sight of the dog. He stopped dead and gawked at Botty. "What the hell is that?" For the first time his words came out slowly.

"It's a, um, fighting Bortic terrier," said Timona. "Very special breed. This one is a champion."

"Looks like it's lost more than a few of its fights!" Solly snickered. "No, don't tell me. I should have seen the other dogs!"

"Absolutely," Timona agreed.

At the door of the next car, the conductor rushed towards them ready to send them back to their proper place in the second-class car.

Timona smiled placatingly. She slipped some folded bills to the frowning man and leaned towards him to utter a few words. The man turned and showed them to a table tucked into a corner of the luxurious car.

Mick had to admire the way Timona dealt with the walls erected to keep out riffraff; she slipped through them as if they were made of mist. Of course, she was helped by the fact that the walls weren't built to keep her out.

They sat at a table that was covered with crisp white linen and set with a porcelain vase of fresh, pale pink roses. Mick gently nudged the growling Botty under the table with his foot. "G'wan, be quiet, you hell hound," he muttered.

A porter handed them menus and Mick was amused to see how it described a hot turkey sandwich as if it were fabulous culinary treat.

Solly ate the way he talked, quickly and with enthusiasm. He also put away an enormous amount of food.

"Timona! I must've gotten all the way to Columbus before I figured out you were left back in New York! Your father didn't know where you were, and Mr. Blenheim was fit to be tied. I had to pay my own train fare! Back to New York, too. And I listened to droning about fossils for six solid hours before I gave Pops the slip. I've been forced to write horrible dull pieces about some dusty political scandal. Ugh. What in God's name have you been up to?"

Timona gave him some details of New York. Mick was interested in how much she left out, though she was careful to mention the Tuckers. She also mentioned the Graves and other respectable folk she met up with.

After she finished, she turned to Mick and said, "Solly here is extremely clever. He's a stringer, a freelance reporter. But he's a smart boy who makes his money coming and going."

She took a spoonful of soup, and then went on. "I pay him to put in and take out particular fragments of his stories. Solly acts as something like a public relations man, but not as falsely hearty, or constantly in one's hair, which my father does not tolerate. And once Solly does a version of a story for me, and I pay him, the editors turn around and pay him again to publish it."

Solly, working his way through his third sandwich, smirked as if he were getting credit for a particularly clever invention. "Don't forget, part of the deal is I get first crack at the Calverson story of the week, Timona!" Solly reminded her. "Speaking of which, down to business! I want to file a story by Thursday so I get my rent taken care of. Here's the idea! You're helping these poor people flee the unhealthy air of the city at a—"

Timona groaned. "Oh no, Solly. How sick-making. No. I know you think you have to include me. But I should be secondary."

"Timona, you always say that and then the editors chop off every word that isn't related to you. All my fine work wasted!"

She thought as she sipped her wine. "All right. It's strictly in New York. I was, er, coshed on the head. And the people came to help me in my time of need. Does that ring true enough, Mick?"

"Coshed on the head? Honest? Timona my fine friend, you never fail to deliver!" Solly practically drooled in delight as he frantically searched his pockets for a better pencil.

Mick finally had to ask. "Do you mean all the stories about you are lies?"

"Of course not. Simply, er, edited. In this case, we'll just leave out the bordello, and the boy's clothes, and the single man's flat. Solly will put in people like the

Tuckers and the Kellys, though I think it best if we change names. "

"Oh, Timona." Solly groaned. "Don't! Please do not say words like 'bordello' and 'boy's clothes' in my presence! McCann is the lucky man with the flat, I take it?"

Mick felt himself blush.

Timona nodded. "But Mick must be left out entirely, Solly. I mean it."

Solly exploded. "I can't bear it! Yes, yes, creating a Calverson fiction is not in the league of fudging an exposure of corruption in government, but it still hurts my newsman's soul to know you're tossing out the meat of the story and leaving me thin broth. A bordello! I know you are!"

Timona blew a genteel raspberry. "Solly, don't you preach to me of your pure journalist's soul."

She turned to Mick as she waved a fork at Solly. "We struck our first deal a few years ago. Sol approached me one night in a Parisian restaurant to say he had written a story about the drug-deal my father mistakenly made. Papa thought the items in question were bones . . . well, let's never mind that misunderstanding. Anyway, Solly was going to turn in his story no matter what I said, but he offered to change details. Very apologetic and friendly. Not at all threatening or unpleasant like the usual blackmailer. And the story he finally wrote was really very good."

Solly the blackmailer beamed at Timona.

She smiled back and said, "Our Solly can turn a word. After that first story I developed the idea that he could do more of the same writing for us. He tends to stick close. Don't you, Sol."

Solly nodded. He tucked a wad of his sandwich into his cheek and said, "When the editors stop clamoring for news about you and yours, Timona, I'll hold a wake!

You shall be invited of course. I will send the very finest engraved black-edged invitation."

The two of them nailed down the basic idea of the story. Mick listened and marveled at how chunks of the story was gently wiggled and rearranged, or ignored. And here he always thought plain truth was important.

Timona finished by saying Solly really should talk to the Tuckers and Lex and Eddy. "They might still think I'm Miss Cooper, by the way. Poor Jenny is mourning right now, but she'll talk about her husband, Lester. I didn't know him well, but he sounds like he was a grand person, worth a paragraph or two at least.

"When you do be write it up, be sure to emphasize the fact that they are not poor because they are lazy, Solly. Pure bad luck. And emphasize their generosity. They didn't have much but they shared everything they owned with me. Their, um, last cup of tea. But mind, Solly, if you throw in one cliché, such as a drunk Irishman," she flashed a sly grin at Mick, "you shan't get a farthing out of me. Oh, and end the story in New York. There are some people I do not wish to meet up with."

"Always are," Solly grumbled.

Timmy ignored him. "You can say I am in the process of rejoining Papa, and that is enough."

"I'll get the rest in later copy? Yes?" Solly said hopefully.

"We'll see, dear." She picked up her bag and handed Solly some money. "Eat as many desserts as you like. I shan't ask for a receipt."

"Charming company you keep," Mick said as they made their way up the train's aisle back to their own car. "A blackmailer who writes lies as fact and a . . ." he almost said "killer," thinking of Griffin but at once changed it to, "an Irish fancy man."

Timona frowned at him. "Do you feel like a kept man? Truly?"

"I feel mostly dizzy around you, *a ghrá*. You keep turning the world upside down."

"Not upside down, really? I prefer to think I occasionally turn things right side round. Speaking of which, do you know I was thinking about you?"

"Ach no, I don't like that tone. I would rather you'd leave me out of your circus, love. I prefer to be a spectator."

"It's just that you said you wanted to work on a farm, but I, um, wonder if you . . ." She shook her head and laughed. "It's so wonderful to be with you, Mick. You're tolerant even when you want me to go to the devil. Another man would have stormed and carried on, but you . . ."

"Yes, and don't ye bother to sweet-talk me, Timmy. Go on. I know you well enough by now. You have a plan in your mind and it'll eat away at you until ye speak of it in your sleep. What is it?"

"A veterinarian. Or maybe a regular doctor. Mick you'd be perfect."

"No."

"But you already know—"

"No." He dropped into his seat and shifted to look out the window.

He could feel Timmy's eyes boring into him. She couldn't hold back, of course. "Why ever not?"

"Damn it, Timmy, it's my life, and I do have some control, I believe."

"Of course. But do tell me why the idea upsets you so?"

He took a deep breath. Here was the moment he showed her another of the chasms between them. "Timmy, love, I told you I left school early. I didn't say . . . well, here 'tis. I don't have so much as a basic education. I was seven years old when I quit."

"How did you manage that?" She sounded interested, and not in the least shocked.

"I had a disagreement with the teacher." Mick said.

Mr. Thurman had flailed the young Mick's behind every time he spoke Gaelic, which he did just to annoy the pompous old stick of a teacher.

Mick went on. "'Twas actually more to do with my family. My father was grateful for the extra help. And in the evenings, Da taught me to read and do sums. He didn't know much more than that, since he left school when he was nine. He did enjoy reading in the English. The doctor my Da worked for had died, and left him some volumes of Shakespeare. That's where I met with *Timon*. But Da's teaching me was a case of blind leading the blind." He laughed without a trace of amusement. "We loved reading 'em, but we didn't know half the words in those plays. Had to invent meanings to fit. And Mam—she can barely write her name."

Timmy was shaking her head. Mick wondered if she was at last appalled until she spoke. "Griffin will be wildly jealous to hear that you just up and left school. He hated school. I don't think it ever occurred to him to simply walk away from boarding school, or even university."

"Nay, Timmy you can't go around telling people I'm an ignorant git."

She stared at him, her eyes wide. "You're seriously upset, aren't you?"

"Timmy!"

"Does it help to know that I never spent a day in a school? My teachers were Griffin and Papa when I was lucky, and governesses when I was less lucky. The governesses attempted little more than improving my manners and handwriting. You've got more formal education that I do."

He laughed, astounded and entertained by her, as usual. "You have an answer for everything."

"Aha! Indeed I do. Mick, I just recalled that your background is better than mine. Did you know that my parents are actually divorced? My mother is still alive, but I think I told you, she is not interested in acknowledging the fact that she has children."

"Oh, poor girl."

"No, no need to sound so mournful. Don't waste pity on me. Papa and especially Griffin, were enough family for me. If anyone suffered, I imagine it was Griffin, for he has memories of Mama. Sometimes that's why I think he occasionally laughs, but so rarely smiles and why he is . . . well, who he is. But don't you understand? You come from a better family, and you've stayed in school longer than I did. Time to knock off the chip on the shoulder, McCann."

She scooted her bottom across the seat to lean close to him. "About becoming a doctor now."

He groaned. "No, no, Timmy. Leave be, woman."

She answered cheerily. "Fine. As long as it's a real no, I'll leave it be. It is the 'I'm-not-good-enough' noes that I disdain."

She was quiet for a long minute. Then she spoke in an unusually grave and hesitant tone. "Forgive me for saying this, and I swear I will leave it be, Mick, but . . but you aren't your father. You are strong. I- I would help in anyway I could."

A reference to her damn money, no doubt. She looked up at him, her large eyes concentrating on him as if she could use her gaze to pour her conviction into him. Casting another of her spells. "I think you should go ahead and dream, Michael McCann," she whispered.

Later as he gazed out the window and she dozed on his shoulder, he began for the first time to imagine life as a country animal doctor.

He didn't have to be a laborer or farm hand. He could fix his mind to something larger.

She must have some kind of power, he reflected, as he felt stirrings of ambition. He knew he could manage it. Even if he did not touch her damn money.

Timona discovered that traveling with the young children and the large entourage was more interesting and a great deal more fun than with her father. And it was a positive pleasure to travel with the capable Mick. Not only did he know what had to get done, he'd do the worst of jobs without comment.

He'd change the baby's diaper, then bound off the train during a half-hour stopover to wash the collection of dirty ones in the pail he'd found, whistling all the while, or laughing at Rob and Lex's jibes about women's work.

As they left the city farther behind, he grew light-hearted.

His mouth quirked into an easy smile, even when he dozed. He opened the window and risked getting cinders in his eyes as he leaned his forearms against the polished wood frame of the train to watch the countryside of hills and forests roll by.

In the middle of the first night, the train stopped to take on water and more coal. Around them everyone slept. Mick disentangled himself from Timona and Eddy who leaned on him as they dozed. Timona watched him leave the train. She followed and found him standing in a copse of trees a few hundred yards from the train, breathing in the soft night air and scent of pine.

He turned and gathered her close. "I had no notion I missed it so much. The fresh green world outside New York. Perhaps I would have lived and died in that city if . . ." his voice petered out. "Thank you," he said and fell silent.

They stood together wrapped in darkness, watching the moon play hide-and-seek behind the clouds and trees, and listening to the sleeping countryside and the hiss and rumble of the train, until the conductor's bell and the shriek of the train summoned them.

Days of train travel made the tightly coiled Solly more like a crazed rodent than a man. He bounded off at stations and barely made it back to the train in time. Timona was used to Solly, but the others screamed encouragement and laughter as they watched his long legs whipping down the platform. From long practice, he managed to fling himself after the train and swing aboard as it slowly pulled away from the station.

Rob, who'd taken a liking to Solly after their interview, reported that he seemed to have picked up a strong interest in the blonde woman.

Timona knew what would come next. She only wished she had seen a good version of the article first. The one he showed her had too much "Timona, Victim of the Cruel Streets of New York" for her taste.

In Chicago, Solly watched from the station window and muttered something that might have been poetry about "a piece of heaven marching amongst them."

Timona looked up from a book she was reading. Solly gazed after the blonde woman who swished her way down the wide, sunny platform followed by a porter pushing a cart loaded with baggage.

Timona leaned over and whispered to Mick, "It has

been at least six months since the last girl, and so it is time he fell in love again."

Solly's plans, which never stayed solid for long, would change. Would he require cash, she wondered or would a cheque work?

Within five minutes, he was begging Timona for a wad of cash and jumped up to trail after the mysterious blonde.

"I'll catch up with you in the frozen north."

"It is summer, Solly. Even Minnesota has a break from ice in the summer. You have my father's address. Send me my rewritten copy or you won't get that rent money," she added sternly.

"Right." He nodded absentmindedly and then took off after his prey.

"Alas, yet another broken heart in store for Solly." Timona sighed as she watched Solly stride down the station platform. "The first one I met was a Russian girl who wanted him to live in Moscow. Solly couldn't bear that idea. He'll be a wretched boy soon, but he tells me he tends to write better when his soul is in anguish. He was in love with me for a few weeks."

"I don't want to know."

"It ended when I bit his tongue. I suspect he thought it was a friendly kiss, but he is such an enthusiastic person."

Mick growled something incoherent or Gaelic or both.

At Uncle Dave's, Mick was the only one who expressed any interest in the flocks of chittering, smelly birds.

Timona asked the dubious Lex to stay behind to help the Tuckers. She pressed cash into his hand.

"Escape funds for you and the Tuckers," she told him

privately. She gave him a paper with an address. "And here is where we will be in Minnesota, for a little while, anyway, if you decide you don't want to go back to the city."

"I'm not staying here. I'm gonna be a railroad man," he informed her. "As soon as I can, I'm getting me a job with the railroad."

She nodded, unsurprised. He had spent most of the trip talking to the brakeman, the conductor, and any other trainman he could corner, including the person Lex described as the greatest man he'd ever met: The locomotive engineer.

She hoped Lex wouldn't disappear with all the money and, after thinking it over, secretly pressed a similar amount into Rob's hand. And then Jenny's hand, too. She gave copies of her father's Minnesota address to all of them, admonishing Henry to write, even if his handwriting was wobbly.

Timona disliked the turkey farm, though she could not help admiring the vast skies and wondering to herself how long an exposure she'd need to capture the scene of clouds with a camera. Only those clouds could convey the wide sprawling emptiness of the flat land.

Jenny stood in the yard and watched, even more grim-faced than usual, as Mick and Timona left her and the children.

At least Uncle Dave looked cheerful. He looked over his dead brother's brood and widow as proudly as if they were already his.

There had been brief talk of leaving Eddy with the Tuckers, but when Timona had seen the terror in the boy's eyes, she knew he still needed Mick, the only adult he seemed to trust.

Eddy wasn't certain how old he was but said he guessed he was about eight. Sallow and thin, the quiet boy with the too-mature face was theirs now. Timona hoped Mick didn't mind that she'd landed him with Eddy, but she didn't want to ask.

On the bouncing, jolting train that was the last leg of their journey, they talked about the Tuckers. "I worry for them," Mick admitted to Timona. "Perhaps Uncle Dave is not the answer. But they couldn't stay in New York, I'm certain of that."

Timona rubbed the steely muscles of his upper arm. She didn't do more than that because Eddy clutched at Mick's other arm.

The boy silently stared out the window of the train, lost in his own thoughts, but unwilling to let go of his protector.

Timona decided not to mention the money she had left with Rob and Lex. And Jenny. Mick still seemed touchy about money. So she said, "If Uncle Dave is not the answer, Rob will write to you and we shall find an answer that suits." She couldn't resist adding, "That is the beauty of money, you know."

Mick scowled at her, as she assumed he would.

She attempted an Irish accent. "Go on, laddie. No need to disdain a *bhean* for having a bit o' gold. Tis not her fault."

"What on earth did you just say, Timmy?"

She giggled. "I tried to tell you to put up with the hardship of staying with me."

His scowl transformed into an easy smile. "Hardship? Not likely."

God, how she loved that smile of his. She searched his face and whispered, "Hard to imagine what life was like before we met, isn't it."

"I can see it too well. My life was empty," he answered without hesitation. "Filled with noise and people, but empty. You may be the princess of the world, but it turns out I am too selfish to give you up, Timmy, *a ghrá mo chrói*. We should marry."

Hardly able to breathe, she clasped his hand. And spoke with unusual seriousness, for she had to bring up her last stumbling block. "But I still think . . . you do not entirely approve of me. And I think I cannot marry someone who does not approve of me."

He was silent for a time "'Tis not you. Never you, now. It's the rest . . . the claptrap."

Relief made her roll her eyes and give a dramatic groan. "You still mean money, don't you, you great lummox?"

"More than that. Your place in the world. The gang o' Calverson boyos."

"Ignore it all, Mick," she urged. "I'm not them."

"It's me that they may not ignore. Nay, Timona Calverson. I won't let them stop us, but I can't ignore it all."

"Purely because you're pigheaded."

"Purely because I'm sane."

Timona, her heart filled with contented joy leaned against him. He had not said he loved her, but he came close. She was nearly certain from the book she'd been reading about Irish Gaelic that *a ghrá mo chrói* meant "love of my heart." She would have to look that up.

She agreed with him, in part, about her blasted life. She almost didn't want the trip to end. It wasn't merely because travel was a familiar world to her, and this was a particularly luxurious form of travel (though her bum ached from sitting so long every day, and she wished the seats were higher so she could lean back).

She worried about their current destination. Her father and Mr. Blenheim. They would want to her to stay with their entourage. But she was happily finished with that part of her life. Now she was going to take pictures and live with her Mick. Only Mick himself had the power to tell her otherwise, and she was gloriously aware that luck was on her side: He seemed to want her as much as she wanted him. Almost as much, at any rate.

She yawned, and leaned on his broad comfortable shoulder. He shifted a bit so he could wrap his arm around her and pull her close. Oh, she did hope Mick didn't want to go exploring the globe. If she never saw another new port of call, or discovered another uncharted corner of the earth, or even visited another one of her father's digs, she would be just fine, thank you.

Timona knew there would be some fuss about this plan of hers. She'd rather not think about how much.

Chapter 17

He should have stayed with the turkeys and the Tuckers. The second he laid eyes on Blenheim, Mick knew life had taken a turn for the worse.

Blenheim was tall, well formed, handsome, and thoroughly aristocratic. Blond, elegant, graceful—athletic, rather than willowy—Blenheim's perfection extended to his face. He had the classic chiseled features of a blue blood.

Perhaps his chin was not entirely strong, but Mick didn't think the man's physical imperfections were pronounced enough. Mick was immediately conscious of his own over-large body, twice-broken nose, and large, blunt fingers. And his riotously curling hair, which badly needed a cut.

Before Mick even got off the train, he suspected he disliked Blenheim. Once the man opened his mouth, Mick knew he loathed him.

Blenheim met them at the door of the train. He helped Timmy down the steps as if she were made of spun sugar, and cooed over her like a slightly disapproving but indulgent mentor.

Right away, Mick caught on to the bastard's hold on Timmy. Blenheim did not fawn on her, the way her other would-be suitors must.

Maybe that was how Mick had gotten his opportunity

with Timona Calverson. He'd been mighty critical of her at first.

He was still contemplating this dismal thought, when Blenheim turned to him and Eddy. "You two. Help with the bags."

Mick could see Blenheim knew who he was. He considered pointing this out to the blighter, but for the merest second the ice blue eyes met his, and dared him to make a scene in the tiny train station.

"Wait. Mr. Blenheim, this is Mr. McCann, and Mr., ah, Eddy," said Timmy. Her voice sounded slow and uncertain. For half a second, Mick thought his heart would shatter. She spoke as if she wasn't sure she actually knew Mick after all.

But no, this was Timmy.

She broke into a grin.

"Did I do that correctly, Mr. Blenheim? I think that's the order to the introductions since you're related to royalty. I would introduce someone to you rather than . . ."

"It is never proper," said Blenheim very, very quietly—but not so quietly Mick couldn't hear, "to introduce one's friends to servants."

The silence was deafening. Until Timmy, bless her, put out a reassuring hand and touched Blenheim's arm. "Oh, Mr. Blenheim, you and Aunt Winifred have tried and tried to explain this, but I cannot fathom it. Truly, just because you are Papa's secretary we can not consider you a servant."

Mick couldn't hold back the guffaw. Blenheim turned ashen, but did not move or utter a peep. Mick had to admire the training that kept the man from exploding on the spot.

He knew Blenheim was his enemy, but he should not have laughed at the man's humiliation. He also knew, though he suspected Blenheim did not, that Timmy was absolutely innocent of malice. She really was trying to reassure this duke's grandson or earl's nephew that he was socially acceptable to her friends, the near-penniless, ignorant Irish farmer and the illegitimate street orphan.

It's something like people who can't sing properly, Mick thought as he walked behind Timmy and Blenheim to the waiting carriage. Poor Timmy knew about rank but could not really grasp the importance of a person's place in the world. It had blared loud and clear to Mick's ear, all his life, a menace to his peace. Like this Blenheim was sure to be.

Saints, it was not a case of poor tone-deaf Timmy. She was the blessed lucky one.

Eddy must have sensed the tension in the air, because he again clung to Mick's arm. In the city, the sensitive boy had always been one of Mick's more frequent visitors and beggars, but now he seemed to be melded to his side. Mick ruffled Eddy's hair with his free hand.

"We shall be fine, Eddy. I promise I shan't leave you." The promise he'd lately repeated so many times had its usual effect. Eddy loosened his death grip, though he still held onto Mick's sleeve.

"An' the kitten?" Eddy whispered. "We'll get him soon?"

"He's safest tucked into his little basket."

The groom helped Timmy into the carriage. She gathered in the growling Botty. Her face appeared in the window, which she lowered.

"Come on, Mick and Eddy," she called cheerfully oblivious to Blenheim's pained look.

Mick came to the carriage and leaned in, glad for the excuse not to sit in the carriage with Blenheim.

"Eddy's worried about his cat. We'll get a ride with the luggage."

Timmy nodded, and tightened her hold on Botty. "I

shall have to keep this boy from leaping out the window to get at you."

"Pray tell, Miss Calverson. What is that beast?" Blenheim walking past, stopped to stare at Botty with undisguised loathing.

"A Corptic terrier," said Timmy.

"I've heard tell tis Bortic," Mick said mildly.

"Of course. How silly of me." Timmy shook her head sadly. "And all this time I have considered myself an expert on the breed."

Blenheim busily ordered everyone in the area to help load the luggage onto the pony cart. Then, ignoring the groom's proffered hand, Blenheim climbed into the carriage.

The groom doffed his cap to the Blenheim and said, "*Póg mo thón*," in a respectful tone. Kiss my ass.

Mick laughed. The groom tipped him a wink, then leapt up to his seat.

It felt glorious to be in the clean, sweet air, after being cooped up in the small railway car. Pressed against Mick's side, even Eddy relaxed and looked all around them at the rolling hills.

The driver of the cart introduced himself as Morrison, then said, with a chuckle, "So you are another man to play the Irish harp, then?"

Mick frowned. The old derogatory reference to a shovel sounded odd coming from the mouth of an Irishman.

Morrison didn't seem to notice Mick's response. He asked, "Planning on staying long?"

"I plan on finding work on a farm eventually."

"It's not a bad outfit," said the driver in Gaelic. "Pay is good. The old man is fairly mad but not a bad sort. Imagine. He offers a thousand dollars to the first man to dig up a dinosaur bone. Only have to watch out for the young Gall." Englishman. "Blenheim is a rare wind-bag of a man. Blown up with his own self worth."

He nodded towards Eddy. "Your son looks too thin. The camp cook will help fill him out. God, I wish she'd help me out. She has the look of a wild one, and makes the finest food I have ever put in my mouth. She can't abide the old gentleman, though."

"Calverson?"

"Himself." The driver spat over the edge of the cart and continued. "I see you came with the blessed Timona. Quite a honey mouth look to the girl. She has some ripe and pretty parts to her, aye?"

Mick growled, "Just a moment Mr. Morrison . . ."

The man mistook his anger. "No, no. I don't mean to offend your boy's precious ears. We've heard a word or two about the fair Timona from the cook, who's fond of the lass, it seems. Of course I wouldn't touch the girl if she were beauty itself.

"Calverson Junior is pure trouble, they say, and I guess he wouldn't take to any bog dweller messing with his sister."

"What are you two talking about, Mick?" asked Eddy.

The driver tsked disapprovingly. "He calls you by your name? I'd flail that disrespect out of a boy. And why don't you teach him your own tongue?"

Mick was careful to answer in Gaelic. "I'm glad he can't understand with some of the nonsense you've been spouting, Mr. Morrison. He calls me Mick because he's not truly my son."

Mick turned to Eddy. "We're talking about where we're heading. Remember what Miss Timona told you about dinosaur bones? We're going see where they actually dig for them."

Morrison glanced over at the dark Eddy. "Now I can see what you mean. Got some spic in him. Or yid? Watch your wallet!" He laughed like a hyena.

Mick growled and hugged Eddy closer. Blenheim might not be the only idiot in the outfit.

The cat began to yowl but Morrison didn't allow them to stop and search for the basket. Mick felt annoyed for Eddy's sake, until Morrison showed a spark of kindness when he offered an explanation.

"I don't want to miss lunch, as you call it. It is called dinner here, and 'tis the largest meal of the day. But I think your cat is just fine. Hark how it is complaining loud and clear, like it was a good strong animal? Don't fret, boy—I was extra careful with the basket as we loaded up."

When they had arrived at the camp, it proved to be larger and more luxurious than Mick had imagined. There were four buildings on the site. The largest was a former farmhouse and had been set up in fine style, said Morrison, for the boss, his secretary, the cook, and now his daughter. Two buildings were barns converted into bunkhouses for the diggers. And the last smaller building housed Sir Kenneth's two assistants.

Mick and Eddy helped Morrison unload the baggage.

"How many diggers are there?" Mick asked, looking around the sprawling compound.

"Counting you, now there's thirty-eight. And there are others too. Grooms and whatnot. You are a digger ain't ye?"

Mick again wished he'd stayed at the damn turkey farm. "I am not a digger. I think."

"You are not? You think?" Morrison pushed back his shapeless felt hat and from under thick gray eyebrows examined Mick with interest. "What are you then?"

Good question.

"I've been a farmer." That was all Mick could say with certainty.

"We're friends of Miss Timona's," said Eddy.

A good enough answer.

Within moments the woman herself appeared and trotted across the yard towards them. The leashless Botty raced ahead of her as if he'd been shot from a cannon.

Timmy gave Mick a hug. Thank God she held back her usual lusty kiss.

She shook hands with Morrison who muttered an astonished, "How do ye do."

"*Dia duit!* That's supposed to be 'hello,'" she said and added, "I have an atrocious accent, or so Mick tells me. He has been teaching me Irish. I'm Timona Calverson. And you are?"

Morrison's eyes were round with fascination "Brian Morrison. Pleased to meet you."

He looked at Mick and then at Timona. And then at Mick again.

"A pleasure to meet you, Mr. Morrison," said Timona cheerily.

She reached for Eddy and Mick's hands. "Sorry to hurry you, but we're just in time for lunch," she told them, and pulled them towards the house, allowing Eddy to stop and scoop up his cat's basket.

She looked over her shoulder. "Thank you again, Mr. Morrison. I understand your meal is ready, too, so you might as well leave the pile of bags where they are. It won't rain, and we can fetch them later."

She stopped for a moment while Mick held open the door for her. She said, "Before we eat, there is something I should mention."

Mick racked his imagination. Was her father in the habit of dining naked? Did Blenheim refuse to share a table with him?

But he didn't get far in his speculations, when she continued, "You must not forget to tell Araminta how wonderful the food is as she serves the meal. Do not stint on the praise. She is an artist, and feels she deserves compliments for every meal. I suppose it is entirely true, for she puts up with the most appalling conditions."

"Araminta? Isn't that your best friend's name, too?"

Timmy looked confused for a second. "Yes, that's Araminta."

Mick couldn't help grinning. What other rich girl would count her cook as her best friend?

He wasn't sure how Botty would do in a real house, so he ordered the dog to wait on the porch. At least he didn't have to worry about people throwing rocks at the dog here. He hoped.

The father did not appear at the meal.

"He's in the middle of something, so I'll introduce you later," said Timmy as she settled in the chair Blenheim held for her.

Mick wondered if the old man had even looked up when his daughter had reappeared in his life. Poor Timmy.

Mick did not suppose Mr. Morrison and the others were eating the same delicate fare, though he thought Araminta could probably make shoe leather taste delicious. But he didn't get to tell her because one of the diggers served the meal.

"Mrs. Araminta asked me to because she is in the middle of writing something down," the nervous laborer explained. He'd scrubbed his hands so much they were a different color than the rest of his tanned arms.

Blenheim, at the head of the elegantly laid table, tsked impatiently at the man's lack of training. With icy and exaggerated politeness he corrected the laborer's blunders. "I appreciate you taking the time to help the cook, but do you think you could hold still long enough for us to serve ourselves? And could you please hold this lower so that I might actually see the food you are offering? Thaaaank you."

Eddy dove into his food as if he were starving. Blenheim clicked his tongue and muttered, "Disgusting."

Mick leaned close to the abashed Eddy and whispered. "Listen, love, remember when I showed you how to use the fork in Miggie's? Show this Blenheim man your best manners."

Eddy turned red and looked near to crying. How on earth did a child this tender survive the streets, thought Mick, not for the first time.

But Eddy aimed a wavering smile at Mick and picked up the fork.

"Mr. Blenheim."

Mick looked over at Timona, who sounded unusually perturbed. "I do hope you are not feeling ill."

"Not at all, my dear Miss Calverson. Why do you ask?"

"Since we've arrived, you have seemed a bit under the weather. Is something bothering you? It is not like you to be uncivil."

Blenheim's perfect brow clouded. "Ahem. I thought I made it clear in the carriage, Miss Calverson, that I do not believe our current . . . ah."

Timmy frowned. Even she must understand the man, Mick thought.

Blenheim wasn't doing a good enough job hiding his dislike of Mick. Blenheim was a fool, but he must have understood if he started an open war with Mick, he would lose his hold on Timona.

Sure enough, within a few seconds Blenheim was making an effort to be polite. He gave a tiny cough, and turned to Mick.

"So, Mr. McCann. I understand that you were a New York City police officer. Did you enjoy the work?"

"'Twas all right."

"Then why didn't you stay with it?"

"The job was about to change."

"I thought the change would be all for the better."

Mick stopped eating and examined Blenheim. "And where did you hear that?"

Blenheim's face turned pale rather than red. "One assumes. I mean people customarily make advancements, you see."

Interesting.

Mick changed the subject. "So, Mr. Blenheim. Do you know Mr. Calverson well? I mean Mr. Griffin Calverson?"

"I have met him twice, and I must say he is a very impressive gentleman. He is one of our future leaders. Though I do not know him as well as I like, I am convinced that should he settle in this country permanently, he would make a superb senator or congressman," said the suddenly effusive Blenheim.

Mick knew the man was delighted by the change of subject. Blenheim babbled to them about Mr. Griffin Calverson's amazing business acumen.

Fool, thought Mick with relish, though he felt more than a little uneasy about what he'd heard. Time to turn into a digger after all. He'd dig down until he understood everything.

Chapter 18

Mick turned his attention from Blenheim to Eddy, hoping to get the boy to eat more lunch, but he had apparently lost his appetite.

After the meal ended, Blenheim excused himself to go pen some important business letters.

Timmy led Mick and Eddy into the kitchen where Araminta sat at the table, writing notes.

She was a tall, voluptuous woman of about twenty-five, with skin the color of rich coffee with a touch of cream. Her hair, black with a hint of cinnamon, was piled on top of her head, a pile of tiny delicate curls. Mick saw her hair had simply been done up in a knot and her dress was faded calico, yet she had an air of impressive elegance. She was the kind of woman who created her own style.

"And may I ask what the devil you are doing in my kitchen?" she said without looking up. Her voice was lovely and husky and she had the diction of a duchess—must impress even Blenheim, Mick thought.

"We have come to offer our thanks for your usual superb efforts," said Timona.

Araminta glanced up then, and a wide smile lit her face and enormous chocolate brown eyes. "Timona, my beloved! You darling girl! How long have you been here?" She jumped up from the table and hugged Timona.

"Mr. Blenheim told me you were making meringues and the man helping you with lunch said you were writing. So I waited to bother you until after lunch," said Timona, her voice muffled by Araminta's embrace.

"Oh, pish," said Araminta. She let go of Timona and looked her up and down. "Food is food, but you are a feast for the eyes."

"You say that now that the meal is over," Timona pointed out. "How is your book progressing?"

"Very well indeed, Timona. You shall have to sample some of my newest concoctions. But where are your manners, girl? I don't recognize either of these gentlemen with you. Will you introduce me?"

Timona drew in her breath as if she was about to say something momentous. In a solemn tone, she announced, "Araminta, I would like you to meet Mick McCann."

"*The* Mick McCann?" Araminta said. She raised her eyebrows as she looked him up and down. "Well, well. What do you know!" She shook Mick's hand vigorously.

Mick wanted to ask her to explain, but by then Timona was pushing Eddy forward. "And this is Eddy."

Araminta dropped to her knees as if she had been felled by an axe. Eye to eye with the boy, she studied his face. Eddy shrank away from her intense scrutiny. Mick didn't blame him.

"You, my boy, need to be fed. I suspect you were too agitated to eat at lunch? Traveling has that effect upon me as well," she announced. She stood up again and put her long fingers on Eddy's shoulder.

"You two get going. Get some time to yourselves. Eddy—I shall call you Edward? Do you mind?" She did not wait for his answer before continuing. "Edward will stay here with me."

"But ma'am, I wanna stay with Mr. Mick and—"

"Oh, you have the most charming accent!" Araminta clapped her hands in delight. "Are you from New York?"

"Yes, ma'am, but you see I want to be with Mr. Mick and—"

"Mr. Mick will return, Edward. But I am lonely and in need of company here in the kitchen. Is that a cat I hear calling us from your basket? We shall give some food to the dear little thing. And some earth for it to do its business. We had best not let it go outside until it calms down. But first will you help me clean this out?"

She held up a pot with the small remnants of a chocolate mousse. Eddy just stared, so Araminta took his small skinny hand, gently pushed his finger across the chocolate, and then pushed his finger into his mouth.

"Oh," he breathed, and leaned towards the pot.

Mick and Timona crept away.

"In your letters did you mention me to Araminta?"

"Of course. She is my best friend."

"And she seems to know that we are to be married. How long ago did you write that news to her?"

"Ah. I told her that we might be married. Perhaps. I might have mentioned it. I think."

"I wonder how long ago you told her we would be married. Probably weeks before you bothered to tell me?"

An amused Mick took pity on her after she blushed and bit her lip. He changed the subject. "However did you meet up with Araminta? I can hear that she is English."

"Two years ago in England, I was at a grand dinner at a duchess's house. Or maybe she was a countess? When I managed to escape for a few minutes, I wandered into the kitchen where I found Araminta in charge of a kitchen full of servants. She was giving an undercook a furious scolding.

"At first I felt she was a tyrant, but then I understood the undercook had boxed a scullery maid's ears. Araminta has always been a champion of children."

Mick chuckled.

Timona said, "She agreed to travel with us because we became good friends and she wanted to see the world and taste its cuisine. But she is starting to chafe at the travel. She wants to settle down."

"Ah, Timmy, I am glad to meet her. She seems a fine woman. But why are we here? No. I know why you are here. Why am I here?"

"You are with me."

"Yes, I suppose that will do for now." He shook his head as if to clear it. "Timmy. Listen. You wanted to reassure the Blenheim. Now what do you want us to do?"

"Mick?"

"Hmmm?"

"Why are you upset?"

"I'm not. Yes, I am. I just don't . . . I don't like this place. And I don't care for Mr. Blenheim."

"He can be rather stern," said Timmy. "I mean about the proper thing to do. I can't understand why he is so unpleasant about you."

"Timmy, you are a blind woman. He wants you for himself."

"Nonsense." Timmy laughed. "He finds me an intriguing student. Before I met you I rather wondered if he and I would suit. But I never loved him, and I know I am far too wild for a man like him."

"You are far too warm for a cold fish like him," corrected Mick, his heart sinking at her words. So she once had an interest in Blenheim, of all people. Blenheim probably knew it, since Timmy was not a one to hide her feelings. No wonder the man hated Mick.

"Timmy. Let us go riding, or let's just walk away. I want to have a look round now Araminta has detached my little leech."

Timmy looked at him, her lips pressed tight, obviously worried. She slowly asked, "Do you resent Eddy? I hope not, for you are so good with him."

He was surprised at the question. "Nay, 'course not. I couldn't truly resent him. He needs to hold on to something. 'Tis good he has trust enough to cling. Most of the others push away, they don't believe grown people any more. I've hoped it means he is still young enough to be saved. I thank you for rescuing him from the streets."

"You saved him, you know, and probably before I met you. I just paid his fare. We will keep him, won't we?"

"I will. And his kitten too."

They found the stable. A groom dozing in the sun woke up and saddled two horses for them.

Morrison must have talked to the other laborers about Mick, for every last one of them stopped work to watch as Mick and Timmy trotted off.

Botty raced ahead, clearly delighted by the feel of dirt under his paws. Mick wanted to gallop away as fast as he could, too. But not with delight. The place felt almost evil to him.

"Oh I want to spring this horse and fly." Timmy echoed his thoughts.

"Best not. There might be holes in these fields that could bring the horses down. Once we reach a road, we'll let the animals go, eh? Poor old Botty will have to do some tracking."

Mick was not an expert horseman. He hadn't had time in his life to practice. He could stay on the beast and probably did not look an entire fool. But Timmy was in another league altogether. She looked as if she'd been born sitting atop a horse.

When they slowed enough to talk, and for Botty to

catch up, Timmy said, "The last time I was in America, I learned to ride bareback. Good way to learn balance, particularly going up and down hills."

"Sounds about right," he said absently.

He was still distracted by thoughts of Blenheim and the other men from Calverson Company.

"Timmy, I am afraid," he said suddenly.

She looked back at him; a breeze blew a wisp of her dark hair across her face. "Of what?"

"I am not sure. Timmy Calverson, I think you should marry me. Soon as we can."

She giggled. "You are afraid. And is that why you want to marry me, so I will protect you?"

"Absolutely. I have seen you with a knife, woman, don't forget. I know you are a *saighdíuir mná*—a soldier woman, my Timmy. It is what we call courageous women such as yourself."

She grinned at him. Then her brow furrowed. "Are we even yet?"

"Hey?"

"I think so. I suppose it would be a bad start if we weren't even. I have asked twice, and now so have you." She stopped to consider the matter. "That first time you asked does not count for you were martyring yourself. Yes. So the answer can be yes."

She rode on for a few minutes, then called back to him, "Did you want to marry in a church, Mick?"

He laughed out loud. "I think the answer to that must be no, Timmy."

"Good."

She pulled out the small, scarred mahogany box that held her beloved compass, and flipped it open to examine it.

After a minute or two, she carefully shoved the instrument back in her pocket, and steered the horse off the dirt road to follow a path through a field.

"Come on then, Mick! Before you change your mind."

"Where are you heading, my explorer?"

She pointed across a field of wheat bending and rippling in the delicious breeze. "Araminta says the town is to the east. In her letter she was terribly sniffy about the place. She claims it does not deserve the name 'town.' Araminta can be as starchy as Mr. Blenheim. But there is a courthouse."

"Are you saying we should go be married now, crazy woman?"

"That would be lovely, but I doubt we can. I think that there are no special licenses available in this country so I suppose we must wait several days."

"But what about your father? What if he does not approve?" Or what if Griffin Calverson had changed his mind.

Timona stopped her horse and twisted in the saddle to look back at him, puzzled. "Why on earth would he disapprove?"

He shrugged. "I have no idea why any father would object to his only daughter marrying an unemployed ignorant oaf of a fancy man that he's never so much as once met." But Timmy didn't hear a word for she had trotted ahead.

Botty swerved after Timona, making his excited huffs.

Mick turned his horse, gave it an encouraging little cluck and tap with his heels, and followed them along the edge of the field planted with tender new wheat. He'd followed Timona this far across the world. Why stop now?

Chapter 19

As they rode back from the town, they decided not to tell anyone. "Except Araminta," said Timmy. "I have to tell her or I shall burst. She is very good at keeping secrets. I think. I haven't had many secrets before and certainly never, never one this wonderful."

"You should tell your father, Timmy," Mick said.

"If I must. But now I'd far rather discuss more interesting topics such as where shall we live." she said.

"What do you require for your home?"

"Someone who will cook, a place for my photography, and you. And now Eddy, too. I travel light. Haven't I mentioned that?"

They agreed on a house near a river or the ocean.

"Wide windows overlooking the sea," said Timona, dreamily. "A house large enough for us, Eddy and lots of visitors like the Tuckers."

Her voice grew sober as she hesitantly asked, "You-you do not mind visitors? I mean who are not like us?"

"You mean Mlylans and what not?" Mick said.

"I have always promised my friends that when I had a place to live they should visit me."

"I would be glad to meet anyone you call friend," a solemn Mick replied, hoping this was true. True, she called charming people such as Araminta and Mrs. Kelly friend. On the other hand, she liked Blenheim.

And there were those other Calverson company types. Not to mention Solly Tothman.

They agreed on other details of their future. More animals. And babies.

"As long as you take care of them all, too, for you have had experience," said Timona. She turned almost all the way around in her saddle and, throwing wide her arms, she cried exuberantly, "Oh, let us start right now. I want it all, all of our life this very minute."

Mick gestured at the field of swaying tall grass they rode through. "Certainly, if you like, I can give you a baby. Would be better if we had a blanket," he said with a leer, just fooling about.

But damned if the woman didn't immediately pull her horse to a stop and slide off its back.

"What a good idea," she said, delighted.

Mick suddenly recalled it had been a matter of days since he had held Timona. And the ground, warmed by the sun, didn't look so bad at that.

They tied their horses to some saplings. Botty collapsed, panting, in the shade of one of the cropping horses.

With a whoop, Timmy flung herself onto the grass. She lay on her back, squinting into the sunny sky. He walked over to her and stood above her. Dress all rumpled, bonnet askew, she grinned and held open her arms to him. "See? A warm meadow makes a perfect bed."

Mick lowered himself slowly to the grass, then without warning he grabbed the yelping, giggling Timmy and rolled her on top of him.

"Nah, I'll be your bed, love."

The grass was cool beneath him, Timmy a warm armful on top. Paradise.

* * *

The heady joy of their ride evaporated as they entered the camp.

A short, white-haired man was bellowing over the rows of digging workers, waving his hands. The king, thought Mick sourly, but it transpired the old man was not giving anyone grief.

"Oh dear. He must be growing anxious, for he is again trying to describe the types of bones he expects they might find," Timmy said. "We'll go give the horses back and then I'll introduce you."

Mick walked back to the site with her, hot with embarrassment as all of the laborers looked up from the pits. Could the men see the grass-stains on their clothing from their lovemaking an hour earlier?

He did not want to yank away from Timmy, who clung to his hand. But he did want to wipe the knowing smirks off the faces of the men who watched them. Or at least fight to prove that he loved Timmy, loved her for her sweet self and not her grubby money.

Of course, he reflected gloomily, he'd have to beat the stuffing out of them and everyone else he ever encountered. Taylor, the rodent man and the other New York crew. Bloody Blenheim. Even Mick's old mate, Jim. Oh. Hell.

Timmy managed to pull her father away from the digging at last. They strolled to a shady spot under some trees near the house.

"Papa, please pay attention, it's important," said Timmy calmly. "I'd like you to meet Michael McCann. You may call him Mick."

Sir Kenneth, a sunburnt, stout man with a moth-eaten mustache and a pop-eyed, goggling look to him, obligingly shook Mick's hand. He grunted a howdy-do. He even went so far as to peer, frowning, into Mick's face.

"Important, you say, my dear? Are you by any chance

an agent of Cope's? Don't tell me you're at Yale with Marsh. Have you seen his newest skeletal restoration—the brontosaurus?"

Timona interrupted. "No, he is not a scientist or dinosaur hunter. I meant to say he is important to me. Mick and I are getting married."

"Eh? What? What? No. No. No. What the devil am I supposed to do? Who will make my arrangements and so on. No, Timona."

He chewed vigorously at the end of his bedraggled mustache. Not moth-eaten after all. "I don't like the idea."

Mick bit back his incredulous laugh. The man did not care who she married, he just didn't want to take care of himself.

"Papa, making your arrangements is your secretary's job. That is why I hire gentlemen such as Mr. Blenheim."

"But I like you better. Much better."

She leaned over and kissed him on the cheek. "That's sweet of you, dear."

"Who's going to talk to the cook? She doesn't like Blenheim now. And she scares the devil out of me."

"You couldn't care less who cooks for you, Papa. You'd eat stones if they were put in front of you. I imagine that Araminta will move on, once I leave. She has said she wants to open a restaurant. It will be a simple matter to find a cook who gets along with Mr. Blenheim."

"But what about Griffin? You know how he is always bothering me with nonsense about money."

"I am sure I can figure out your budgets even after I am married. And you can sign your name, dear. That's all Griffin usually wants from you."

"But you are so good at packing my tools, Timona. No one does a better job sharpening them, too. And who will talk to the dashed locals? I like 'em well enough when the work day is through, but I can't stand 'em poking round into my digs. And when someone wants me to make a speech, you always write it up. You're the best writer, better than that droning Blenheim and . . ."

"Papa," she put a hand on his arm and rubbed it soothingly. "I promise we will find a solution for each of these problems. Solutions that will satisfy you. Why don't you draw up a list and I shall look it over with you."

For the first time the old man relaxed. "Good plan. Good plan. A list, eh? So what did you say this man's name is? Are you truly old enough to marry, my dear? God bless my soul, how the time flies. Does he know even the *first* thing about the terrible lizards?"

"This is Mick McCann," Timona repeated patiently. Mick wondered if the man had always been like this or if it was advancing age.

Sir Kenneth said, "McCann. McCann. McCann. Irish, eh? The bogs. You know some mighty interesting things have been found in those bogs. I met a man once in England who said he was doing research on a boat dragged up that was estimated to be more than a thousand years old. Post-dates my area of research, however . . ."

Mick glanced at Timmy who aimed a broad smile at him. That was it? The end of the man's objections to her marriage?

Five days. That was all they had to wait.

Chapter 20

Timona and Mick walked into the house, and Eddy ran out of the kitchen yelping with delight. He went straight to them and threw his skinny arms around Mick's waist for a hug. The boy had often clung to Mick, but had not often shown happy affection. Mick raised his eyebrows and looked over at Timona. They exchanged pleased smiles.

Mr. Blenheim strolled into the front hallway where they stood.

"Miss Calverson, may I speak to you a moment?" He waved an elegant hand toward the parlor.

She sat down on the new horsehair couch, and wondered why anyone would want to own a piece of fashionable furniture if it forced you to keep your feet planted on the ground for fear of sliding off.

"Yes?" she said, hoping against hope that Mr. Blenheim was not going to start complaining again. Had he always been so particular?

Mr. Blenheim drew up a chair, and sat down near her.

Mick stood in the doorway, one arm around Eddy, who still leaned against him. For a few moments she watched them, the tall mountain of a man supporting the skinny urchin. The amazing joy swept through her again. Her family. They would be her family. Forever.

She felt like leaping up and dancing with them around the room. Perhaps she would, once Mr. Blenheim was finished speaking with her. A jig was a jolly sort of dance. Maybe Mick could teach her. The dances Mr. Blenheim had taught her were pleasant but too staid and stately for her heart just now.

Mr. Blenheim smiled at Timona. He did have a very attractive smile, though Timona had long ago noticed the words that usually followed that sedate look were usually not as agreeable. He would often begin with phrases such as "Miss Calverson, I fear you do not understand," or "Miss Calverson, I am hesitant to mention this, but . . ."

Yes, she was right. In a low, serious tone, he said, "Miss Calverson, I do not know how to word this, but I think it is bad for the morale of the men if you show preferential treatment for one of their kind."

Timona had to think for a moment about what Mr. Blenheim meant. But she had come to understand Mr. Blenheim more clearly in the last few hours, now that she saw how he treated Mick.

Araminta had long ago declared Mr. Blenheim was frightful, but the cook was a critical person too. As critical as Mr. Blenheim, Timona had pointed out at the time.

But no, Araminta was correct. Mr. Blenheim was not critical and perceptive like Araminta. He was merely a dreadful snob.

Timona had learned how to squelch people during her years as a celebrated female. She disliked doing such a thing to a person she liked. Or had thought she liked.

She drew herself up. "Mr. Blenheim, I assume you are referring to the fact that Mr. McCann is Irish. Am I correct?"

Blenheim blinked, obviously taken aback. Timona had not shown him cold behavior before.

"Well, ah, Miss Calverson, you must understand that society's . . . and, er, it is more that the men might think . . ." He glanced over at Mick as if the sight of Mick offended him deeply.

"Mr. Blenheim. My friends are not your concern. I believe we have discussed this matter before, sir?" He'd been quite upset when she made it clear that Araminta was her best friend.

"Timmy. The man has a point." Mick's voice was thoughtful.

Timona wanted to bellow at Mick. What was he doing? How could he believe that he belonged anywhere but with her?

Mick whispered to Eddy, who let go of him. Mick walked into the room. He crouched next to Timona, took one of her hands and looked up into her face.

"Seems best to me if I take up residence with the laborers, Timmy," he said softly. "At least for the time being."

She stared into his china blue eyes, so pale in the light they looked translucent around the dark middle. His lovely, slightly crooked nose, sunburnt face—she wanted to reach over and pull him to her. She longed to kiss him and feel his arms around her. She moved her hand in his and his grip tightened.

"Soon enough," he whispered, almost as if he could read her mind.

"You will eat with us?" she whispered back.

Mick glanced over at Blenheim. He straightened up, and spoke aloud. "I think it best I eat with the men, most times. If Miss Araminta does not mind, I'll join her in the kitchen now and again for lunch or dinner."

"That's fine then," said Timona at last. "I frequently eat with Araminta."

Blenheim coughed. "Miss Calverson. I do think that you have been showing such an improvement in our more elegant dining experiments. It would be a terrible pity if you were to allow your sentiment to take precedent over your self-improvement."

Not much call for a farmer's wife, or perhaps a veterinarian's wife, or a photographer's husband, for that matter, to know which fork to use with the oysters, thought Timona. But she thought Mick was right to be cautious. She would not let Mr. Blenheim know that fact yet.

"When my father skips meals, as he so often does, I am sure you are welcome to join us in the kitchen, Mr. Blenheim. We can all practice elegant dining," said Timona. She knew his terror of Araminta would keep him out. Now that she thought about the matter, though, she suspected he was simply a man who judged people by their race.

Mr. Blenheim sighed heavily, but did not respond otherwise. He stood up and pulled out one of his odious cigars. Since Araminta hated smoke in the house, he would have to take the thing outside.

"I am glad we could sort this out amicably," he said to Timona.

"Indeed," she said coldly, and gave him a curt nod. He blinked at her again, registering astonishment. Good, she thought and wondered why she ever thought him remotely attractive. Though to be fair—and Timona tried always to be fair—he was a wonderful dancer. And he read aloud beautifully. Though not as beautifully as Mick.

Blenheim chose to take his meal in the dining room that evening, so the kitchen was a relaxed place during dinner.

Araminta fed them an exotic dish she called goulash, and for the first time since they arrived back in the camp, Timona felt carefree. Araminta, Mick, Eddy, and Timona ate and chattered together.

Araminta liked Mick—she was bound to. And Timona's friend adored small Eddy, who blossomed astonishingly after spending one whole day in a real house with kind adults.

"Shall Eddy stay with me here tonight?" asked Timona, hopefully.

Mick took a bite of goulash. As he chewed, he listened to Eddy talk to Araminta about his New York friends, mostly fellow paperboys. Eddy did not sound at all homesick, thank goodness.

"He asked if he might stay with me in the barracks with the men. If you don't mind I think I will keep him there. He has shown some fear of men in the past, and if he actually asked to stay, perhaps 'tis a good sign."

After dinner, Timona showed Eddy some of the drawings her father had done of dinosaurs. Sir Kenneth was a skilled draftsman, and had put together a fine portfolio. Sir Kenneth wandered over, and insisted on showing them and explaining all aspects of every picture. Soon Eddy was yawning, as was everyone else.

By the time they'd gone through the drawings, Mick was the only one who still showed interest. "I have to put the boy to bed, but I wish I could see the photographs Miss Timona has taken of your work, sir."

"Another day, another day, Mr., er, McClennan," promised the happy Sir Kenneth. He obviously loved an appreciative audience.

Eddy wandered off, allowing Mick and Timona a few minutes to talk.

Timona walked a few steps from the house to look up

at the enormous display of stars. "I missed that sight in New York."

"As I recall, you liked the sight of buildings against the sky. I suppose it's a gift you have. You seem content wherever you land."

In the dark twilight, he could see her gleam of a smile. "Do you really want to marry me, Michael McCann?"

"With all my heart. You are the light of my life, Timona Calverson. You bring me joy such as I had never had even imagined before you tumbled into my life."

"I don't know if I can wait five entire days. I will miss you too much."

He gave a low whistle and said, "And you have called me insatiable."

"Oh, you know very what I mean, you rascal." she said. "I can't even hold you or kiss you first thing before I am even awake. I detest empty beds."

"I know. It has been too long since we shared a bed, Timmy." They were at the back door. He pulled her into his arms and gave her a long, slow kiss. "Here you go, then. Good night."

She placed her hands on the sides of his face and pulled him down to her for another kiss.

"And good morning for before you're entirely awake," he whispered. After another soft, languorous kiss, he pushed her from him. "You'd best go inside before I have you right out here at the kitchen door."

"Yes, as I recall you are good at doors. Though I usually prefer beds," said Timona thoughtfully. "I suppose that means I am an old-fashioned girl."

"Timmy, I do not think anyone on earth would describe you so," he said.

"Ah, as if I would care how anyone described me," her voice quavered with laughter and something else.

"Good night, wild woman." With regret he watched

her go back inside. It was best for he knew that the diggers were his best chance at finding help. Though he was not looking forward to what he suspected would be a chilly welcome.

The group of men who lived at the dig were a mixed lot. Morrison, a fine source of information, had given Mick the run down. A few men came from cities such as Dublin. There were some laborers, even a man who'd been a cop, like Mick. But mostly they were drifters and worse, including a couple of men who once had been part of the Whyos, one of the most violent mobs of Hell's Kitchen.

Mick wondered if Blenheim or whoever did the hiring knew they had at least two former convicts on the job site. Morrison reported that rumor had it one of the men, named McNally, might be on the run, wanted by the police.

A couple of Germans also lived in the building. The rest of the workers, Danes mostly, lived in the area and went home at night—though they tended to stay for supper, and show up early for breakfast. Araminta's cooking was one of the best things about the job.

Morrison warned Mick that word had gone around that McCann, Miss Calverson's "companion," was going to sleep in the bunkhouse and that several of the diggers were ready and waiting to take on the man they had decided was a rich girlie's plaything.

As soon as he walked into the barracks, the men fell silent, then began to speak in a loud, drawling voices, glancing in his direction.

Mick knew that he was going to face a tussle.

He could go one of two ways: Plow right in and get it over with, or dance about, using his damnable influence with the Calversons to get the trouble makers fired and the rest silenced.

It was an easy choice, as far as Mick was concerned. He'd grown accustomed to the violence of New York, and was not easily intimidated by thugs. To settle the matter, Mick was happy to be prodded into a fight. He felt nothing but relief to get the damn subject on the table, so to speak. Best to go with one of the larger men of the group, just to be more impressive and to avoid looking like a bully.

He stood up from his cot and walked over to the bulky fool who had just called him a "fancy man."

Mick smiled into the man's face. "C'mon. Let's go outside with it then, shall we? I'll be glad to show you how a fancy man fights."

An interested group formed a circle to watch the evening's entertainment.

Mick waited until he saw most of the laborers were there. Then he pulled off his shirt, the signal to begin the fight.

Despite his size, Mick could move fast, which meant he often managed to fool opponents—like this idiot of a man. Mick missed his nightstick, which would have settled matters faster, but he quickly enough had the burly laborer stretched out on his back. The man lay groaning on the ground while Mick only had a ringing ear and a bloody lip to show from the brief fight.

Mick knew that, for now, he'd be as close to acceptable as possible. And the men would leave his pack and his things—including Eddy and Botty—alone.

The one drawback was young Eddy lost some of his new confidence at the sight of the dustup. Mick had to pull the boy's small cot close to his own so Eddy could put a hand on Mick's arm if he needed to. He managed to convince Botty to climb onto the bottom of Eddy's bed, to provide the boy with another source of comfort.

As Eddy slept, Mick lay on his bunk and spoke in a low voice to the man on the other side of him.

Mick was delighted to find that the large man, Frank Travis, was the ex-constable from Ireland.

"Tell me, Travis, have you seen anything odd since you been here?"

"Nothing," the man reported. "Other than old man Calverson, of course. Do you have something in mind you're worried about?"

"Maybe. Probably I just don't like this place," said Mick.

"Give it a chance," urged Travis. "I love it here. It's a good, peaceful area, this Minnesota. Oh, I long for a quiet life again."

They talked about crime, mobs, homesickness, and beer. At last Mick fell asleep, making plans. If his suspicions were correct he could use some help.

Early in the morning, Blenheim opened the door to the bunkhouse and called out.

"Is there a McNally in this group?"

Interesting that he would pick the name of the possible criminal. Mick sat up and looked around.

No one else stirred.

"I will see McNally in the main house. After breakfast. Without fail."

Blenheim slammed the door in disgust.

Mick spoke then. "If there is a McNally here, might I have a word with him before he goes to see that thundering pain in the ass Blenheim?"

Breakfast was served in another converted barn. Everyone sat at long wooden benches to eat.

Mick went to breakfast with the laborers, and sent a

reluctant Eddy to the main house kitchen, with his apologies for Araminta and Timmy.

Over the bowls of thick porridge, he turned to his new friend, Travis. "Do you think, for some spare cash, you could lend me a hand? It might require a bit of risk, though."

Chapter 21

That morning, while Timona went over lists with her father, Mick went into town with Araminta, ostensibly to help her haul back supplies. When they finished, he asked her to stop at the station so he could send a telegraph.

The message cost almost two dollars, and Mick, who hadn't expected it to be so expensive, had to borrow 25 cents from Araminta.

Araminta uncrumpled one of copies Mick had started, then discarded.

"'Look into job offer to me,'" she read aloud and looked up. "Are you and Timona leaving us?"

"Nah. See? It's to Griffin Calverson."

Her whole face wrinkled, as if she smelled something gone bad. "That man. I have absolutely no patience with him. I do hope you are not expecting him to find you a job?"

"Of course not." Mick couldn't help sounding indignant.

She nodded approvingly. "I knew I was right to like you, McCann."

They walked out of the train station. Mick helped Araminta into the wagon, then vaulted into the seat next to her.

Before he picked up the reins, Mick hesitated and

rubbed his nose. "Er, Miss Araminta. I wanted to ask you. You know Timona well. D'ye think she is doing the right thing? Marrying me I mean? Will I make her happy?"

"That's a good question."

"Ah, damn. You have your doubts, then?"

"Not at all, McCann. The answer is of course it is the right thing for her to do. I merely meant that it is a good question because you are not worrying about your happiness, you are worrying about hers. Keep that up, and you'll do fine."

Araminta patted his arm. "You can't do any worse than that blasted father and brother of hers. Timona needs a home, and she tells me you are it."

He snorted. "There's the pity of it. I can't provide her with much of a home."

"She doesn't think of home like most people, Mc-Cann. She once told me she has traveled so much, home has come to mean the people she is with, not the place she lays her head."

Mick sighed. "She is a rare wonder of woman, isn't she. I do not understand how I managed the luck to—"

"Mick, I have grown tired of our bout of sentiment. I will force you to walk home if you start waxing poetical about Timona. She is my dearest friend, but I warn you, a person can bear only so much."

He laughed. "Shall I grow lyrical about my love's friend and her cookery?"

"Certainly I can listen to that kind of lyricism all day."

The next two days passed far more pleasantly than Mick expected. Mr. Kendall, her usual assistant, was still on holiday, so he and Eddy helped Timona carry and set up her bulky equipment and tripod when she decided to take photos of a cliff, and when she took pictures for her father of the work site. She gave them lessons on photography, and allowed a delighted Eddy to look through the camera at the upside down images.

Sir Kenneth spent much of his time on his hands and knees, crawling around the two pits. While he crawled, the men ceased their work and picked up decks of cards.

"An easy job," Morrison told Mick. "I would not mind if the old gent stayed in the area for years. Maybe I'll follow along with his band for the next dig."

Morrison and Eddy had become unlikely buddies. Mick could only hope that Eddy wouldn't pick up Morrison's way with slurs. At least Morrison insulted everyone equally. Poles, Yanks, Swedes, Africans, English—name a nationality or race and Morrison knew and used the nastiest possible name and reputation for it. Other than that, he seemed to be a amiable soul.

While Sir Kenneth roamed the site and Timona waited to take pictures for him, Mick squatted on his haunches to show Timona and Eddy how to play the penny whistle he'd bought in town.

They were interrupted when Blenheim came out to the dig to summon Timona.

"I have the receipts you asked me about, Miss Timona."

She frowned and then nodded. "Oh, yes, last month. The strange entries in the household books."

Timona turned towards Mick. "Perhaps you might be interested in seeing them," she said. "After—"

Mick gave her a warning frown. "No, I thank you, Timona. I will take a walk with Eddy."

Mick had discovered a river, and took Eddy to a shallow sandy edge to teach the boy to swim. Botty stood on the mossy bank and wheezed at them. Eddy whooped and screamed with delight. Next, Mick coaxed him to use some soap. And when they rested, Mick whipped out a pair of scissors from the satchel he carried and gave Eddy a hair cut.

"Now when we get back you'll see, lad, how beautifully you clean up. Miss Timona will barely recognize you."

Eddy squinted thoughtfully at the handfuls of curling dark hair lying on the grass. "Suppose I might be a gentleman when I grow up, Mr. Mick?"

"If that's what you want, sure enough," Mick said solemnly.

"Then I could marry Miss Timona."

"Ah, there you will be out of luck, I'm afraid."

Eddy took the news philosophically. "Then I can marry Miss Araminta. Yeah, that would be good. She cooks better anyway."

The next afternoon, Mick and Eddy again returned to the slow moving, shaded river. Mick cut branches and with some string and hooks from his pocket they made fishing lines. Eddy watched as Mick dig in the cool, soft earth on the river bank for worms to use for bait.

The sheer joy of doing nothing much, and being outside as he did it, filled Mick with surprising and unfamiliar joy. Even as a young boy he had spent his daylight hours toiling at work. Too bad Blenheim and Sir Kenneth seemed determined to take Timona away from the lazy fun. He would love to see her naked and splashing in the river. She likely swam like a fish.

Mick and Eddy lay on their backs with their bare feet dangling in the cold water. A shadow passed over the sun that warmed Mick's face.

He opened his eyes and looked up into the serious faces of three of the laborers.

"McCann," one of them said. "There's a slight problem."

Mick stretched, and slowly got to his feet. Eddy had fallen asleep, so Mick and the other men ambled a few feet away to keep from bothering him.

"Fact is," said another one. "We've been hired to beat the crap out of you."

"Oh?" Mick wasn't terribly surprised.

The three men nodded.

"Blenheim?"

They nodded again. Surprising only that the man was stupid enough to be so direct.

"Bloody fool," one of them offered.

Everyone nodded this time.

"Well," said Mick. "Let me take Eddy back to the house first. He doesn't care for brawling. After that, I'll see what I can do to accommodate you lads."

Mick woke Eddy. They collected their shoes and fishing poles. Then Mick and the men walked Eddy to the house. Mick went into the kitchen with Eddy. The scent of warm gingerbread filled the air. The boy's eyes opened wide at the wondrous spicy scent.

"What is that smell?" he whispered.

"Food fit for the gods, if I know Miss Araminta. Save me a piece, please," Mick said to Araminta. "I'll be back soon."

He went out to join the three men who waited by the kitchen door.

"Come on then." Mick led them to a spot out of sight of the house. He turned to face them, his hands clasped tight behind his back. "I think it best if you do some obvious damage to my face. You'll get your pay and I'll be able to walk. Oh. I'd appreciate it if we leave the nose alone."

One of the men laughed nervously. "Ah, well, after I

watched that dustup the other night, I'm glad to hear you're not going to fight."

The largest of the group took a couple of well-aimed punches. They all agreed it did the trick. Mick's face looked very decorative.

Mick pulled out a handkerchief and held it to his bleeding mouth.

"If only I could be sure that this is the worst Blenheim'll want to do," he mumbled indistinctly. "But I fear there's even worse to come."

The three men stood around uneasily watching as Mick gingerly probed the inside of his mouth with a finger.

"Any loose teeth?" the puncher asked.

"Nah. Just a hell of a cut. It'll be a day or two before I'll eat."

"Sorry, McCann," the man said. "There's anything we can do to make it up to you?"

"Don't you worry, there will be. And you can be sure I'll ask it of you. Don't fret yourself a moment about this." He waved at his face and the eye that was fast swelling shut. "But please don't let me forget that when this nonsense with Blenheim is over, I owe you all pints."

He started to smile at the man who'd hit him, but the pain in his mouth turned the expression into a grimace. "And maybe we can see how you and I do in a fair tussle, hey, lad?"

Chapter 22

Mick showed up at dinner with a black eye and bloodied swollen lip but refused to discuss the matter.

"A disagreement," was all he said, when Timona pressed him.

Eddy was not feeling well either; Araminta said that she suspected he had probably eaten too many pieces of gingerbread that afternoon.

"What with my injuries and the lad's belly, I think we'll call it an early day." Mick excused himself right after dinner, and took himself and the boy over to the bunkhouse.

Timona wandered about the farmhouse for a few minutes after they left, feeling the absence of Mick and Eddy. She worried about Mick's battered face. And she missed him. The air was thinner when Mick's large, warmhearted presence left the house.

Then she remembered a stack of photographs her friend had just sent from Colorado, along with an article deriding a new photo plate made of paper.

She took her riches into the bedroom. She had got out a magnifying glass, and was just examining the details of a landscape before a thunderstorm, when there was a knock at the door.

Mr. Blenheim stood in the doorway, very properly

staring at the wall and not looking at her sprawled across the bed.

"May I speak to you in the library?" he asked in a respectful tone.

"Where's Papa?" asked Timona. The slightly shabby room Blenheim called the library was her father's favorite room in the house.

"I believe he is visiting the digs." Mr. Blenheim waited and Timona realized he wanted her to follow him down the stairs immediately. She sighed and rose from her bed.

She hoped that he did not want to discuss the receipts again. He had apparently misplaced quite a few and she did not wish to hear another long-winded explanation about the complexities of debits and credits and interest. Mr. Blenheim tended to use long words for simple concepts that she had dealt with since Griffin had left her father's entourage. She feared Mr. Blenheim attempted to impress or bamboozle her. She did not particularly care either way. The sums in question were not worth squabbling over.

Mr. Blenheim offered Timona a glass of wine. She sat back on the library's sofa, and waited for him to begin.

He didn't speak. Instead, he drank his glass of wine and watched her solemnly. Just as Timona was about to ask why he had summoned her, Eddy's friend, the gray-haired Mr. Morrison, knocked and entered the library, his shapeless hat in his hand.

Mr. Blenheim straightened up. He cleared his throat delicately. "When Mr. McCann showed signs of having been in an altercation this evening, I was worried there might be a problem with the work crew. I wanted to know what had happened to your, ah, guest.

"So I have been asking a few questions." He waved a hand at Mr. Morrison. "This worker here says that it is not the first time Mr. McCann has been assaulted."

Morrison nodded glumly then said, "I'm right surprised Mick, Mr. McCann, I mean, looks so bloodied, sir. Last time he was the one who did the knocking about. As I told Mr. Blenheim a couple a days ago, I saw that brush up. But I don't know nothing about this 'un."

"Tell Miss Calverson the cause of the earlier dispute." Blenheim ordered.

Morrison twisted his hat and drew his mouth up tight.

"Please go on," said Timona, filled with dread. She sipped some wine to steady herself, and recalled Mick's sore mouth of a few days earlier. He claimed he'd walked into a tree while exploring in the dark.

"It was yourself, ma'am. Rather what Mr. McCann is to you if you'll pardon me. Lies, I'm sure."

"And what names did the men call him?"

"Umm, I think 'tis not proper to repeat."

"Morrison. Miss Calverson should know the truth."

Timona wished Mr. Blenheim did not sound quite so pleased.

"Umm. They call him a fancy man."

"Is that the worst of it?"

"Ah. They called him, ah, whore."

Mr. Morrison stared at the rug by his feet.

Then he looked up for a brief second. "But the thing is, I thought for sure the lads liked him now, ma'am. He's not afraid of real work. And that night he knocked the man down, most o' us come to think he's a not a—"

"That is all. Thank you, Morrison."

Morrison nodded miserably. He shuffled from the room. In the silence, Timona could hear the slam of the front door as he left the house.

"Do you understand? Miss Calverson?"

"It is bad. Dreadful," she said faintly. She sipped the wine, and wondered why Mick had not told her.

But maybe he had. Didn't he say he loved her, but

was scared of all the rest? Perhaps this was what he meant. The problems that would plague him when he became part of her life. Why else wouldn't he tell her this evening about the black eye?

Her fault. It was entirely her fault he was called a kept man, but she could only pray the name-calling would cease when they were married. Two more days. Or was it one now? She was so upset, she couldn't think clearly.

"Mr. Blenheim. I thank you for looking into the problem. But I believe the situation will improve when I am married to Mi—"

"Pardon? What did you say?"

She blinked. Mr. Blenheim had shouted, very unlike his usual correct self.

"I will marry Mr. McCann. Soon."

He looked positively ill. He gulped down the rest of his wine. Then looked at her glass.

"Please excuse me. I will get both of us more wine," he said. The decanter was empty, so he had to go to the kitchen to refill it.

Mr. Blenheim must be very upset to be willing to venture into Araminta's territory. Perhaps there was some truth to what Mick said—that Mr. Blenheim wanted Timona for himself.

"I will fetch it," Timona volunteered, dully.

Araminta sat at the kitchen table, reading. She looked up and frowned at Timona.

"What ever is the matter?"

"It is just that . . . Mick. Oh, it is hard for him to be with me, Araminta. People despise him. I want nothing in the world but his happiness, but perhaps that can not include me."

"If that Blenheim louse has—" began Araminta.

Timona shook her head. "Not just him. It's not fair, and oh it is so complicated, isn't it?"

"No, it isn't," said Araminta crossly. "Are you coming down with something, Timona? You seem remarkably maudlin."

Timona heaved a sigh. She filled the decanter and trailed out of the kitchen.

Blenheim was waiting by the kitchen door. Cooperative and contrite, he escorted Timona back to her chair and took the decanter from her hands.

"I apologize for startling you when you spoke of your engagement," he said as he handed her the refilled glass. "The news is a complete surprise to me. And, if you will forgive me for speaking the plain truth, perhaps I exclaimed a few minutes ago because it so inappropriate a match."

She started to get up. This talk was not what she wanted to listen to just now.

"Please. I beg of you to sit down, Miss Calverson. I promise not to insult your future husband. But might I just share a few thoughts?"

She sank down again, still hot with sorrow and guilt. She drank half the glass in one gulp. Poor Mick. Beaten because he dared to care about her. She should have married him in New York. She drank some more wine.

Mr. Blenheim was talking. "A fellow like McCann is not bad, per se. But he has lived all of his life in a simple style. He is not used to riches and the complications of prosperity. Now I'm not saying he will succumb, but many men thrown into affluence, without the right upbringing, without discipline . . . they allow themselves to become lax creatures."

Timona felt thickheaded. She remembered something that nagged at her. "Mr. Blenheim, I am sure I heard you just promise that you would not insult Mr. McCann."

Blenheim looked surprised. "I am simply stating facts. He will lose what might be termed his natural dignity. His figure, already large—though, I admit, well-proportioned—will undoubtedly grow soft, even fat. It is a well-known problem with men who are not bred to the life of luxury."

Timona gave a tiny groan. Mr. Blenheim was off on his speech about rank and class, subjects dear to his heart. Very well. She supposed she could put up with it. She drank her wine and half listened.

Was he telling the truth about Mick? She did not think so. But then again she found it hard to imagine people would want to attack a person just because he loved the boss's daughter.

She was not sure she understood people as well as she had assumed. The thought made her profoundly sad for some reason. The wine contributed to her sorrow, no doubt. She tended to grow melancholy when she drank wine.

And this was very strong wine.

Mr. Blenheim poured more into her glass.

Oh, her heart ached profoundly, for if she didn't understand people, perhaps she didn't understand Mick.

He had never said the words aloud, but she was almost certain he loved her. Perhaps love wouldn't be enough to overcome the problems of her blasted money.

Well, she thought drowsily. They could give it away. The money. Buy houses and beds in New York for people. Better beds. That seemed like a fine solution. And beautiful quilts that would flap on the clotheslines, brightening that dark sky in the tenements.

And if that wasn't enough . . . She could slit the

throat of anyone who hurt her Mick. That would work, too.

Blenheim was still talking. She wondered why he sounded so very far away now.

"Miss Calverson?" he was saying, "Timona?"

She opened her mouth to tell him she was listening, and to please continue his lecture, but nothing came out. She was suddenly too tired to speak. She leaned her head on the arm of the chair. How had she managed to slide down that far? It didn't matter. She was glad for a place to put her head while she took a short rest. It would serve the purpose though the spot was not nearly as comfortable as Mick's broad chest.

Before she fell asleep, or maybe later when she woke for a moment, she groggily wondered why Mr. Blenheim told her, "Thank goodness you've arrived. You were absolutely right. And there is not a moment to lose."

Chapter 23

In the morning, Mick and Eddy ate breakfast with the crew. Eddy showed no ill effects from too much gingerbread. After Eddy put away three bowls of porridge and half a loaf of bread, they started towards the house. As they walked past the excavations, one of the youngest diggers scurried over with the mail he'd fetched.

He handed a letter to Mick, and peered over Mick's shoulder as he opened it. "I've never seen one afore. It's a night cable. The telegrapher left a message with the post office for me to fetch it, cause he knew we'd be going to town this morning. It's from the New York office of Calverson. Who d'you know there?"

"All sorts of pleasant people," said Mick absently as he read the note.

Mick was not going to offer more information so the digger wandered back to the work site. The night cable was from Griffin, who answered Mick's telegram. No, he hadn't gotten the job for Mick. But he thanked Mick for alerting him. He had looked into the situation. And it was interesting—

Mick stopped reading to pull open the door to the farmhouse.

Botty skittered ahead to the kitchen, where he would

pick a fight with Eddy's cat and beg for treats from Araminta.

Eddy trotted after Botty.

Mick was through the door when Blenheim came out of the library. Instead of pointedly ignoring Mick, as he usually did, Blenheim grabbed his upper arm.

Mick easily shook off the man's hand, then began to gently shove him out of the way.

"McCann. I have a message for you. From Miss Calverson."

Mick froze. He folded Griffin's cable and pushed it deep into his trouser pocket. "Aye?"

"She has been talking about going to Colorado."

"I don't recall such talk."

Blenheim ignored him. "Last night she made the decision. She is already on her way. She left early this morning, off to visit her friend there—that is to say, her new friend."

Blenheim flapped a piece of paper at Mick, who impatiently grabbed it from him. These Calverson underlings were always showing him papers.

The letter was an invitation from the photographer to Timona to come to his studio and see his work. Mr. Jackson had enjoyed seeing her in New York and was eager to continue their growing friendship.

Blenheim took back the paper and said in a faintly bored tone, "I am afraid she has dashed both of our hopes, Mr. McCann. She is off on yet another of her mad crushes on an inappropriate man."

He looked at Mick with thorough disdain and what might have been a touch of pity. "You were not the first, you understand. The girl is spoiled, has had too few restrictions and far too little direction in her life. I was attempting to give her the proper training when she strayed into your, er, life in New York. So you see . . ." He gave a discreet little cough.

"I am not sure I do see. Why doncher tell me straight out, Mr. Blenheim?"

"Miss Calverson is finished with you. She is a tender-hearted girl, and is reluctant to hurt you. We have had this problem before—had, er, discussed her 'friends' before. She believes these friends are none of my concern. Alas, they so often become my responsibility when she grows tired of them."

Mick felt chilled to his core, reminded again of his inferior position in the world. The other man's blasé arrogance was enough to bring it to full flower.

Add in his own familiar refrain: Timona Calverson, amusing herself with the natives. Using him, Mick, the "big brawny man," as a bored rich girl's diversion, a plaything.

The worst of every misgiving and fantasy he'd had about the woman he loved all rolled into the moment. Mick nearly passed out with the cold that clenched his heart.

But even as the thought grew plain enough to understand, he stopped himself. Better to despise Blenheim and his own imagination than doubt Timmy. Doubting her would bring an end to the existence of happiness.

Blenheim was still nattering at him, "She left word with her friend, Araminta, about another reason she is leaving you. Go ahead, talk to the cook."

Mick pushed past the man, and went straight to the kitchen.

Araminta was feeding wood into the kitchen stove. She straightened up at once when she saw Mick, as if she were expecting him.

"Araminta. What is this rot Blenheim is jabbering? Did Timona say anything to you about—about leaving me?"

She brushed her hands against her skirts. "I am not

certain what is going on, Mick. Timona was in here last night for a couple of minutes, talking nonsense of how marriage to her wasn't fair to you.

"And then Blenheim showed up early this morning, even though he knows he is to stay out my kitchen. He proceeded to question me about what Timona said when she came into the kitchen last night. I haven't seen Timona since, by the way. She missed breakfast. She does sometimes, but I am worried. After I finish up this batch of biscuits, I am going upstairs to find out what is going on."

"Bloody Blenheim," mumbled Mick. "Please keep an eye on our Eddy will you and keep him here for the time being? Blenheim seems to have forgotten the lad exists, thank the Lord."

She nodded. "So do you suppose Blenheim is out to cause a serious problem?"

"The devil of it is, I don't know a thing for sure. I dare not beat it out of the idiot either, for perhaps he is not alone in this. Keep your ears and eyes open, love. I think she's honestly not here. But please, check to see if her bag and other possessions are gone. Her compass is in that battered box. She wouldn't willingly leave for more than a day without that. I'll get back as soon as I can."

He paused at the door, wondering if he should tell Araminta of his suspicions, but he decided there was no point making her any more worried than she already was.

After all, Mick had taken a few steps of his own. Timona would be safe. He hoped.

He couldn't change his mind and decide to go back to the kitchen to tell Araminta his fears. He wasn't given the time.

* * *

Blenheim waited for him in the dining room, directly in Mick's path as he left the kitchen. The two men stood for a moment in silence, eyeing each other.

Blenheim spoke first. "As Sir Kenneth's assistant, it is my job to keep order on the work site. It has come to my attention that you have been creating dissension among our workers. You have been involved in brawls."

"Have I? How did I manage this, do you suppose?" At least Mick now understood the point of yesterday's exercise.

Blenheim ignored him and pulled an impressive gold watch from his waistcoat pocket. "Mr. McCann, the situation has reached the point that I must tell you to vacate the premises. There is a train heading south towards Chicago in about an hour. In order to smooth your way for you, I have ordered my assistant to go to the bunkhouse and pack up your things for you. Mr. McNally?" He called out.

Mick already knew Blenheim was going to take full advantage of the criminal, McNally, but what did Blenheim want with the man?

A thoroughly ugly behemoth lumbered into the room. He carried Mick's pack. He tossed it hard at Mick, who caught it with a grunt.

Blenheim nodded with satisfaction. "Let us be off then. We don't want you to miss your train, do we?"

The huge assistant gave Mick a shove towards the door. "Go on then. No point in kicking up a stir, McCann. I been told to take care of you if you do," he said. He had a slightly servile, apologetic manner, peculiar in such a large creature.

"That's all you been told, McNally?" said Mick, sneering.

"Aye." He lapsed into Gaelic. "The Englishman has offered me a huge sum of money. Twenty thousand dollars, but for what I don't yet know—"

"I don't want to hear any of that Irish garbage spewing from your mouth, McNally or you'll find yourself out of work. We are going now. Please escort Mr. McCann and this rat of a dog to the carriage."

The three of them marched into the yard, Botty staying close to Mick's heels. When Mick hesitated for a moment, Blenheim nodded, and the assistant again gave Mick a push.

"Right then, McCann, don't make me need to get rough with you," he said. "I'll be up with the driver, sir, iffen you need me," he added to Blenheim.

Mick had the growling Botty under his arm, and was pleased to see the animal had enough taste to bare its teeth at Blenheim.

The Englishman grew pale.

"Put the dog on the floor, or I will have McNally shoot it," said Blenheim, shrinking away from Botty.

Hell. Not a good sign that the usually suave man acted so nervous.

"Do that, and I'll rip your guts out," said Mick pleasantly.

Blenheim glared at Mick, then must have remembered he was a gentleman. He brushed some imaginary dirt off his sleeve instead, likely to demonstrate how unaffected he felt.

After that, neither of them spoke during the drive. Blenheim stared out the window absently humming to himself and tapping a well manicured finger on the polished window frame.

At the station, Mick reluctantly jumped down. He had not thought he needed to take action yet and, for the first time, he was at a loss of what he should do next.

Blenheim didn't get out of the carriage, but he leaned out the open window. "I almost feel sorry for you, McCann. Dragged across the country by a woman you thought actually cared for you, then abandoned like a child's plaything. I daresay you'd have done better to stay in New York. Here."

He pulled out a roll of bills and tossed them into Mick's open hand. "Enough to get you to New York and then back to Ireland. Sir Kenneth is known to be very generous to his daughter's cast-off, ah, 'friends.'"

Mick looked down at the money. If he hadn't needed cash he would have thrown the dollars back in Blenheim's bloody smirking face.

Blenheim's assistant called out in his slightly apologetic manner, "You'll be fine, McCann."

"Shut up, McNally." Blenheim thumped the roof of the carriage. "Drive on," he shouted.

The driver slowly backed and turned the vehicle in the rutted small yard. Before he flicked his whip at the horses, he twisted back to look at Mick. He touched his cap at Mick who didn't have the heart to lift his hand in acknowledgment.

Mick watched the carriage roll away, a sick and heavy lump of fear in his chest.

Chapter 24

Mick watched Blenheim's carriage until it was out of sight, but he couldn't make out its direction. Probably back to the Calverson site.

He turned and walked into the squat wooden train station, Botty so close to his heels he almost tripped over the dog.

"D'ye mind sending another of them messages, lad?" He asked the station master, who was also the telegraph operator.

"Sure," the operator—a young, excitable type—sat up. He reached under the grill for the paper Mick shoved through.

Mick eyed him for a moment. "You don't go blabbing round town about these matters, do you?"

"Of course not," the man said, a shade too indignantly.

Mick didn't have a choice. He'd leave out the details and concentrate on the most important part.

"Come as soon as possible. Stop. Mick. Stop."

The station master read it aloud then looked up eagerly. "To Calverson? And the same location as the last one? I have it right here. In New York City?"

"Aye," said Mick. "And just in case, I have the address for the same man in Chicago. Send one to each place. Do ye have a horse I could borrow or hire?"

"You'll have to go into town for that," said the man. "I'd lend you my horse since it sounds awful important, but she's thrown a shoe."

It was only two miles into town. And then ten miles from town out to the Calverson place. He hoped he would be in time. Or that his suspicions were wrong.

If only he had been able to talk with Travis . . . but it didn't do to make Blenheim any more alert, or more of a nuisance than he already was.

Mick was in a hurry to get going, but had one last question. "Any Calverson Company men get off the train lately?"

The station master pursed his lips. "Not any who said as much."

"Spotted any men who are dressed better than the sort you usually see? What ye might call a city man, a banker type."

"Oh sure, one yesterday," said the station master. "A grim-looking fellow at that."

Mick almost smiled. "Brown hair, green eyes, and mustache on him?"

"No, sideburns though. A big guy. Dark hair, I believe."

Oh saints, thought Mick. He sprinted all the way to town.

Mick was right to worry. By the time he made it to town, hired a horse from the livery stable, convinced Botty to let him haul him on the saddle, and galloped back to the site, Blenheim had vanished.

Sir Kenneth scribbled at his desk and shrugged when Mick asked about the secretary.

"Er, not here," was all Sir Kenneth could said about him.

Araminta was not in her kitchen, so Mick went out to

the work site. Some of the laborers leisurely dug about. A few played cards or sat on the grassy banks of the pits, smoking.

Under the sandy loam they had hit solid rock. A digger who had done some mining in another part of Minnesota thought this stuff might be iron ore.

One of the men spoke up. "Yesterday, Miss Calverson begged us to look busy a longer while yet. She said she wanted to stay in Minnesota a few days more at least."

Timona. Today they could have been married. Mick's insides curdled as he realized he had never so much as told Timona he loved her. He'd been so careful not to trap the girl into an unequal marriage for so long he'd forgotten . . . No. He did not have time to fret over such matters.

Eddy and his cat were watching Morrison.

"Araminta sent me out here," Eddy said. In a singsong voice, he recited what she'd told him. "She got a message and had some kind of important business she had to take care of and she might be a while. She asked me to please stay out of Mr. Blenheim's way, and I haven't even seen him."

Morrison sat on a rock, carving a dog for Eddy from a block of wood. He held up the carving and squinted at it. He said, "No point in pretending to work when Calverson isn't around. Old duffer said he was going to be in his office for the afternoon and we weren't to disturb him."

A man stretched out on the ground on his back using a rock as a pillow piped up, "The way I heard it, the father has some land in California. Miss Calverson said we should put on a show for him because the father will board a train for California the moment he hears we won't find none of his old bones."

"Have any of you seen Travis?" Mick called out to the whole group.

Someone called back, "I believe he left about a coupla hours ago, maybe."

Hell. Mick only hoped he could find out where Blenheim and the mysterious city slicker he was almost certain was Taylor had gone. And now, come to think of it, he hoped he didn't have to worry about Araminta, too.

He should have said something to her.

Mick had to push down the panic and anger. He forced himself to concentrate.

He'd search the area. The carriage they used about the place was a small affair, no room for luggage. It was gone.

A train or a good long-distance, for-hire carriage would attract too much attention in such a small town, so he had to hope they had not gone far. The carriage would not be suitable for a journey longer than, say, twenty miles.

They would probably hire a reasonably luxurious house. Mick already figured out Blenheim was not a lad for roughing it if he didn't have to, and he obviously had a free hand with Calverson money.

The location would have to be distant enough from other houses.

A Dhia, it could be miles away.

Enough concentrating, time for action. He raced over to the group of Danes who knew the area best.

He didn't know exactly what the Calverson men planned to do, but he suspected time was running out.

After talking to the locals for a few minutes, Mick placed his fingers in his mouth to produce a shrill whistle. The men looked up and Mick began shouting out an explanation, hoping he sounded convincing.

He folded his arms across his chest and put on his best authoritative cop manner. As he shouted, he kept an eye on the house, and prayed Sir Kenneth didn't hear him. He wished he could talk in Gaelic, but he needed the Danes and Germans too.

One man would stay behind to tend to Sir Kenneth and Eddy. The rest would help with the search.

Mick squatted down. With a stick, he drew a primitive map in the dirt. The men gathered around and listened as he gave instructions.

Even the interruption caused by Solly Tothman's arrival did not stop Mick's planning.

Within a half an hour he had the group organized and dispersed.

Then he turned to Solly, who was complaining that he didn't want to wander all over the countryside.

"I'll take a tour! Not now though! After I visit Araminta, and see what's cooking."

"Come on then, Tothman. Araminta is not here just now. You find Timona, and you've got yourself a headline."

Solly perked up. "What? Do you mean she's gone and done it again?"

"Perhaps," said Mick grimly. "If it's true, well, this will be the very last time any one kidnaps my Timmy."

Chapter 25

Timona was groggy and her head felt as if it weighed far too much. Had she been ill? Some grief filled her, she knew that for a certainty.

She had a vague memory of waking up once before and someone feeding her a horrible concoction. She had fallen back to sleep almost at once.

She moaned. And felt vile.

"Good, good, you shall be fine!" said a hearty voice nearby. "Miss Calverson. Timona. Can you hear me?"

"Mr. Blenheim?"

"Yes, and I am delighted to see you are better now. Er, you are better, aren't you?"

"I don't think so. I believe I am going to be sick."

"Oh good lord," he said. She didn't open her eyes. Someone was prodding at her arm. No, it was a basin prodding at her. She tried to reach for it, but couldn't. Her hands were tied to something.

"I shall return when you feel more the thing, shall I?" Mr. Blenheim sounded nervous. She opened her eyes and saw he was backing away from the bed on which she lay.

Without obvious twisting, Timona yanked at the cords that bit into her wrists. She carefully breathed in and out on counts of three. She held back the nausea and was able to speak. "Why are my hands hampered, Mr. Blenheim?"

"We thought it best, Timona. Please, call me Horace."

She continued counting. "Why, Mr. Blenheim?"

"I think in light of the fact that we have known each other for several years, and I hope you will regar—"

"Why am I tied up?"

He cleared his throat "We know that you are most expert at, ah, shall we say, escaping. And it is best if you do not leave just yet. We have a proposition to lay before you."

Suddenly Mr. Blenheim was kneeling before the bed, his face was quite close to hers. The scent of his bay rum cologne and cigars was almost enough to push her over the edge. She had to count as she breathed again.

"Miss Calverson. Timona. From the first time I took your hands to show you the steps of the quadrille I have known that we are a perfect fit. You are graceful, beautiful, desirable—all that any man could ever want."

Her eyes widened. "What on earth are you talking about?"

"Will you marry me, Timona? I have put off asking too long and I—"

"Mr. Blenheim! The answer is no."

"You must hear me out, Timona."

"Mr. Blenheim. You know that I am engaged to Michael McCann . . ." She wondered if that was still true. Something happened last night. Or whenever it was.

His sharp laugh cut her short. "Mr. McCann will soon be on his way back to his native land."

He pulled out a note and held it above her head. She squinted at it, then querulously said, "I can't read what it says. You hold it too far away."

"I shall read it to you then. 'My Dear Mik.' Spelled

wrong, Miss Cal—er, Timona. And I might add the handwriting is deplorable. 'Word has come to us that you have involved yourself with a heathen sinner of a woman.' I shall insert a period here, though the writer seldom bothers with details such as punctua—"

Timona's heart pounded, but she managed to sound cool. "Mr. Blenheim. Read it or do not read it. But please refrain editorial comments."

"Very well. '—involved yourself with a heathen sinner of a woman who has never been baptized and has no virtue from what we hear. We beg of you to come home to us, Mick, and leave behind the wicked country and the woman that has drawn you to sin. If you must stay, then Theresa still waits here for you. I thought perhaps when you had enough for her fare you might send for her. I have long prayed and hoped you would wed . . .' and so on. And more tripe such as this. It is from his mother, of course.

"Mr. McCann left word for you, my dear Miss Timona. He told me he was worried about his mother. He said that he still cared for you, but he knew he was not breaking your heart, since he knew that a woman like you was too cosmopolitan, too sophisticated, to care for a man like him for long."

Timona couldn't remember what had gone on the evening before she ended up here, but she knew it had to do with Mick leaving her. And that last line of tripe Mr. Blenheim uttered did sound rather like Mick at his worst.

She had managed to hold down the nausea but now she didn't particularly care to try.

"The basin," she gasped.

"Pardon me?"

"The basin, Mr. Blenheim."

He put it near her head and fled the room.

She hoped he would stay away until the dizziness

passed and she could collect her thoughts. They had scattered like so many terrified rabbits. No, Timmy Calverson, she scolded herself. Do not give in to the illness. She took some deep breaths.

Mick gone? Mr. Blenheim had tied her up. She grinned; this was a fairly good sign that his word could not be trusted.

She spat out the last of the dreadful taste in her mouth. The fear lifted from her heart as she recalled something Mick had once told her.

His mother could sign her name, and not write a word more.

Thank goodness. If the man lied about that, the rest must also be a pack of lies. She lay flat again, as far from the basin as possible. She was now ready to face whatever nonsense Blenheim had in mind for her.

If only she had married her Mick when she could, but no, she had to thumb her nose at the penny press. If she were married, what she suspected was an absurd attempt to get her money would—

There was a soft knock at the door. A young woman entered before Timona could call out.

"Hello, Miss," she said brightly, without looking at Timona. "The gentleman said you were feeling poorly."

"I am better now, thank you. But do you suppose you could help me undo these ropes."

"No," said the woman firmly. "I can't." She picked up the basin and strode from the room. She came back, carefully wiped Timona's mouth and helped her take a drink of water. She left as Timmy tried to explain that she was an innocent woman being held against her will.

"'Tis not my business," said the young woman. "I am being well paid and that is my business, so I'll bid you good evening."

Evening. Timona must have been out for at least several hours. But the thick ache throughout her body, particularly her limbs, and the coldness in her hands might mean she had lain here longer.

A few minutes later, Blenheim reentered. He fetched a chair from the corner of the room and sat down near Timona.

"How long have I been here?" she demanded.

"Ah. Well, this is the second day. I think we gave you too large a dose of medication. I was not sure how much to administer because, I assure you, I not done such a thing as this before, Miss Timona."

"Huh," she said, unimpressed.

He pulled out a cigar. "Do you mind if I smoke?"

"Yes."

He pulled out a tin of matches. "Now Timona, you must grow used to it. I warn you that I shall smoke indoors when we are man and wife."

"I am not going to marry you."

She did not like his confident manner or the way he smiled as he answered, "Very well. I believe we can offer you some alternatives."

She waited. And wished she could scratch her nose.

"If you won't have me, perhaps one of my business partners will suit you. Though I must say I feel I am the best of the three of us. I would actually be a good husband to you if you so wished. There is also Mr. Taylor. I believe you met him in New York."

Blenheim puffed on his foul cigar and seemed to wait for her response.

"Yes, I remember him," she said and regretfully discarded the idea of asking Mr. Blenheim to scratch her nose.

Somehow she was not amazed to hear Mr. Taylor was involved in this scheme. He had struck her as less subtle than most crooked businessmen. The kind of person more drawn to kidnapping than, say, embezzlement.

Hell's bells. Perhaps he indulged in both. That might explain the reason for her current predicament.

"Our other partner is far less well educated than Mr. Taylor or myself. We picked him from this crew of diggers because he is Irish and you seem to have a taste for that sort of crudity. He is a criminal but we have firm control over him.

"We threatened to expose his record to local authorities, which helps keep him from doing everything he wishes. Since we do care about you, despite your uncooperative nature, we would make sure he would not injure you the way he did his previous wife. He is willing to work with us on this matter."

"How much will you pay him?" asked Timona.

"I have always maintained that you are intelligent despite some of your, ah, unfortunate choices," he said admiringly. "It is a matter of money. Mr. McNally will take a mere twenty thousand dollars and passage to some secluded spot. With you. Or, if you were willing to sign some papers that would put your financial affairs into our hands, without you."

"Timona, if you would choose me, let me say I would be honored by your preference. I would forgive your little transgression with the Irishman. I am prepared to pretend it never occurred. We could start afresh. I would be happy to continue our work of smoothing over your rough edges and turning you into a rare diamond. I trust you see that both of our interests would be served."

"This has to do with the missing receipts doesn't it?"

"Ah. Well, we did decide it would be best not to allow you to alert others. And there is the matter of testifying against your husband." He flicked the cigar into a small porcelain ashtray. "We had to move quickly and I am still hazy on the details. Mr. Taylor could explain if you wished."

Timona decided to skip right to the threats and find out if McNally was the worst threat they could manage. She thought of poker, a game she had occasionally played with Solly and some of his friends.

"Mr. Blenheim. I will not marry you or any of your partners. I will not let any of you have a farthing of my money. But I promise that if you let me go immediately, I shall not speak of this matter or your botched receipts. With anyone. Including my brother, Griffin."

There, she thought. I'll see your McNally and raise you a Calverson.

Mr. Blenheim definitely paled. But a moment later he smiled.

"Mr. Calverson has no reason not to trust me, Timona. And I have taken the liberty to send a message from you to him which he also has no reason to disbelieve. You are on your way to meet your friend Mr. Jackson in Colorado. No. I cannot think of how Mr. Calverson might, er, be brought into the matter before we have settled it among ourselves."

"I am patient, Mr. Blenheim. And I am ready to wait a very long time. Eventually someone will be alerted to the fact that I am missing. You shall have to lay down all of your cards, sir," said Timona, still unable to resist poker.

"We have the perfect witness to your wedding," he said, sounding far too smug. Then he called out, "McNally."

The door opened and there stood Araminta. Her mouth was bound shut. They would have to, Timona thought with a flash of love for her outspoken, brave friend. She would never submit to threats. She saw they had had to bind her with so much rope she could barely walk.

Mr. McNally, a huge ape of a man was behind Araminta, holding her by her hair. Araminta's eyes were wide with anger, but Timona thought she could discern fright. Her friend was not used to this sort of treatment.

"Araminta," Timona called out. "I am so sorry that you are involved in this idiocy. I promise you that—"

The door slammed shut.

"There, you see?" said Mr. Blenheim. "And you do understand that no one but yourself would bother about a being like her."

"Because she is a Negress?"

"Exactly so. In this country, she is not important."

Timona exhaled impatiently. "You should do your research, Mr. Blenheim. Araminta is the granddaughter of a wealthy British banker."

He smirked. "Who cast off his daughter when she delivered the little half-bred savage. I shall wait right here while you consider the full implications of the situation."

Oh bother, thought Timona. It had been worth a try.

"A simple ransom," she coaxed. "Much simpler to negotia—"

"Marriage," said Blenheim firmly. "We feel it covers all potential problems. Once you agree, we will lay out our other conditions."

Timona lay thinking for several minutes, but she was stumped. For the moment.

Blenheim hummed to himself and examined the immaculate fingernails on his slender, immaculate hands.

"Let Araminta go," she said at last. "I shall marry one of you."

Chapter 26

Blenheim untied her to allow her to prepare herself for sleep, then tied her to the bed again. Timona spent a bad night fretting, mostly about Araminta, and occasionally about what they had told Mick. She prayed he did not think she had abandoned him.

The next morning, the men brought Timona into the parlor, her hands still tied, and lashed her firmly to an elegant purple velvet couch. She looked around with interest. This was quite an expensive, modern house. Not the usual pit of misery one was dragged when one was kidnapped. Where in heaven's name were they?

Her attention was dragged back to the three men as they argued amongst themselves about who should be the lucky groom.

"I have suffered. I deserve something," Taylor rumbled angrily.

"Surely you gentlemen will see that paying me off with just the wee amount you mentioned would save yourselves a great deal of trouble," McNally pointed out.

"Oh, pray do be quiet. I do not care which one I marry," she interrupted them at last. "Any one of you idiots will do. Understand it will not be a real marriage. I shall sign over the money you want. You will allow me and Araminta to leave. And, yes, I agree to your escort to 'ensure we do not do anything stupid' for several days. The arrangements are straightforward enough. Get on with it."

"But I rather thought," bleated Blenheim. "That you might come to care for me."

"On second thought," said Timona. "I will marry either Mr. Taylor or Mr. McNally. Not Mr. Blenheim. But, no—now I recall how badly Mr. Taylor behaved in New York, so I choose Mr. McNally."

Mr. McNally actually looked pleased. Mr. Taylor appeared to be in his usual dark fury.

They escorted her back upstairs to "prepare" herself.

"I cannot use the chamber pot with my arms tied," she pointed out.

"Chamber pot," said Blenheim, horrified.

Timona was amused. She knew ladies did not use the phrase, but that wasn't the source of Blenheim's horror.

"Miss Calverson. Of course we have water closets here." He showed her to the room and demonstrated the sanitary ware as if he had invented it himself.

"Perhaps I might even indulge in a real bath," she said speculatively. "Would you mind?"

Blenheim pulled out his watch. He sighed. "I had wanted a bath and lit the fire under the water heater. I suppose I can allow you to use some of the hot water. A half-hour. No more."

After they untied her and locked her in the small room, Timona turned on the water taps. She couldn't resist giving herself a quick wash but without getting undressed. She needed the thunder of the water in the tin tub mostly to cover any sounds as she carefully slid open the window. No squeaks or thumps. The rambling, recently built house was a solid one, thank goodness.

She quickly stripped off her silk stockings then wrapped them around a solid-looking pipe in the room. Gripping tight to the stockings to keep from falling, she leaned far out of the window to examine the outside. At once she saw she could easily inch out to the edge of the window ledge to shimmy down the water disposal pipe.

She turned off the water filling the tub, and climbed onto the window ledge.

After she landed softly on the grass, Timona pushed herself tight against the house so no one looking out the downstairs windows would spot her. She would have considered her options, but she had none. If she fled to seek help, they might hurt Araminta.

She hitched up her skirts and crept on all fours towards the back door. She must take care of her friend now.

What would they do to Araminta if they discovered Timona's escape before she had a chance to get to her? Timona had never had to worry about someone else the other times she had been kidnapped.

She put her ear to the kitchen door. She couldn't hear anything so she carefully turned the doorknob.

Mr. Taylor stood by the door as if he had been waiting for her.

He dragged her into the house. He stood close behind her and pushed both of her arms painfully up so she couldn't move.

"I thought you might attempt this sort of nonsense. But tell me, what do you suppose you could accomplish," he hissed into her ear.

"I should think that is obvious."

"You think you are so much better than us mere mortals, Miss Calverson."

She thought this over for a second or two. "I don't go

about kidnapping people, so I suppose I do think I am better than you."

"You are wrong. You are not worthy of the title 'woman.' You are filth." Still speaking quietly through a clenched jaw, he marched her to an empty servant's room on the first floor, next to the kitchen.

He shoved her hard into the room, then closed the door slowly. She saw the hand holding the doorknob was white-knuckled and trembling as if he were forcing himself not to slam it shut.

In a choking, low voice, he began. "I have been waiting for a long time to show you what I think of you. The way you spat on convention. You turned your back on what a real lady should be. Did you even know I loved you?"

"No," she said faintly. He was very angry. And, she finally realized, dangerous.

His dark face was flushed with angry passion and a vein running down the center of his forehead pulsed. "I loved you for years."

"But you haven't known me for years, Mr. Taylor." She inched away from him, hoping he only wished to scold her.

"I have known you, Timona. I read anything I could about you. I went to work for the Calversons mostly for the sake of you. I have loved you for years, I tell you. And you repay my devotion by taking up with a- a piece of trash like McCann. And you let him humiliate me. In public."

She thought it best to not argue with him.

Thundering at her was not enough for him, unfortunately. He was coming toward her.

She was ready.

But so was he. Taylor seemed to know how she would defend herself. He circled left and she followed, when, like a flash, he reached out and hit her on the right side. When he slapped her face hard, she spun from the impact. He grabbed her arms and again yanked them behind her.

There was a horrible snap and pain flooded her.

"It's dislocated, Mr. Taylor. My shoulder. It hurts."

"Shut up," he said and ripped at the front of her dress.

He wasn't stupid enough to put his mouth anywhere near her teeth, but he put it almost everywhere else.

Timona kicked out. He swiftly grabbed her bare foot and jerked it, which threw her down on the floor near the door. He knew not to go directly at her where she could get at him with her knees or head. Instead he let go of her injured arm.

He grabbed the wrist of her good arm, and yanked it up by her head. Still clutching her hand, he used two fingers to yank pins from her hair. When a handful of hair hung loose, he wrapped it tightly around his fist. Now he could hold her wrist and head down with just one hand.

Through the horrendous pain, Timona felt a flash of indignation. The man fought as unfairly as she did.

Noise. She would make noise. She opened her mouth and he stuffed in a handkerchief almost as soon as her first shout left her mouth. The handkerchief seemed clean, at any rate.

She drummed her feet on the floor hoping the thumping would attract one of the other villains. Taylor reached behind him, grabbed her foot and twisted.

The combined agony of her ankle and shoulder nearly sent her unconscious. But it was worth it because she heard footsteps pounding down the hall outside the room, growing louder.

Taylor reached over to the door, getting onto his knees to lock it.

She managed to twist her body sideways and drove

her hip into what she hoped was a tender spot. It must have been because he yelped with fury. Good. That shout would attract more attention.

As he worked at yanking up the bottom part of her dress, his grip on her hair loosened. She made the mistake of lifting her head from the floor.

He saw what she was doing. With his palm on her forehead, he slammed her head back down on the hard wooden planks.

She heard two loud thumps, then saw black.

Chapter 27

"Miss Calverson." Someone was talking to her. "I am sorry. The bastard locked the door."

The voice was Irish. Mick?

Oh, no, God no. It was that ghastly McNally. But at least Taylor was off of her. A blanket covered her now. Her shoulder throbbed with sharp pain, her ankle hurt, her mouth felt dry as desert sand, and her heart ached. Hell's bells, but she was sick of being abducted.

"No more," she said groggy, but furious. "Enough is enough. Let me go. I want to go, I want to go . . ." She was going to say home, but who knew what that was. Timona had briefly had a home, but she vaguely recalled he had left her.

She began to cry in bottomless anguish. Hard sobs shook her until she couldn't breath.

Araminta helped her in a sitting position and stroked her back. "She never cries. Never. I fear she must be suffering from a serious injury. At the very least we will need a doctor for her shoulder." Araminta spoke in an alarmed tone, not angry as Timona would expect.

"Oh Araminta, I am so sorry they have bothered you. Ouch. My arm pulled from the socket, I believe. Mick would have known what to do," Timona managed between sobs.

"Ah, now that's the plan," said McNally.

Timona still crying, opened her eyes. "P-pardon?"

McNally said, "You mean McCann, don't ye? He should be along eventually. And now I recollect that little boy of his said he was good at healing injuries."

She sniffled, hiccupped, and gaped at him. He pushed back his greasy dark hair and gave her a hideously ugly smile.

"I thought you heard me explain, miss, but you must be groggy still. I'm not McNally. My name is Frank Travis. Now you're wide awake I can explain. Miss Araminta knows all about it.

"A few days back the *boc mór*, er, Mr. Blenheim, asked around the diggers for McNally and McCann said that I should go in his stead. McNally thought perhaps they were going to fire him because he's on the lam, so he was more than willing to let me be him."

"But I don't understand, why you?"

"I'm formerly of the police. Nothing like New York City, you understand. I was a constable covering a few villages in County Kerry. But McCann thought I'd be better at keeping you safe should the Calverson boys have something in mind for you. I'm a fair size bigger than McNally, you see.

"And I'd be an experienced witness no matter what nonsense they were working on. I was holding off until the judge or whoever they bribed to do the ceremony showed up, ye understand. Wanted to gather in the whole nasty bunch of them at once.

"Your friend Miss Araminta said you wouldn't mind waiting that long. 'Tis very sorry I am that I didn't do so good a job at keeping you safe, Miss."

She beamed at him through eyes swollen with crying and the blow from Taylor. "You are an angel, Mr. Travis. Don't let anyone ever tell you otherwise."

"He is certainly strong," Araminta said gloatingly. "He put Taylor down and out fast enough. And

Blenheim, that fearful coward, did not even put up a fight."

"Ah. I think the door might have smashed Taylor, not me."

Araminta gave Timona a handkerchief. With her good hand Timona rubbed at her face and blew her nose.

"And here is some brandy for you, my dear," said Araminta. Timona was about to say that one wasn't supposed to drink after receiving a blow to the head. But the bash wasn't so terrible. And she really needed something for the pain in her shoulder. She reached for the brandy and gulped it down.

She dozed and woke to the sound of a door slamming. A familiar voice spoke in English and another shouted angrily in Gaelic.

"Mick," she croaked.

He kissed her gently, next to the bruise on her cheek and then on her mouth.

Considering how rough Mick had to be to reset her shoulder, she more than deserved such tenderness. He'd directed McNally—no, Travis—to pull on her arm until there was a grinding click. He had held her tight in his arms as McNally pulled the shoulder into the right spot.

Then Araminta had handed over the strips of cloth she'd made and Mick bound her shoulder and arm firmly. In less than an hour the earthshaking, nauseatingly sharp pain had lessened to a horrible ache.

"That'll do for now. We must get a real doctor to look at you, though," he said.

Her ankle was sprained, but not badly, Mick told her.

He kissed her again, then turned to the others. "Araminta, love, please give me ten minutes with her.

Could you make some of your ambrosial coffee perhaps? Get Mr. Travis here to help you with the stove. Tis the least he can do. Maybe the men out on the porch can help."

"Men?" asked Timona. "Oh, did I hear Solly's voice outside?"

"Aye, you did. Your blasted Tothman has come. He insisted on trailing after us. I asked a couple of the diggers along in case I needed help, but then had 'em all stay put on the porch so's they don't go messing about with what's known as the crime scene. Mostly it was to keep that damn Solly from coming in and pestering you, Timmy."

Mick stood up and pulled a random handful of bills out of his pocket and handed them to Frank Travis. He gave Timona a quick crooked grin. "Blenheim gave me all this cash, sure I am that he'd be overjoyed to know I'll use it so well."

He turned his attention back to Travis. "Would you thank the men most kindly and send them on home? This'll be for their troubles. I wish you could shuck us of Tothman so easily, but we'll have to deal with him later, I imagine."

Timona smiled, recalling how Mick ordered the Tuckers about on the morning of the fire. He did inspire confidence and action.

When they were alone, he cradled her close. "Timona, I am so sorry."

"Why? Do you mean you were the ringleader of the gang? You want me to marry one of those men? I won't, you know. Not even for you. Not even McNally. Or rather Frank."

He refused to return her smile. "I thought Travis would be enough to protect you. Ah Timmy, my lovely girl, I wish none of it happened to you."

"Mick, the only time I truly felt despondent was when

I thought you were gone from my life. They—they read me a letter they said was from your mother. But then I remembered you told me she couldn't write."

She studied him. He looked down at his hands and his face seemed pink.

"Mick?"

"They are great ones for waving papers about in a person's face for proof, aren't they? I should say 'weren't they,' for they are finished with their plots and stratagems, thank goodness."

"Mick, why are you blushing?"

"Ah, aye. Um, the letter. 'Twas from me mother. I saw it was missing and knew Blenheim must have lifted it from me pack. My sister Nora wrote it for my mam."

Timona pushed herself away from his chest. "Then who is Theresa?"

Mick grinned. "Mam's friend's daughter. My mother long ago decided we should wed. 'Tis a big joke with me and Theresa but the mothers refuse to believe we don't suit.

"Blenheim didn't read you the whole letter. There's a bit from Nora herself and she writes that Theresa's going to Dublin in the fall. My sister ends her part of the letter by saying she will join her unless I and my sinning woman send for her instead."

"Oh. Shall we take Nora?"

"Timmy, we don't have to decide any such nonsense now."

"How on earth did your mother know about me?"

"Nora wrote that a fancy English businessman tracked down the family and informed them I was living in sin."

"A Calverson employee," Timona said glumly.

"Aye. He wanted to bring Mam over here to deliver the message herself. But she'll never step foot farther than the edge of the village."

With her uninjured hand, Timona stroked his shoulder. "Oh Mick, I wish they had left you and your family alone. I am sorry it has been so difficult to be with me."

"You won't hear me complaining. Hell, I'm not the one with injuries, my poor dearie."

"But they have been so dreadful to you."

"Not so bad. And entertaining. Hear this for sheer lunacy: Taylor paid a considerable sum of Calverson money to buy me a job. Remember the one I didn't take in New York? If I'd taken it, turns out they would have fired me and had me thrown in jail for corruption. And you remember the article they showed us?"

"*Cac capaill,*" she said with a damp smile.

"That's the one. Written by Taylor. He forgot to make all the right changes about me being busted for corruption when I didn't take the bait."

"But I don't understand. When I saw Griffin in New York, he . . ."

"Go on," Mick said.

"He mentioned that in New York police and others almost always pay Tammany for their advancement."

"Yah, but there's so much grand talk of late about cleaning up the system. And they were setting up the whole job to make an example of me. They planned to nab me for bribing my way into advancement. A shrewd plan—it would have gotten rid of me and had the Calverson company sitting pretty with the Tammany bunch, supplying them with a good scapegoat to make the press happy."

"How did you figure all that out?"

"Oh, I figured out none of it. I long ago had Griffin marked as the man who got me the job, as a sort of a favor to his sister's . . . Ah. Well. But I must say Blenheim is a blunderer. He mentioned me grand new job at lunch our first day here. When he said he did not know your brother well, I believed him and I thought it

about time to ask your Griffin for help. He very obligingly did a bit of snooping.

"Oh, and when I wrote to Griffin I used the telegraph
as if it were merely a letter. I'm catching on to the ways
of the rich, you see."

Mick brushed back a few strands of her hair from her
face and kissed her again.

"Is that really all they have done to you?" she asked.

"Yes, that's all. Nothing to what they've done to you,
love."

"Oh, Mick. When did you learn all of this? Why
didn't you tell me?"

He drew in a deep breath and slowly let it out before
answering. "Timmy. I didn't want to bring you into it. I
wasn't sure if it was my dreadful prejudice against
Blenheim and his rich university-boy kind. I had to
know they wished us harm. 'Twould be carrying tales to
you if I told mere suspicions. A dolt I was to stay mum,
I know. I am sorry."

She smiled. "Mick. If I so much as brought home a
guest for dinner I would tell you. Much less if I was setting up some kind of elaborate plan for your protection
or detecting a plot to kidnap you."

He kissed her jaw and gently skimmed the bruise on
her cheek with his forefinger. "I promise. Next time I
ferret out a plot to kidnap you, I'll tell you. I did plan
to say something once I knew for certain. But you'd
been snatched away by then. If only I'd been there to
follow or stop the buggers! Oh, I am sorry, love. I know
I should have told you. I didn't want you to think I was
as bad as Blenheim. A reverse snob, I think you've
called me."

With her good arm, she pulled him down. They both
forgot their injured mouths for a long kiss.

She snuggled close to him. Everything would be all
right now. No. Not quite everything.

She looked up into his face, her brow furrowed. "Good Lord. I have just thought of Griffin. Does he know about this nonsense yet?"

Mick shook his head. "Not yet, but he will, and too soon. I sent a telegram for him yesterday since I knew he'd want to, ah, straighten things out and I wanted to see him in person first. I worry about your brother for your sake, ye ken. He is not likely to sit back when it is his own company's men that did this to you."

She rubbed her face on his shirt.

"Mick. He might do something horrible and—"

"Listen, my darling. This will be hard, and perhaps long, but I think we can get through this. I have a fine list of witnesses from here to New York. McFee, Colsun, Padraig, and other good people heard the threats and nonsense in New York if we need to make a case there—that day I wrote all the names in my memo book. While we were at Colsun's with 'em, I palmed a middle page of that rubbishy article they wrote. So if Taylor penned the dirt himself, the way I think he did, there's some handwriting to compare. Better even than countering with your own pet reporter's story, aye?"

"You're jealous because you want your own pet reporter."

Mick chuckled and smoothed back a few strands of her hair from her face. "Here we have the diggers, not to mention Travis and Araminta and even your blasted Solly. But just to be sure, well, I'm thinking your camera will help provide evidence. I have your equipment out in the cart. I believe I remembered the right plates to use. And I have the stuff that flashes light. But you must tell me what to do."

She leaned back against him. And he told her the details of his plan.

Chapter 28

Timona lay with her eyes shut, listening to the murmur of voices on the front porch as Mick sent Travis off to get the sheriff.

A soft voice by her ear made her smile and open her eyes again. "Time for the photos, love. What do I do?"

Mick took photos of Timmy in her ripped dress, making sure her bruises showed. They took a picture of the bed where she lay with the ropes clearly displayed.

Solly was practically incoherent with the riches, and only managed to stop talking after Mick threatened him with violence if he didn't hold his tongue.

Even Araminta was full of delight as she recited the list. She settled next to Timona who lay on the purple couch. "Your testimony, Timona. My testimony, Frank Travis's testimony, a list of witnesses as long as my arm, and Mick's little book of names. It will be enough," gloated Araminta, who looked positively bloodthirsty. "I can hardly wait. Good-bye, you bloody Blenheim. And terrible Taylor too."

"I'm using that!" Solly chirped. "You know the editors absolutely adore alliteration, Araminta!"

After they finished with the pictures, the sheriff arrived. Travis had given him a rough idea of the kidnapping and the others filled him in on other parts of the plot.

Mick jerked a thumb towards the back room. "You'll find Taylor and Blenheim tied up in there. When they start their big noise about being important men with Calverson Company, tell 'em you expect Griffin Calverson any minute. And he already knows all about them. Should shut their mouths fast."

He helped Timona to her feet and said, "I'm taking Miss Calverson to a place in town. The Calverson outfit is too far away for her to travel just now. I promise you a doctor will take a look at her and then give you a report."

The sheriff, a large man with serious dust-brown eyes frowned. "I have some more questions."

But Mick was heading out the door, his arm wrapped tight around Timona to support her limping steps. "You can find me in town if you need to ask any more questions. Wait a day or two at least. We're not going anywhere."

In the supporting circle of his arm, Timona took a deep, shuddering breath of pure happiness. She ached all over and throbbed with pain. But she was home. For the moment, that seemed more than enough. It was perfection.

They sat outside the small but grand and newly built brick courthouse and town hall. Mick and Araminta perched on the wide granite stairs out front. They scribbled furiously, making copies of the notes from Mick's book and his and Travis's descriptions and lists of witnesses.

One for the law, one for Griffin Calverson.

Timona rested on an iron bench near them, her face turned towards the sun. Solly sat next to her and cajoled her for details of the kidnapping, since Mick refused to allow him to help with the copying. Timmy seemed able to ignore Solly, but Mick could not.

"Cease the palaver, Tothman, no more bothering Timona, or I shall turn you inside out," Mick growled at last.

Solly sighed lugubriously. He was silent for several whole seconds together, then said, "Fine, then, listen! I shall turn the tables and relate my own adventures, Timona." And he launched into the story of his latest failed *affaire de coeur*, as he called it. Apparently the grand passion hadn't lasted more than several hours.

People strolling down the wooden sidewalk of the short main street stopped to stare. Mick idly wondered what passersby made of the four of them: A pretty young woman who'd obviously been beaten, a jabbering string bean of a city slicker, a shabby Irishman with a black eye, and an imposing, beautiful Negress. And Botty who slept with his head on Mick's foot.

Araminta paused writing and nudged Mick. They looked over at Timona sprawled on a bench in a position Mick saw was most unladylike but entirely appealing. She lay with her injured foot up, her eyes closed.

"We really should find a place for her to stay," Araminta said to Mick.

"Already have done," he said. "While you fetched her a proper dress from the dry goods shop, Solly and I went over to the local hotel. I booked a room. More of a large house than hotel, but at least there are no Calverson types about the place. I'm about fed up with them. Yourself excluded, of course."

She grinned. "Of course. But why didn't you simply allow her to go directly to the hotel?"

He picked up his memo book from New York. He frowned at it, trying to discern his own notes. "She said she'd much rather not. She went on about how she has to stay busy after she has one of her 'adventures.' She gets an attack of the nerves, I'd say. Besides, I need her here," he said absently.

When they finished their copying, Mick helped Timona stand up, and they started towards the front door.

"Come on then, love, we want to drop off the package for the sheriff to pick up. Or is it the local prosecutor, we want, Tothman?"

Solly started a lecture about different municipalities' methods of dealing with crime, when Mick held up a hand. "Never mind."

He held open the door for Araminta. Then he smiled down at the woman holding his arm for support.

"And since we're here, Timmy, will this do? Or did you want a grander wedding?"

"Oh, please. Yes, this will do," she said. "Mick. This is perfect. And I don't even give a- a damn whose turn it is to ask whom."

"Now do you see?" he said to Araminta, an exultant grin plastered across his face, a smile so wide it almost hurt. "That is just why I needed to drag her along."

He reached into the back pocket of his dusty trousers and pulled out a tattered piece of paper, the application for a marriage license.

Any strain from her discomfort vanished from Timona's face as she beamed at Mick and then at Araminta. "Will you be my maid of honor, Araminta?"

"Ha. You understand that I would slay you if you asked any one else."

Mick's own blissfully happy smile diminished slightly as he eyed Solly. "I suppose you shall do as the other witness."

"I'll put that in the story! God! Please let me be best man!"

Timona answered. "Yes, of course, Solly. The wedding, yes, and maybe some sinister hints of a plot, if you must. But you leave out all specific mention of the unfortunate mess with Mr. Blenheim and Mr. Taylor for now. We don't want to run the risk those men might go free."

"Timona, I remain your faithful correspondent. As long as I will get that too. I want the exclusive on it!"

Timona considered for a moment. "Yes, you get it, especially if you stay in town and chase off any of your wretched brethren, as you call reporters. Stay away from Papa and the compound, Solly, or I shan't grant you an interview ever again."

"Will I eventually get the photographs from the scene for the newspaper artists to copy? Promise? Cleaned up, naturally. You'll look as lovely as usual, Timona. And only a bit disheveled!"

"You get it all," Mick growled. "Now put a stop to your blabbering, lad. I wish to get married."

Timona giggled and they made their slow, limping way toward the judge's office, watched all the while by a disapproving clerk.

Chapter 29

After the short ceremony, and a long conference with the deputy sheriff, Mick handed the second heavy package of evidence to Araminta.

"I trust you with the glass plates of Timmy, rather than handing them over to that ham-handed sheriff's assistant."

"Mick! I'll hold them for you!" Solly exclaimed.

Mick merely gave him a long look, then turned back to Araminta.

He spoke in a low voice. "You'll be seeing Griffin before us. Could you give him this? If 'tis at all possible, could you explain how Timmy wants to use the regular, er, forces of law for this affair?

"It should even up the score, tell Calverson, since he cares about that sort of thing. And we'll take a few days for ourselves Timmy and I. We will come back to fetch Eddy and face the music. *A Dhia*, Araminta! I didn't even ask you. I hope you won't mind if we leave Eddy with you?"

"Of course. I adore that boy. And it will be good for him to see that when you leave you come back. I shall give him your love."

"Thanks for that." Mick scratched at his unshaven chin. He hadn't slept in a day or two. "Saints. I expect Griffin any minute. Ah well, if anyone can face up to the man, you can, Araminta. Tell him Timmy is not his responsibility now. She is mine. As I am hers."

Timona, who'd been shaking the hands of municipal well-wishers, now leaned on Mick. She must have overhead the last few quiet sentences for she frowned up at him. "I think we should tell Griffin, Mick. Really. He won't bite."

"Yes, you are right, *a grhá*. 'Twasn't cowardice on my part." He grinned. "Eh, not entirely. More, I wondered could it wait. It can. So we tell him face-to-face."

"No, please, I insist. Allow me to. Mick, Timona," said Araminta. "It would be my pleasure to explain this to Mr. G. Calverson."

Mick saw the meditative smile on her face and almost had it in his heart to feel sorry for Griffin. Araminta seemed to hold a special grudge against Timmy's brother.

He forgot Griffin, he forgot everything when Timmy pulled on his arm.

He bent down so she could whisper in his ear. "Remember the first time you nursed me, Mick? I believe the best cure was lying in a bed in a room alone with you, for a month or two. Or at least a few days and nights. Might we find a room somewhere?"

He nodded and whispered. "We already have a room for just us. And this one has a very good bed indeed."

They smiled at each other. She took a step towards him and grimaced. He swept her up into his arms. "Still as light as a bag of feathers," he remarked to no one.

"This is so undignified," she squeaked and tried to wriggle out of his grip, but he had a firm hold on her.

"Stop squirming, Mrs. McCann. D'ye wish me to sling ye over my shoulder as I did the first time I came upon you? . . . I thought not."

He nodded to Araminta, Solly, the now-grinning clerk, and the others who stood in a semicircle, watching. Every worker in city hall seemed to have heard all about the strange events a few miles outside of town.

Mick overheard their muttering. Another Timona Calverson adventure. Right here in their small town.

Mick supposed the stationmaster couldn't keep his mouth shut. He knew Solly couldn't.

"So. Well, er. Good-bye, all," Mick said to the group and strode towards the door.

Timmy wrapped her uninjured arm around his neck.

"I shall see you soon, Araminta," she spoke over his shoulder.

"Not too soon, I hope," said Araminta with a grin.

Timona smiled back. "Do not allow Griffin or Solly to be nuisances. No, don't bother to look so amazed and hurt, Solly. I know you will be after Araminta to feed you. Just, please, leave Papa alone. Maybe he won't even notice Mr. Blenheim is gone. If he does, he becomes your responsibility. Oh, and, Araminta, please don't let anyone unload my photo equipment from the cart until Mr. Kendall returns."

Mick nuzzled her ear and quietly growled, "Say your farewells."

"Good-bye! And thank you, darling Araminta, for everything."

The door creaked shut behind them.

Mick's boots thudded on the wooden sidewalk as he carried her from the courthouse, along the main street, past the three storefronts, to the hotel at the end of the block.

The hotel's bell clattered at their hurried entrance, bringing the startled hotel clerk to his feet. Mick nodded a brief hello and Timona grinned happily to the man. Botty raced after them.

"Welcome, Mr. McCann, oh, and Mrs. McCann," the man said. "Er, I'm sorry but we don't allow dogs in the best room."

"He'll stay in the hall," Timona called over Mick's shoulder as Mick bounded up the stairs, taking them two at a time.

Mick cursed under his breath as he tried to open the bedroom door, keep a firm clutch on her, and shove Botty into the hall.

Timona didn't bother to stifle her giggle. "I can walk," she pointed out.

Mick smiled down at her. "Ah. But I think it best if you save your strength for your cure."

His face filled with tenderness and passion. Something in her chest twisted, and sweet heat spread and settled all the way down to her belly.

She remembered the night she'd met him and fallen in love with his friendly grin. Good thing she hadn't seen his face beaming with love, or she would have spontaneously combusted. A woman had to be acclimated to smiles this powerful.

In the room, he carefully shifted her from his arms onto the tall bed then hoisted himself up to stretch out next to her.

She had turned onto her side to face him when a thought struck her. "Oh, Mick! I forgot to ask Araminta to give Eddy a kiss from us. She'll probably remember but what if—"

Mick stopped her words with a gentle but firm kiss. He ran his fingers through her hair, loosening it from the makeshift bun she'd made. He kissed her cheek, then nipped at her ear.

She frowned, wondering if she should have sent a comforting message to their child.

Mick must have sensed her distraction. She could hear the mix of passion and amusement in his whisper, "D'ye know what? Even with your poor arm and cracked head and my beauty of a black eye, this is a honeymoon. So give over worrying, my Timmy."

Timona's frown vanished. She pushed her face against the lovely dip where his throat met his collarbone and felt his pulse beat against her lips. It had been too long since she'd been alone with her Mick.

She gave over worrying.

About the Author

Kate Rothwell grew up in Washington, D.C. She went to art school in Boston, where she met her husband. Besides writing, Kate has worked as a parts runner in a garage, an artist's model, a bartender, a feature writer, a food prep chef, and editor of a newspaper for children. After a few years in Maryland, she and her husband headed north to Connecticut, where they still live with their three boys and a maniacal dog.